Honour & O|

A Victorian Crime Thriller

Carol Hedges

Little G Books

For Avalyn Grace

About the Author

Carol Hedges is the successful British author of 16 books for teenagers and adults. Her writing has received much critical acclaim, and her novel Jigsaw was shortlisted for the Angus Book Award and longlisted for the Carnegie Medal.

Carol was born in Hertfordshire, and after university, where she gained a BA (Hons.) in English Literature & Archaeology, she trained as a children's librarian. She worked for the London Borough of Camden for many years subsequently re-training as a secondary school teacher when her daughter was born.

Carol still lives and writes in Hertfordshire. She is a local activist and green campaigner, and the proud owner of a customised 1988 pink 2CV.

Diamonds & Dust was her first adult novel. Honour & Obey is the sequel.

The Victorian Detectives series

Diamonds & Dust
Honour & Obey
Death & Dominion
Rack & Ruin
Wonders & Wickedness

Acknowledgments

Many thanks Gina Dickerson, of RoseWolf Design for another superb cover, and to my two patient editors.

My biggest thanks however, go to my readers. There was never going to be a second book but the overwhelmingly positive reaction to Diamonds & Dust and the incessant requests for a sequel could not be ignored. This is the result and the author can only hope it lives up to your expectations!

In particular I should like to single out the following: Lynn (3), Michael, Jon, Peter, Terry, Val, Ros, Anne and Ali and so many others too numerous to mention. This book would not have been written without your encouragement.

Finally, I acknowledge my debt to all those amazing Victorian novelists for lighting the path through the fog with their genius. Unworthily, but optimistically, I follow in their footsteps.

Honour & Obey

A Victorian Crime Thriller

"In the beginning was the deed."
Johann Wolfgang von Goethe

London, 1861. An evening in early spring, and it is raining. But this is not the sweet spring rain beloved of romantic writers. This is rain on a mission. Relentless rain that falls with a steady patience as if it has got all night. Rain with the volume turned up.

Rain corrugates windows. Rain drums off roof tiles, the water falling in torrents from leaky gutters. Rain whips the surface of the muck-encrusted streets into thick brown soup. Rain coats ancient brick buildings in a slimy sheen of wet. Rain glugs and gurgles into drains and culverts.

Stand awhile in the shelter of this doorway and listen. The noise of the pelting rain is almost drowned out by the great cacophonous cauldron of sound swirling around you. Horse-drawn omnibuses clip and clop, and slide on their steel wheels. Arguments break out amongst the shapeless huddled crowds hurrying to and fro. At the corner, a ragged soaked drunk raises his voice in discordant song. Church bells ring the quarter-hour in disunited chimes. A dog howls. It is an evening not to venture abroad, you might think. But you would be wrong.

In the building opposite, a door suddenly opens and a young woman appears. The building is old, brick-banded, and run-down in appearance. The paint is peeling and several of the lower windowpanes are cracked, and streaky with rain. It bears the hallmarks of a lodging house, where rooms can be rented cheaply and the landlord lives elsewhere.

The young woman wears a neat but shabby dress, a shawl and an uninteresting bonnet. She carries a wrapped bundle under one arm. Her complexion is pale and pinched, bespeaking a lack of regular nourishing meals. She glances up at the sky, grimaces, then sets off determinedly. Her name is Violet Manning and she is a dressmaker.

You will meet her again, very soon. But not as you see her now.

And the rain keeps on falling. It falls upon a semi-detached villa on the outskirts of New Camden Town. The villa is owned by Mrs Lucinda Witchard, widow of the late Nathaniel Whitchard, owner of a piano factory. In its time. the house has known the laughter of children, the bustle of family life. Now it is a boarding house for professional gentlemen, overseen by Mrs Witchard (widow), who has a false front of black curls, a false set of yellow teeth and a false smile.

At Mrs Witchard's, for a moderate outlay of cash, the professional gentleman can avail himself of a bed, use of ablution facilities and privy, together with breakfast and an evening meal. Mrs Witchard's cooking is in a class of its own. Her cabbage is always boiled for exactly one hour. She makes pastry you could tile roofs with, and her gravy possesses a thick, glutinous quality rarely seen outwith the river embankment at low tide.

Mrs Witchard's lodgers have just finished their evening meal of scrag-end of unidentified animal served with soggy potatoes. Now she is busy clearing away the plates, helped by the undersized maid of all work.

"Knives and forks in the basket, girl," she snaps. "Then scrape them plates into the pig bucket."

The maid comes from the local Foundling Hospital. She has a name, but Mrs Witchard prefers to call her "girl." It saves time. She drops the cutlery into the basket and eyes the plates hungrily. Several of the lodgers have left unappetising scraps of food.

"Hurry up, girl," Mrs Witchard commands. "I 'aven't got all day."

The Foundling scrapes the plates into the rusty iron bucket. Her stomach rumbles. Footsteps sound in the hallway. Mrs Witchard darts to the door. One of the lodgers, the new young man who only arrived recently, has just descended the stairs and is heading for the front door.

"Going out, are you, Mr Err ...?"

Mr Err is indeed going out. He has on a long dark overcoat and his hat is pulled low over his face. He makes no reply, merely opens the front door and disappears into the pouring rain.

"Manners!" mutters Mrs Witchard.

She goes back to clearing the plates, and persecuting the Foundling.

Evening lengthens. Lamplighters begin their rounds. Shop windows are also lit, displaying their rich contents to the rain-soaked passers-by. The magic light of a million gas-lamps draw the flâneurs – both men and women – like moths to its flickering flame. For there are particular pleasures to be had at night, when the streets become a glittering gallery of images and goods.

Sometime later Mrs Witchard's lodger will return, will let himself in with his key and will quietly climb the stairs to his room. Sometime later the brightly lit shops will shutter-up, and the streets will empty out. Sometime later, Violet Manning will be brutally murdered, and her body will be dumped in an alleyway.

****

The early morning fog is thick as heavy velvet curtains as Detective Sergeant Jack Cully, accompanied by two police officers, hurries across London. He is heading towards the elegant shopping area of Regent Street – or, more specifically, one of the many slum alleys behind Regent Street – where an 'incident' has been reported.

The detective division of the Metropolitan Police was formed in June 1842. Based in Great Scotland Yard, it was created to investigate and co-ordinate murder hunts, and other serious crimes that cross the city boundaries. Vilified by the press, and implicitly distrusted by members of the public, the division has nevertheless built up an exemplary record in solving crimes and catching criminals. What Jack Cully is about to encounter, however, is going to challenge even the finest deductive abilities of this elite force.

Cully reaches his destination and pushes through the inevitable crowd of nosy onlookers who always materialise magically out of nowhere whenever there is anything grisly to gawp at. Guarding the entrance to a narrow, piss-stinking alleyway is a police constable, arms folded, a grim set to his mouth. He eyes Cully and the two accompanying officers, recognising them as members of the detective division.

"The body's just back there, sir," he says, gesturing over his shoulder.

Cully steps past him into the alleyway.

The young woman is sprawled against a brick wall. Her dress has been partly pulled up, revealing the milky blue-white skin of her calves and a pair of battered boots. Her throat has been slashed with a long, razor-like cut from one side of her neck to the other, and her head has been beaten in with some heavy object. Brain tissue has oozed out, matting her fair hair in thick clots. Feeling suddenly un-tethered from reality, Cully stares down at the bloodied skull, squashed and bruised like overripe red fruit, and feels the bile rising in his throat.

One of the accompanying officers is sick.

"Meaningless violence," the other murmurs, shaking his head in disbelief.

But, Cully thinks grimly, there is no such thing as meaningless violence. All violence has meaning – for the perpetrator, if no one else. He gets out his notebook and begins to go through the meticulous police rituals that always accompany the discovery of a person found dead.

First of all, he notes down the relation of the body to the surrounding objects (in this case a bonnet and a parcel). Then he notes the position and attitude of the body, after which he makes further notes concerning the place where the body has been found and the surface upon which the body is lying. Finally, he writes a detailed description of the woman's clothes.

Having thus completed his preliminary investigation, Cully closes his notebook and steps up to the constable guarding the crime scene.

"Has she been ...?"

The constable shrugs.

"She doesn't look like a ..."

The constable shakes his head.

"Dressmaker," he says laconically.

"Aren't they all?"

Cully has lost count of the number of whores he has arrested who've given their stated profession as dressmaker.

"This one actually was."

"How do you know that?"

"Callouses on her thumb and sides of the first two fingers, sir. Dead give-away."

Cully winces at the ironically apposite phrase.

"And there's a bundle of sewn shirt sleeves and collars."

Cully writes this down.

"Have you arranged for ..."

The constable nods. "Should be here any second, sir."

"The finder?"

"At the Marylebone police station. Giving a statement."

Cully makes a further note. He checks his watch, and writes some more. Then he studies the surrounding area carefully, before he returns to the young woman's mangled corpse once again. He spends some time staring down at it. Finally, he glares at the crowd milling at the entrance to the alleyway, their faces alight, their eyes agape.

"For God's sake cover her face, man," he hisses to one of his constables, as he thrusts the notebook back into his coat pocket and prepares to head back to Scotland Yard.

****

Sisters Lobelia and Hyacinth Clout wake in their Islington town house. Ears straining, they lie on their backs in their respective bedrooms at the top of the house, like two carved stone effigies on two tombs.

Silence.

Absolute silence.

No imperious little bell summons one of them to the close, stuffy bedroom with its drawn curtains and dim light where Mama lies, dying (as she has lived) with contempt and loathing for the world in general.

For Mama is dead.

Only in dreams do they once more view the massive, saggy, bedridden body heaving itself upright, once more see the expression of disapproval, once more hear the rasping voice that could, with just a couple of words, instantly cut the ground from under them, reduce them once again to snivelling, cringing children.

For Mama is dead.

Only in nightmares do they find themselves stumbling along endless corridors, spilling barley-water, tripping over Turkey carpets, rushing, rushing, but never quite reaching the door to the sickroom where she, the invalid, waits impatiently for them.

No longer.

For Mama is dead.

And with her has died all the guilt, and the shame, and the constant reminders of that bright summer day, so long, long ago, when three children went out to play, but only two returned home.

****

Detective Inspector Leo Stride has returned from a few days' unwelcome holiday spent in the dark dour northern house of his wife's family. Now he sits in his office, staring with disbelief at his desk, which was empty when he left, but is now completely swamped in paperwork.

Stride feels his heart sink. So much paperwork to read. So much paperwork to ignore. So much paperwork to pretend he hasn't received, so he won't have to do anything about it. A knock at the door heralds a temporary relief. Jack Cully enters, his expression sober. Stride glances up.

"Trouble?"

Cully nods.

"A murder."

Stride rolls his eyes.

"Man or woman?"

Cully grimaces, recalling the poor bashed-in head and the helplessly sprawled body.

"Young woman."

"Where?"

"Alleyway off Carnaby Street. She was a dressmaker."

"Ah. One of them."

"No – this one really was a dressmaker. She had a bag of shirt collars and cuffs. It looks as if she was on her way to deliver them. I thought I might go around a few of the big stores in Regent Street. Could be someone's missing their order and might know who she is."

Stride nods.

"Good idea. I'd like to come with you but ..." he gestures despairingly at the overflowing desk.

"That's quite alright, I understand. The chances are I won't discover anything, but I thought it was worth a try." Cully glances down at Stride's desk but tactfully forbears to comment.

"Anything is worth a try at this stage," Stride agrees.

He picks up a folder from the top of the pile, and gloomily flicks it open with a sigh.

****

The rain has faded from the streets like a bad memory as Cully leaves Scotland Yard. He whistles up a cab and gives the driver his destination. All the way there, Cully tries to see the pattern. To understand the question that precedes how: Why?

By the time Cully arrives at the opulent shopping paradise that is Regent Street, the sun is glittering off shop fronts and bouncing off the plate-glass windows. He prepares to work his way from store to store. It is a long street and there are many stores, so it looks as if he is going to have to work like a dog. But fate unexpectedly throws him a bone in the form of Marshall & Snellgrove, the fourth shop he comes to.

Entering the shiny atrium, Cully approaches one of the counters, explains his mission to an assistant who, after a whispered consultation with another assistant higher up the retail food chain, instructs him to 'wait there while Mrs Crevice is sent for.'

Cully waits. While he waits, he watches the customers. There is something about the expressions on their faces – a snatching quality to their eyes. Cully has never got the hang of this new phenomenon called shopping, and the past few hours has reinforced his opinion.

He can think of nothing he'd like to do less than stroll around a big department store staring at things he does not need. Buying necessities like food or drink is one thing. Gawping at luxuries is another bucket of fish altogether.

Eventually the floor manager reappears, followed by a thin, angular, middle-aged woman dressed in high-necked shop black. Her face wears a sourly disapproving expression.

"This is Mrs Crevice. She is the superintendent in charge of the sewing-room staff," he tells Cully.

Mrs Crevice's thin lips pleat in on themselves. Her eyes, black pinpricks in an angular, pointy-chinned face, measure him up silently.

Cully clears his throat and repeats the sad tale of the previous night. Mrs Crevice hears him out in snooty silence. Then she asks snippily,

"How many collars and cuffs?"

"Two dozen."

"Sewn or unsewn?"

"I believe they are sewn."

"Violet Manning," Mrs Crevice says.

Her mouth scissors itself closed.

Cully stares at her.

"A piece-worker. Recently taken on. They were supposed to be delivered last night. Where are they now?"

"On their way to Scotland Yard with the body of the young woman."

Mrs Crevice's sharp nose quivers.

"I should like them returned as soon as possible, please. They are the property of this store. It is the start of the Season, and there are orders to be fulfilled."

Once again, Cully marvels at the inhumanity of his fellow man. Or in this case, woman. Not a flicker of pity or concern for the poor murdered girl has crossed the hard-faced woman's features.

"I will arrange it," he says. "Meanwhile I should like to speak to your dressmakers, if I may. Perhaps one of them might be able to give me some more information about the young woman, as she was in your employ."

Mrs Crevice considers his request.

"You will have to be brief. They have a lot of work to do."

Cully is escorted to the back of the store, then through an insignificant baize door and down a flight of uncarpeted dusty stairs to a dimly-lit basement. Here, rows of women sit at long cloth-covered wooden tables, mechanically sewing.

At one end of the room, completed and half-completed dresses hang on mannequins. At the other, swathes of material with patterns pinned to them are laid out, awaiting the pattern-cutters.

Mrs Crevice claps her hands. Conversation dies.

"This is a detective from the police. He wishes to ask you something. You may stop sewing temporarily."

A couple of the women instantly lay their heads onto the table and appear to fall asleep. Cully relates the events of the previous night, keeping details to a bare minimum.

When he finishes speaking, there is a shocked silence. This is followed by a sharp cry of pain, like a wounded animal. All eyes swivel round to a slightly-built young woman sitting at a corner of one of the tables. Her face is white, stricken.

Cully nods encouragingly.

"Yes, Miss?"

"It is Violet Manning. She lodges ... lodged in Bonnet Box Court ... off Carnaby Street."

"Thank you, Miss ..."

"Benet. Emily Benet."

Cully smiles encouragingly.

The young woman fixes dark eyes pleadingly on his face. They send him a subliminal message: *Ask me, but not here.*

Cully thinks fast.

"I wonder whether Miss Benet might accompany me to the Yard," he says. "I could talk to her on the way, and hand over the sewing."

He sees Mrs Crevice purse her lips ready to refuse the request, so adds quickly, "This is a police matter, madam. We are talking about a murder investigation. To refuse to assist the police in pursuing their lawful inquiries could be considered a criminal offence."

Mrs Crevice gives him a look so stiff you could have ironed sheets on it.

"In that case she may go. But she must be back here by midday prompt, or her wages will be docked."

Cully waits while Emily Benet collects her shawl and bonnet. Then he and the young dressmaker leave by a back entrance that is as shabby, sordid and run-down as the front entrance is grand and impressive. As soon as they get out into the fresh air, she collapses against a brick wall, her hand to her side.

Concerned, Cully stops.

"Are you alright, Miss?"

But Emily Benet is far from alright. Her shoulders are shaking with sobs. Her whole body is racked with them. She sways to and fro, as if suffering the effects of an inner storm.

Helpless, Cully stands and watches. Female grief is something he is familiar with, it comes with the job, but not at such close and intimate quarters and on such a passionate level. Eventually, the sobbing ceases. The young dressmaker raises a white, tear-soaked face to his.

"Are you sure it is her? Quite, quite sure?"

Cully describes, as best he can, the features and dress of the murder victim.

"Ah," she utters a low cry. "I recognise the description. It really is Violet."

For a moment, Emily Benet sways on her feet. Automatically, Cully reaches out a hand, but she steadies herself.

"Violet was my best friend," she says. "We came to London together to find work. She rented the attic room next to mine. When I left this morning, I gave her a knock, just like I always do, to say I was off. I didn't get any reply, so I thought she must've slept in."

"I'm so sorry," Cully says.

"What happened to her?" she asks.

Cully bites his lip. He cannot share what he saw; the details are far too shocking for any young woman to hear – let alone a close friend of the poor deceased girl.

"A passer-by found her," he says. "She was already dead."

She raises wounded dark eyes to his face.

"It isn't just that. We both know it. But you aren't going to tell me any more, are you?"

Cully looks away. There is a brief awkward silence.

"Was it bad?" she asks.

He nods.

"Oh, poor Vi," she whispers, her voice breaking. "Oh, poor dear friend. How did this happen to you? And why was I not there to protect you?"

Cully waits for the next fit of sobbing to pass.

"Can I see her?" she asks.

"I'm afraid in the circumstances that I don't think it would be permitted," he says.

Her lips twitch.

"I see. I understand."

She tries to walk, but staggers, reaching out to grasp a railing to steady herself.

"Would you like a cup of coffee?" Cully asks, offering the only comfort he can think of.

The young woman heaves a sigh that seems to come from somewhere deep within her soul.

"Thank you, that is very kind. Perhaps it might fortify me."

Cully leads the way to one of the many street food stalls and purchases a mug of black coffee, carefully selecting the one with the fewest stains.

She lifts the chipped white mug between dry swollen fingers, drinking the hot dark liquid in quick gulps.

"That's better," she nods.

Unconsciously, her eyes drift to the plates of ham sandwiches, temptingly arranged on the wooden trestle table.

Cully may be way back in the woods as far as women are concerned, but he has worked the streets of London long enough to recognise real hunger when he sees it. He is seeing it now. And they have a longish walk ahead.

"May I also buy you a sandwich to go with your coffee?" he asks, adding delicately, "It must be some time since you breakfasted."

The young dressmaker gives him a wryly amused look.

"I start work at eight o'clock. I don't have time for breakfast."

Cully recalls the nicely cooked breakfast prepared by his generous-hearted landlady *("Can't have you chasing all them criminals on an empty stummick, Mr Cully")*. Silently he hands over the few coins and she selects a sandwich. Cully politely watches the passing carriages while she eats it with great relish. He waits until she has finished eating before he enquires:

"Are you ready to go on?"

She nods.

"Yes. Let us go on, officer," she says, wiping her fingers on her overall. "If I cannot see her, I can at least be near her, can I not?"

Awkwardly, because he isn't used to it, he offers her his arm. She hesitates, then lays her hand lightly upon it. Cully directs their steps towards Westminster.

****

Sisters Lobelia and Hyacinth Clout, who have never worked a day in their lives, let alone a day that begins at 8am on an empty stomach, have enjoyed a substantial breakfast. Eggs, bacon, toast, and the remains of a cold fowl from the previous evening. Now they sit in the morning room, dealing with correspondence.

Later, because the period of mourning for Mama has now elapsed and they are free to re-enter society, they have let it be known that they will be 'At Home' to friends and acquaintances – though the latter greatly outweigh the former. Mama did not encourage what she sardonically referred to as *'girlish gatherings.'*

Lobelia, who at 29 has long since lost any 'girlishness' that she might have originally possessed, works steadily through the pile of cards of condolence that keep on arriving. Mama was a leading light on so many charitable committees. Her loss is keenly felt and her absence is greatly lamented. That's what the various writers say. It is only here, in the maiden bosoms of her immediate family, that such emotions are tempered somewhat by a sense of relief.

Meanwhile, younger sister Hyacinth, at 22, still retains a good complexion, though drained by many hours of night-watching at the dying invalid's bedside. She chews the end of her pen and stares pensively into the middle distance. She should be composing a suitable response to the chairwoman of the Committee for Wayward Girls Who Need Immediate Chastisement. But she is not.

Last week, while Hyacinth was exchanging her library book, she had made a most astonishing discovery. Somebody had carelessly left a copy of the *News of the World* on one of the reading tables. Of course, it was out of date: this was Monday not Sunday, nevertheless she had snatched it up eagerly. Mama did not allow the reading of *'trashy public papers'* within the confines of the house.

Returning home with the discarded newspaper and another of the sensationalist novels that she loved, Hyacinth had retired to her room, away from the prying eyes of her sister. The newspaper had been a revelation. So many scandalous and horrific events were taking place right under her nose, and she never knew!

But it was when she turned to the pages and pages of advertisements that Hyacinth's feet hit the

Damascene Road. Amongst the advertisements for hair restorer and cure-all pills and poor unfortunate women seeking employment as governesses, were several advertisements from respectable-sounding gentlemen, all wanting to meet ladies wishing to engage upon the business of matrimony.

Hyacinth's mouth had actually fallen open. The idea that people paid to insert marriage advertisements was totally beyond her comprehension. Mama had always made it clear that marriage was a lowering business, with many unpleasant and demeaning sacrifices to be made on the woman's part, and few, if any, rewards. She never specified precisely what the sacrifices or rewards were, but the impression had been unequivocally conveyed.

Mama had also drilled into both daughters that true contentment and spiritual grace came from staying at home and looking after the one who had bestowed upon them both the inestimable gift of life. Lobelia had been happy to acquiesce, but Hyacinth, who (unbeknown to her Mama) possessed some of the rebellious spirit of her late but not much-lamented father, had never been entirely convinced.

It seemed to her that to be unwed meant a life of mindless and repetitious drudgery and boredom. She based these observations upon the novels she read, and by observing the lives of the many middle-aged church spinsters of her acquaintance.

Lying awake in the dark, Hyacinth had resolved that she no longer wanted to eke out her days in the stuffy house, polishing the old-fashioned furniture, cooking endless meals, attending endless charitable committee meetings and growing sourer and uglier as the years passed.

But where to find a husband? She knew no eligible men. There were a couple of curates, but they were of that limp and lettucey temperament that set her teeth on edge. Besides, marrying a curate would merely be a sideways transference of her current life, with added enforced sanctimony into the bargain.

So, she had studied each advert carefully, noting the age of the man in question, his list of accomplishments (and they were all very accomplished) and his requirements. After much internal debate, and a lot of false fits and starts, she had decided that one advert seemed to fit her situation exactly.

Thus, she is now covertly penning her response to the Editor, who has the address of the gentleman in question. Inspiration drives her fingers across the page, perspiration bedews her furrowed brow. Shading her letter from her sister's piercing gaze, Hyacinth writes:

Dear Advertiser,

I am a young lady of 22 years, recently orphaned and from a good Christian family. I am well educated, can keep house and am accustomed to respectable society, though I have not frequented it much of late, due to the onerous nature of my nursing cares and duties.

I am of average height with dark hair, a cheerful disposition and a pleasing countenance. I do not dress extravagantly. I currently reside with my older unmarried sister in the family home.

She signs the letter *"A London Lady,"* then slips it into an envelope, including (as instructed) four stamps, and a note of her address for the editor to send on any response. With trembling hand, she addresses the envelope, her mind racing at her own audacity.

"Are you quite well, Hyacinth?" The harsh voice of her sister breaks into her reverie. Startled, Hyacinth glances up.

"Oh. Yes. I am quite well, Lobelia."

"Your colour seems a little heightened. I do hope you are not coming down with anything. I trust you are not going to spoil our first At Home."

Hyacinth smiles brightly.

"I could do with some air, now that you mention it. Maybe a walk to the post box would clear my head. Shall I take your letters and post them with mine?"

She picks up her letter, places it under her sister's letters, and goes to find her bonnet and shawl.

Mama vincit omnia?

Not any more.

****

Breakfast is also well and truly over at Mrs Witchard's boarding house on the outskirts of New Camden Town, if the unappetising combination of watery eggs of a greenish hue, burned toast, and weak gritty coffee could be called breakfast.

The house, seen in the damp light of sunless day, presents an equally unappetising aspect. Tiers of melancholy windows, black-framed and dreary, are set in a grimy peeling plaster facade. One of the lower windows bears a flyblown card with the word *'Lodgins'* written in faded ink. The house is reached via a narrow yellow clay and gravel path, sloppy with rain.

Soon, the unbreakfasted Foundling will appear with a big scrubbing brush and a bucket of lukewarm water to scrub the step, and a chalkstone to whiten it, because appearances, however deceptive, are everything, and must be kept up at all costs.

Upstairs on the third floor, Mrs Witchard's new lodger has locked his door. Now he sits at the grimy window overlooking a neighbouring pigsty and the outdoor privy. On the table next to him, is a small brown bottle. He stares at it for some time, then reaches for the morocco case next to it and draws out a hypodermic syringe.

His fingers adjust the delicate needle. He rolls up his sleeves, revealing an arm dotted with small puncture marks. For a moment he hesitates, then with a quick and practised motion, he locates a vein and thrusts the sharp point home, depressing the tiny piston.

He waits for the reddish-brown liquid to flow through his veins. As the shadows in the corners of the room begin dancing their victory jig, he thinks about the previous night. He should have known it was dangerous. He should have thought through what he was about. But he hasn't thought about anything for weeks. He is tired of thinking. I forget my name, he whispers to the empty room. I forget all my names.

****

Meanwhile Cully and Emily Benet are still walking towards Scotland Yard. As they progress, Cully carefully questions the dressmaker about her friendship with the dead girl.

"I met Violet at Mrs Snow's – the lady we were 'prenticed to," she tells him. "We were both sixteen and our parents had paid her the premium to teach us the dressmaking business. It was either that or become governesses, and we neither of us fancied that profession.

"We shared a room together and it wasn't long before we were the best of friends, and were making big plans to come up to London when we'd learned our trade. We thought we'd start a dressmaking business together.

"We used to talk about the beautiful gowns we'd sew for all the rich society women, and how we'd see our names mentioned in the fashionable papers." She shakes her head. "We were so innocent then."

"But you did come to London," Cully prompts.

"Oh yes – well, there was nothing for us in St Albans. So we set off to make our fortunes in the city where the streets were paved with gold. Only they weren't, and we didn't. Nobody told us how much it'd cost to set up a little business – the rents, the materials, everything was completely beyond our means.

"And we had no one to help or advise us. In the end, we decided to hire ourselves out as store dressmakers, live as cheaply as we could, saving every penny of our wages, and one day, if we worked very hard, perhaps our dreams would come true."

Cully steers her carefully across the street.

"You don't have to tell me if it is all too much for you," he says.

"No, I want to. You've been so kind. We both got regular work – me in Marshall & Snellgrove, and Violet in Peter Robinson. It was long hours, but we managed. Vi even got to be chief bodice hand. And then, just after Christmas, she suddenly lost her job. There was a floor manager in her place who kept trying to force himself on her."

Cully stares at her, his expression shocked.

"When she refused him, he reported her – made up some lies about her stealing from the store, something she'd never do, and she was sacked. It affected her badly. She got very low, didn't want to leave the house, wouldn't eat. Then she got a letter from home: her parents were going to emigrate to America. Her father had business contacts and they'd decided to make a new life for themselves and her brothers. That was another blow."

"Couldn't she have joined them?"

Emily shakes her head.

"You don't understand, Mr Cully: Violet wasn't close to her family. She told me she never had been. I met them once when we went home for Mothering Sunday. Her mother was only interested in the boys, and her father was only interested in making money.

"After she received the letter, it was as if something had broken inside her. She withdrew into herself. I managed to get her some piecework to do – just to stop her from sitting and brooding. It brought in a little money, barely enough to pay her rent and let her eat, but better than nothing. And now ..."

And now they have arrived at their destination.

"What's going to happen to Violet's body?" she asks.

Cully shrugs.

"I suppose, if she has no family in England, that she will have to be buried on the parish."

Emily turns to face him, her eyes widening in horror.

"A pauper's funeral? In a public grave? Oh no, that cannot happen; she was my only friend. I should like to make sure Violet has a decent funeral, if it can be arranged somehow."

Cully doubts very much that Miss Benet, whose clothing and demeanour shout out penury and hardship, could afford to pay for even the most basic funeral, but he does not say this. Instead he pushes open the door to the outer office and leads her towards the wooden seat, known as the Anxious Bench, where those seeking news of their nearest and sometimes dearest customarily wait.

"If you could sit here, I shall fetch the sewing articles," he says.

She sinks onto the hard seat, burying her face in her hands. Cully exchanges a quick meaningful look with the constable on desk duty, and hurries away.

****

Detective Inspector Stride stands in the police mortuary, a cold basement room smelling of chemicals, and damp, and unhappiness. The body of Violet Manning has been brought in. Now that the preliminary examination has taken place, it lies covered in a black cloth on the table.

Once again Stride marvels at the cool detachment with which his medical colleague can deal with the bruised battered remnants of humanity that wash up here on a daily basis without a flicker of emotion crossing his face. It is all Stride can do not to throw up his breakfast.

"Very interesting," murmurs the surgeon, nodding thoughtfully.

"So, what can you tell me?"

"The young lady has been the victim of a particularly violent attack," the surgeon says, consulting his notes. "The wounds of the upper part of the throat, dividing the carotid artery, are the most probable cause of death. Given the position and depth of the wound, I am prepared to say that this death was homicidal, not suicidal."

Stride restrains his natural impulse to tell the police surgeon that he is making a statement of the bleeding obvious. Instead, he merely nods a couple of times.

"A few other notable features," the surgeon continues, "there are severe cranial injuries resulting from blows struck to that part of the body. There is haemorrhaging from the fracture of the meningeal artery and the subsequent effusion between the *dura mater* and the skull. I conjecture these blows were made by a hammer of some sort. Again, great force has been used. It is almost as if she has been attacked by a wild beast – if such an animal could perform the actions I see before me."

Stride folds his arms.

"Who knows what actions the human mind is capable of," he says bleakly.

"Yes indeed," the police surgeon agrees. "And have we not witnessed many prime examples of it in our time, Detective Inspector?"

"Well, thank you for your information."

Stride turns to leave.

"Not so fast, Detective Inspector."

Stride halts.

"Also extremely unusual, are the marks upon the upper thorax."

Stride waits. They were all the same, police surgeons. Liked to take their time, keep you waiting, let you know that they were in charge.

"I noticed when the body was first brought in that the dress had been cut about across the bodice. Examining the area more closely, I discovered a particular set of incised wounds just above the left breast. I may be wrong, but it looks very much as though the murderer has made a clumsy attempt to extract the victim's heart."

Stride stares at him in disbelief.

"I can show you, if you don't believe me," the police surgeon prepares to lift the cloth.

"No, I believe you," Stride interjects quickly.

"And there is one other most unfortunate aspect of this poor girl's murder." The police surgeon beckons Stride over and whispers a few words in his ear.

"Are you sure?"

"Oh, absolutely sure. There can be no doubt about it whatsoever."

Stride nods curtly.

"Well, well. That is as you say, very unfortunate. Let me have your full written report when you've finished. The sooner we catch this bastard, the better."

Jack Cully is waiting in the office.

"I've just seen the young woman's body, Jack," Stride tells him. "Bad business."

"Her name was Violet Manning," Cully says. "There's a friend of hers in the outer office."

He relates what Emily Benet has told him. Stride listens intently, making the odd note.

"Can we give her the sewing?" Cully asks. "It's not as if it is part of the enquiry."

Stride waves a hand towards a small wrapped bundle on the desk. "Go ahead Jack."

Cully picks it up.

"One other thing," Stride says, glancing up from his notes. "You mentioned a floor manager in a department store where the young woman previously worked?"

"Miss Benet said he was responsible for her friend Miss Manning getting the sack."

"He might have been responsible for something else as well."

Stride tells Cully what the police surgeon told him.

"Miss Benet never mentioned it," Cully says, raising shocked eyebrows.

"No, maybe not. Probably didn't know. Not the sort of thing you'd necessarily share – in the circumstances. Might explain why she was sacked though."

"Should I tell her?" Cully's brain throws up a picture of the white-faced woebegone woman waiting in the outer office.

Stride strokes his chin with thumb and forefinger.

"I think discretion might be the way to go. After all, if she didn't know, maybe she wasn't meant to know. And once the cat is out of the bag, as it were, there will be no prospect of her arranging a decent Christian funeral, will there? Ask Miss Benet if she knows the man's name, though. Then let's jog along and see what he has to say."

His face a study, Cully picks up the bundle of sewing and goes to find the young dressmaker who is still sitting exactly where he left her, hands folded in her lap, eyes on the floor. She looks up as he approaches, her expression warily hopeful.

Cully gives her the sewing.

"What happens now?"

"Now I shall put you in a cab back to your place of work."

She pinches her lips together.

"I mean about Violet's body. About the funeral arrangements."

"The surgeon who is examining her will make a report. Then the body will be released. I can arrange for it – for her," he corrects himself, cursing inwardly at his clumsiness, "to be taken to an undertaker's, if you let me know the address."

She stands up, holding herself erect.

"Then I shall send word where she is to be taken. Thank you, Mr Cully; you have been very kind to me, but I do not need a cab. Indeed, I prefer to walk. It will give me time to think things out. Good day to you."

And clutching the small bundle of sewing to her as if it were a precious child, Emily Benet straightens her slender shoulders and pushes open the street door. Cully watches her walk out. She does not look back.

****

Three o'clock finds Hyacinth and Lobelia Clout sitting uprightly side by side on an overstuffed sofa in the darkly-wallpapered drawing room. Dressed in unbecoming mauve and surrounded by portraits of deceased male Clout family members, many in military uniforms, they are ready for the arrival of their visitors.

Refreshments are laid out on a side table, awaiting Hyacinth's ministrations. There is a plate of ginger biscuits and a large freshly-baked seed cake cut in slices. Hyacinth has done all the cooking since the last servant walked out, after declaring that she was not going to work her fingers to the bone for a rude selfish tyrant like Mrs Clout even if she was dying. (The Clout household has, over time, gone through a lot of servants on this basis.)

After the departure of the latest one, Mama had decided not to allow any more sinful and Godless girls over the threshold on account of the *'insolence and corruption'* they might bring with them. Since the maternal decree was issued, Hyacinth had been forced to assume the role of unpaid cook, maid and skivvy.

Occasionally Lobelia had helped out, though her proper place, as she stated, was by Mama's suffering side. She always rolled her eyes upwards as she declared this, as if addressing unseen angels gathered around the invalid's bed, although technically, her sentiments would reach the chamber pot under the bed first.

Why is it always called a morning call when it takes place in the afternoon, Hyacinth wonders, staring down at her ragged cuticles. She is supposed to be focusing on the afternoon, but she cannot help speculating on the progress of her letter. She is about to suggest that, as older sister, Lobelia might care to let in the guests for a change, when there is a knock at the front door. Lobelia folds her lips over her rather protuberant teeth and sits even more upright. Hyacinth does not move.

"Door, Hyacinth. Our guests arrive. Let us not keep them waiting."

Gritting her teeth and promising herself that as soon as she is married to whomever, whenever, there will be servants to answer the door, Hyacinth rises and goes out into the narrow hallway. She opens the door with slightly more force than intended, causing it to bang against the inside wall.

On the step stands the black-clad, beak-nosed, gimlet-eyed pillar that is Reverend Ezra Bittersplit, accompanied by his sharp-faced, skimpy daughter Bethica. Hyacinth curses inwardly. Bethica smirks.

"Good afternoon Hyacinth," the Reverend says, regarding her sternly. "A little more Leviticus 4:16, I think. Yes?"

Hyacinth pastes on a polite smile and ushers them into the hallway, relieving them of their outer garments. She used to be in awe of Reverend Bittersplit. Now she merely regards him as an interfering nuisance, thanks to his regular presence in the house while Mama was dying. And his endless Bible verses, which she is beginning – oh, irreverent thought – to wonder whether he just makes up on the spot to aggravate her.

Lobelia rises and steps forward to greet the guests, extending the requisite three fingers. All are seated. Polite conversation is embarked upon. More guests arrive: Mrs Gadgett and Mrs Taylor (two of Mama's charity committee women), followed closely by Miss Phyllis Larkin. The latter has not brought Mother Larkin, she announces in hushed tones, as she has 'one of her heads'.

Lobelia talks and smiles and nods. She seems enervated by the company, though it is all Hyacinth can do to sit still and feign interest. Apart from Bethica, who is eyeing the seed cake speculatively, not a single visitor is anywhere near her age. And Bethica doesn't count – Hyacinth has hated her since Bethica tattled tales to Mama about her behaviour in Sunday School when they were younger.

Eventually, Lobelia sends her sister the signal that it is time to serve the refreshments. Hyacinth pours hot water from the kettle into the teapot, then fills the bone china cups that were never used during Mama's lifetime. To her embarrassment, she manages to slop tea in the Reverend Bittersplit's saucer, eliciting a shake of the stern clerical head and a murmured reminder of James 4: 24.

She hopes Lobelia hasn't seen, or there will be 'words' when the guests have gone. Hyacinth then hands round the cream, the sugar, the plate of biscuits and the cake, noting that Bethica takes the biggest piece.

When all are served, Reverend Bittersplit raises a clerical hand.

"Let us pray," he intones.

The guests bow their heads. His voice rising and falling, Reverend Bittersplit embarks upon a long prayer invoking the spirit of the deceased, pausing at her invaluable contribution made to Good Works, before passing on to the Sinfulness of Mankind and the Heathen Nature of the World in General.

Hyacinth thinks: The tea will be getting cold.

Finally, the long prayer draws to an end. Everybody falls upon the refreshments as if they are manna in the wilderness. Hyacinth ends up sitting next to Phyllis Larkin, who speaks to her in hushed tones about the problems associated with some knitting pattern she is following.

Hyacinth smiles and nods. She does not knit, but it has been drummed into her from an early age that is part of her duty to care, to be interested, no matter what her feelings may be. Her main feelings towards Phyllis are pity. Mother Larkin is known to be an even more exacting martinet in her requirements than Mama was.

Were this not enough, Phyllis' two brothers have left home and started families of their own, so the entire duties of care fall upon their sister. She has never married, and now, judging by the worn-out, cowed look of her, she never will.

The clock ticks very slowly.

By the time the last guest departs, Hyacinth is so exhausted from being polite that she could lie down on the Turkey carpet and fall asleep. There is not a scrap of food left, and she has been so busy attending to the guests' needs that she has not eaten a thing.

"A very successful afternoon. Mama would have been pleased, I think," Lobelia declares. She glances round the room. "There is a great deal of clearing up to be done," she observes. "I think you had better make a start at once. I am going upstairs to lie down for a while. The afternoon has really taken it out of me, I fear."

"Why is it always my job to clear up?" Hyacinth asks mutinously. "Why can't you help me? Why must I do everything?"

Lobelia breathes in sharply. Her expression changes in an instant from limpid exhaustion to ice-cold fury. She strides quickly across the room, bringing her face to within an inch or so of her sister's.

"Because," she hisses fiercely, "I did not let go of the perambulator handle. I did not break Mama's heart."

She glares at Hyacinth, then, after allowing a few seconds for her words to hit home, she flounces out of the room, banging the door behind her.

****

Meanwhile Stride and Cully have arrived outside Peter Robinson's department store, its plate glass windows elaborately arranged with an assortment of brightly-coloured Spring shawls. A row of feathered straw bonnets perch temptingly on wooden stands.

Stride eyes them balefully.

"Fripperies and fal-de-lals," he says scornfully.

"Seems to be popular enough," Cully indicates the number of coaches outside the store, awaiting their owners' return. There is also a group of big-calved footmen loitering by the entrance. They are smoking, and passing the time of day by eyeing up the women walking by.

"Some people nowadays have more money than sense," Stride mutters.

He elbows his way through, and approaches the gilded doors.

"And now to find the gentleman in question. If he is a gentleman. Either way, we have some questions."

If Mr Francis Frye is surprised to be unexpectedly accosted on the shop floor in the middle of a busy afternoon by two plain-clothes detectives from the metropolitan police, he shows no sign of it. A big man in his early forties, he exudes confidence, his broad shoulders straining the seams of his well-cut black suit, his hair and moustache well oiled.

He regards Stride and Cully's approach with an air of detached curiosity. His stance says: *I am master of all I survey*. Behind the long wooden counter, a couple of pretty shop girls steal curious glances and whisper to each other. He cuts them a quick glance. Master of them also, the glance suggests. Yes, indeed.

"Gentlemen – how may I be of assistance?" he asks, after Stride has introduced them.

His speech has the careful intonation of somebody who has risen from a slightly lower class and is working hard not to slide back down.

"We'd like to ask you some questions, if we may," Stride says.

"Oh? What sort of questions?"

Stride glances round.

"Perhaps we might go somewhere more private?" he suggests.

"Naow gentlemen, I'm sure my conscience is as pure and clean as them girls' pretty faces," the man says, smirking at his female audience, who colour up and titter.

"As you please, sir." Stride shrugs indifferently.

Pauses.

"Violet Manning," he says.

He studies Frye's face without appearing to do so.

"What about her?"

"Ah. You knew the young lady?"

"She used to work in the sewing-room. Got chucked out for stealing cloth."

"Stealing, eh?" Stride says slowly, never taking his eyes of Frye's face. "Oh dear. Oh dear. From what I gather, she didn't seem like the sort of girl to steal."

"Well, she must've been. Mrs Locuster found some cloth in her bag."

"I see. Doesn't mean she stole it though," Stride says, his gaze now transferred to a point just beyond the big man's left shoulder. "Somebody could easily have put it there. Somebody who wanted her out of a job and out of their lives. For whatever reason."

Concern leaks into Frye's face.

"Listen," he says, lowering his voice, "whatever the little bitch told you, it ain't true."

"No, sir? And what do you think 'the little bitch' told us that isn't true?" Stride's expression is a perfect study in unreadability.

"I'll have you know she threw herself at me. I never gave her any encouragement. I'm a happily married man. She knew that perfickly well."

"Did she, sir?"

Frye frowns. "Look, I don't see what this is all about, inspector. I haven't clapped eyes on the girl since she left."

"And you're not likely to now," Stride cuts in. "Violet Manning is dead. Brutally murdered sometime last Wednesday night. Just a stone's throw from this shop."

The colour drains from Frye's face.

"Now you look here, officer," he blusters. "You can't pin this on me. I was at 'ome. Ask the wife. Never stirred from my own fireside all night."

"Alright, we shall ask her. Make a note of that, Detective Sergeant Cully, if you would."

Cully makes an elaborate play of getting out a notebook. He writes down: *I was at home all night ... ask the wife,*" deliberately repeating the words out loud as he writes.

Several passing customers pause and regard the trio curiously.

"Look, I don't know what your game is," Frye hisses in a furious undertone, "but I'm telling you fair and square, as God is my witness, I never laid a finger on that girl from the moment she walked out of the shop."

"No?" Stride's words crack like a whip. "But you laid more than a finger on her before, didn't you? According to our police surgeon, Miss Manning was two months gone with child when she died. And her best friend says she wasn't keeping company with anybody. So it doesn't take a mathematical genius to work it out. Does it? Sir?"

"Maybe we should ask the gentleman's wife?" Cully suggests innocently.

Frye staggers back, all the bluster and bravado leaked away.

"Alright, so maybe I may have ... only the once, mind ... but she wanted it as much as I did, and I never killed her. Never. You have to believe me."

Stride gives him a long hard stare that goes slightly beyond the comfort zone.

"Actually, sir, I don't have to believe you. But we shall leave it for now. We will be checking up on your alibi. And we may wish to question you further upon this matter."

"Sadly, Miss Manning has no family, so her friend will have to take up a subscription to pay for the funeral," Cully remarks, to nobody in particular.

A couple of meaningful seconds slink by.

Then Frye digs in his waistcoat pocket and produces a half-sovereign. He thrusts it at him.

"Here," he mutters, "take it. Be damned with the whole rotten business. I wish I'd never set eyes on the girl."

Stride and Cully make their way back onto the street.

"Charming man," Stride remarks. "Makes me even less keen to patronise his store."

Cully pats his pocket.

"At least Miss Benet will be able to bury her friend decently now," he says.

Stride gives him an amused glance.

"Taken a shine to young Miss Benet, Jack?"

Cully shakes his head.

"Certainly not. I'm just sorry for her situation. It seems hard for a young woman of decent class to have to make her own way in the world."

"She isn't the first, and she won't be the last," Stride remarks. "And from what you've told me, she appears to be a young lady who is very well able to take care of herself."

Cully says nothing in reply. But as he threads his way through the crowded shopping thoroughfare, he cannot help recalling a pair of dark brown eyes with gold flecks, the colour of Autumn leaves, fringed by thick black lashes. And the gentle pressure of a small hand upon his arm.

****

The detective division of London's Metropolitan Police was set up to provide a dedicated team of professional men to investigate crimes committed in the Metropolitan area.

Now, four days after the gruesome murder of Violet Manning, two of the division's finest are cudgelling their brains to make sense of this particular crime.

They are reluctant to admit, even in the privacy of Stride's office, that they do not have a thing to go on. Mr Francis Frye's bad-tempered shrew of a wife has been visited, has been closely questioned, and has agreed that her husband was at home on the night of the murder, why do you need to know, officer?

Both men are fervently hoping Frye's life will be a little less pleasant as a result of their visit and the information they had 'accidentally' let slip. They have also been round to the tiny attic room where Violet Manning eked out her last days, and picked over her few possessions in search of anything that might link her to her killer.

It had not been a happy occasion. Emily Benet had stood in the doorway, white-faced and silent, watching their every move intently, as if the room needed chaperoning. The only time her face had broken into a wan smile was when Cully handed over the half-sovereign, telling her it had come from a special police fund kept for occasions such as this.

Since then, nothing.

"All the lurid stories in the newspapers, and still nobody has come forward with any evidence," Stride complains.

"I'm not sure the sort of people who would know anything about it read the newspapers," Cully says. "Or read, full stop," he adds in an undertone.

"You hardly have to read the trash," Stride counters, "the newspaper sellers have been full of it. Everywhere I go, small boys bawl at me about *Ghastly Murder* and *Dreadful Strangling* and *Baffled Detectives*. It's as much as I can do not to throttle them."

Stride taps the desk with the blunt end of a pencil. He has seen many murders in his time at the Yard, each horrific in its own way, but there is something about this particular one that disquiets him. It seems both random and ritualistic at the same time. Disquiets, he thinks, that is the word.

"Was it just a case of mistaken identity?" he wonders aloud. "She was in the wrong place at the wrong time?"

Cully shakes his head.

"Impossible to tell on such little evidence."

"Motive, then," Stride says. "Can we determine a motive at this stage? Because after we've eliminated robbery and rape as possible motives, we've got very little to go on."

Again, Cully shakes his head.

"Perhaps we just have to bide our time and hope something will happen," he remarks.

"Yes," Stride says grimly. "That's exactly what I'm afraid of."

****

London at night. A strange entrancing place, a parallel existence to the daylight world. A city of gaslight, redrawn in lines of artificial light. It bewitches and seduces, bestowing a different temporality of light and blind shadow. A place given over to the imagination. A place to dread, and a place to dream.

And here, a few days later, is Mrs Witchard's lodger. His coat collar is turned up, his hat pulled well down over his face. He stands in the shadows of a shop doorway, out of the gaze of the lamplight's searching eye, studying the late- night shoppers, the revellers and flâneurs, that saunter up and down Regent Street without a care in the world.

Suddenly he starts. He feels a shock like an electric current shoot through his body. She is there. Right in front of him. Parading bold as brass with the rest of the idle crowd. She passes by without noticing him. It is her. He recognises that face, all passion and virtue. Her hair which seems to absorb all the light, yet radiates it back like gold.

He squeezes his eyes shut, remembering it all. Her voice, her soft skin, the way her eyes darkened as he entered her, her false declarations of love. Followed by broken promises, threadbare excuses, missed meetings, until finally the unanswered letters and the closed door.

The monstrousness of rejection.

It was hundreds of years ago. It was yesterday. Everything about her was impossible – except for his love, which was so great, so overpowering, that it could never have been satisfied.

A voice in his head tells him what will happen, how it will happen. He breathes in. Nobody will find me, he thinks, nobody will ever know my secret. He feels the adrenaline circulating through him, bright as mercury. The sense of being invincible. He walks faster. Losing your life is not the worst thing. The worse thing is to lose your reason for living.

****

Emily Benet opens her eyes. It is early morning. Primrose-pale spring sunshine filters through the thin curtains. For a moment she lies still, warm and cosy. Then her eyes well up. It is always like this. First thing in the morning and last thing at night she thinks about her friend, and the heartache returns and the tears flow.

It had been high summer when she and Violet arrived in London. Hot day followed by hot day. Or so it seems, looking back. They were always outside, walking arm in arm, gawping at the marvellous sights and sounds of the great city. They'd visit the bazaars, examining the dresses, turning them inside out to criticise the stitching, commenting on the poor-quality lace. "One day, we shall be famous for our beautiful dresses," Violet had said. "We shall have great lords and ladies waiting in their carriages outside our shop door. You'll see, Em."

She and Violet. Sharing a cake, dipping their fingers into a paper cone, licking off the cream as they told each other stories of the great future that lay ahead of them. She and Violet running through the park, hats blowing off, ignoring the scandalised glances of the portly matrons and snooty servant girls. She and Violet waltzing along the pavement in the summer rain, blinking the drops out of their eyes. A time to laugh, and a time to dance. She cannot understand how it is possible to feel this much pain and still go on living.

Emily gets up. She pours water from a jug into a basin and washes her face. One day, perhaps there will be a time to laugh and a time to dance again. Now it is a time to weep and a time to mourn. She takes down the plain black dress hanging from the curtain rail, and prepares for the ordeal ahead of her.

****

There is precious little laughter taking place at the headquarters of the detective division either. A second young woman's body has been found in an alleyway off Regent Street in the early hours of the morning. News of this arrives in the form of a night constable's report, placed on Detective Inspector Stride's desk first thing.

Now Stride is hastening towards the scene of the crime. This is precisely what he hoped would not happen. A one-off murder is bad enough. Two murders in almost the same vicinity can't be so easily dismissed.

He enters the alleyway, encountering familiar smells of bad drains and poverty and damp. A young woman's body is propped against the wall. She could have been asleep, but for the telltale gaping throat, the dark spilling stain on the front of her clothes.

Two constables lean against the wall opposite, smoking. Their faces are chalk-white.

"Put them out," Stride commands abruptly.

He stares at the slumped body, remembering what he was told by his boss when he first joined the detective division from the rank and file. What separates a good detective from a mediocre one is his ability to see and deduce from what is in front of him, and not make assumptions based on what isn't.

So, he thinks. *What do we have here?*

Young woman, possibly early twenties. Fair hair. Plainly dressed, which eliminates one group of young women. Worn shoes. No gloves, no wedding ring. She must have been placed against the wall: her bonnet is still on her head. If she'd fallen, it would have come off. So, what does that say about the bastard who did it?

He turns to the constables, "Who found the body?"

"Local drunk. On his way home. Turned in to have a piss. Frightened him stone cold sober."

Stride runs his eyes along the high brickworked sides of the alleyway.

"And this alley leads where?"

"Angel Court. Row of tenements, mainly rented. Families and home-workers. We're making enquiries. So far, nobody heard anything or saw anybody."

Stride is not surprised. In his experience, when something like this happens, people keep their heads down and their mouths shut. The police are still not trusted or liked. Co-operate and you could be cold-shouldered. Or worse.

"Keep asking," he says. "Get a constable on each entry point. Stop everybody who uses this as a cut-through. If she's local, someone might know who she is and where she lived."

He takes another long look round, committing as much as he can to visual memory. Then he makes a series of detailed notes. He intends to compare the notes with Jack Cully's notes from the previous murder, although he has a sinking feeling in his gut that they will say exactly the same thing. As will the police surgeon.

They have a replicate murder. He had hoped, prayed it would not happen. Sadly, that ship has sailed. A headache like an iron hoop is tightening around his forehead as he makes his way back to Scotland Yard.

A few hours later Stride and Cully hurry over to the mortuary. The body has recently been brought in and lies on the mortuary table, covered by a sheet.

"Ah gentlemen, there you are. Interesting ..." the police surgeon says happily, glancing up as they enter.

Stride wonders yet again why police surgeons always derive such lugubrious pleasure in their work. It seems as if the more grisly their task, the more delighted they are.

"Of course, I have only made a very preliminary examination of the body," the surgeon continues.

He lifts the lid of a rosewood case, revealing a fearsome set of medical instruments resting on a bed of red velvet.

"The superficial marks of death are remarkably similar to those of the young Manning woman."

He glances up at Stride.

"Same *modus operandi*."

Stride nods grimly. Another thing about police surgeons that gets his goat is their inclination to sprinkle any conversation with medical or Latin words. Stride's education involved a lot of pavement pounding. It was a classical education, but not in the same sense.

"Would you care to take a look?" the surgeon asks, bending down to peel back the sheet.

"It's fine; I believe you," Stride says abruptly, turning his face away.

The police surgeon regards him with an expression of wry amusement.

"Dear me. Too near your luncheon is it, detective inspector?"

Too near many things, Stride thinks.

The police surgeon lifts an ebony-handled knife from its velvet bed.

"I think you will find the murder weapon will resemble one of these. Which is again interesting, as these are specialist surgeon's instruments. Not, I would have thought, readily available to the *hoi-polloi* for purchase from their local cutler's.

"I may be wrong, of course," he continues, in a tone of voice that suggests he is pretty sure that he isn't, "but I venture to suggest that the perpetrator of these crimes is not a member of the low criminal classes. He has access to medical equipment and a detailed knowledge of anatomy."

Stride and Cully stare silently at the knife, as if willing it to speak.

"Well, if I can't interest you both in a little lesson in dissection, I may as well get on," the police surgeon's eyes swivel back to the box on the table.

"Yes, why don't you do that," Stride nods, tearing his fascinated gaze away from the shiny curved steel blade.

"You will receive my full report when I have finished. But I think it is safe to say that we are looking at the same perpetrator."

They return to Stride's office.

"I feared it the moment I saw her," Stride says gloomily. "So, you know what this'll mean? The vultures from the popular press will be gathering at our door once again."

Cully glances into the street where a small crowd is assembling outside the main entrance.

"I fear they are already gathering," he says. "I can spot Dandy Dick's waistcoat from here."

Stride grimaces.

"Well, they will have a long wait. The day I talk to the press is the day you can stew my boots and serve them up to me on a plate, with gravy," he says, reaching for his notebook. "Let's go out the back way. We need to find somebody to identify the poor young woman. That, at this precise moment, is slightly more important than dealing with Mr Richard Dandy, chief reporter on *The Inquirer*. Or his friends. Or his waistcoat."

****

London is changing. A constant shifting of register from old to new, from demolition to construction. There are attempts to make the city a rational place, building the new upon the chaos of the past. But the city is not predictable. Holes and corners remain that defy rationality, where the raw underside of a place that is old and familiar still exists, like a slippage between real and unreal.

Nowhere is that slippage more in evidence than in a dark and dusty shop just a stone's throw from Tottenham Court Road. It is hard to tell what exactly the shop specialises in, for the dusty windows are crammed with so many items, all jumbled together higgledy-piggledy.

Here are broken watches, brass candle-holders, a pair of lace gloves with a hole in one thumb, soiled buff boots, and a set of carpenter's tools. A tailcoat keeps company with some fire-irons, a battered straw bonnet consorts wantonly with some nankeen trousers.

However, a black-faced doll hanging in the window indicates to the passer-by the nature of the establishment. It is a dolly shop, an unlicensed pawnbroker, specialising in the sort of goods that the more regular pawnbrokers wouldn't touch.

This is the empire of Morbid Crevice, beloved spouse of Mrs Crevice and every bit as hard-faced and stony-hearted as she is. And here is the shop owner himself, emerging from the dimly-lit back room, wearing a rust-coloured suit and a sour expression.

He carries a wooden pole to lift down the shutters before opening up for business. Here too is Tonkin the shop boy, whose job it is to run errands, tidy the stock, and generally act as the recipient of Morbid Crevice's ill-temper.

Like the Foundling, Tonkin owes his former existence to the kindness of a charitable Hospital, upon whose steps he was discovered at a very early age. After a half-starved and frequently cuffed infancy, he moved on to the kindness of his current employer, to whom he was 'prenticed at ten years old. He has been with him for six years.

From Morbid Crevice, he also derives other fringe benefits: his accommodation (a bundle of rags under the counter), his clothing (which is made up of items that have been pawned but never redeemed), and whatever scraps of food are casually thrown his way.

Thus, on this particular day, Tonkin faces the vibrant world of business and commerce without breakfast, and wearing a rust-coloured jacket (several sizes too big and rather deficient in the button department). and a pair of trousers slightly too short in the leg.

He also wears boots that once saw better days and had matching laces. Tonkin has lost count of how many times he's been told how lucky he is and how grateful he ought to be. The telling is usually accompanied by a box on the ears to make sure he understands.

By mid-morning the steady stream of customers coming in to pawn their goods and chattels in order to buy enough food to survive the weekend, has trickled to a halt. Tonkin is dispatched on an errand. Clapping a battered top hat on his head, he ventures out into the teeming, bellowing, traffic-filled streets.

The noise is deafening. Hoofs and wheels strike granite slabs, drivers curse and shout as they force their way through, and the street vendors cry their wares in a mixture of sounds that seem to Tonkin to rise up above the blackened chimneys like strange music, backgrounded by an accompaniment of church bells chiming the half hour.

Glancing around for something interesting to stare at, Tonkin spies an undertaker's hearse pulled by two shiny horses. It is making slow but steady progress through the traffic, heading in the direction of St Pancras. The hearse is followed by a lone mourner: a young woman dressed in black.

Tonkin pauses, watching intently as the sad little procession passes. The young woman's face is almost luminous in its pallor. Her eyes are two inky smudges. Tonkin doffs his hat as the coffin goes by, noting how many other people have also stopped as a mark of respect. There is a murmur of sympathy but the young woman seems unaware of it. She follows on, holding her head erect, carrying her silent sorrow as if it were a badge of honour.

Tonkin waits until she is swallowed up in the swirling traffic. Then he goes about his business. It is the usual one: calling upon certain slum tenants who have not paid their rent. For as well as his shop, Mr Crevice is also a landlord. A landlord of the greedy, grasping, squeezing, farthing-extracting school, and woe betide any tenant unfortunate enough to fall into rent arrears.

Such a one has to face the wrath of Tonkin, who has been taught, at the end of a fist, the way to threaten and cajole money from hapless tenants. He also carries The

Ledger – a battered black-bound book in which all the rents, missed rents and general misdemeanours of the tenants are written down. Tonkin cannot read much, but he has seen the power of The Ledger on enough occasions to recognise its importance.

Slipping down a side passageway that runs between two houses and is so narrow that he is forced to walk sideways and move in a crablike manner, Tonkin arrives at a small square, surrounded on all sides by rickety tenement dwellings. It is euphemistically called Paradise Place.

The once flagged courtyard has now disintegrated into a thick slurry of greasy mud, dotted with heaps of rubble, broken furniture and the carcass of a dead dog. There are lines of grey washing strung on poles, and thin columns of smoke rise from blackened chimney pots into the leaden sky.

Tonkin mounts the worn stone step and bangs on the rickety door of number four, calling out loudly that he is here for the rent, and he won't go away until he has it, this being the greeting he has been taught to utter upon such an occasion. A couple of grubby pinafored children briefly look up from whatever they are doing, then turn away with an air of resigned indifference.

Number four is the home of the Claphams, a married couple with five children. After a deal of knocking and shouting, the door is reluctantly opened by a half-grown girl with a pinched face and hard eyes, who invites Tonkin to "Bugger off. T'ain't convenient."

At her back, a herd of smaller children stand and stare like stupefied sheep. Tonkin however, is practised in the art of gaining entry. He inserts a battered boot over the threshold, then leans hard against the door, forcing the girl back into the musty hallway.

"Where's yer Pa and Ma?" he asks.

"Gone for a jug o' beer," one of the little ones pipes up, to be instantly glared at by its big sister, who bids it to "Mind yer tongue or I'll pull it aht wiv red-hot pincers."

"Then I'll wait, h'if you don't mind."

Tonkin pushes past the children and enters the main living room, which, like most of the rooms in Paradise Place, has developed its own internal weather system. The walls are damp, and the fire in the grate has drawn off some of the moisture from the plaster, creating a small local fog. There is very little furniture, and no beds to be seen. From the evidence of the piles of rags, the family sleep about the room however best they can.

"Nice gaff," Tonkin says, folding his arms.

"Yeah, proper posh, innit?" the half-grown girl says. "Lives in the lap o' luxury, we does. Now why dontcher piss off and tell your boss we ain't got anythink more to give him, coz what we 'ad, we've pawned at his place, so he's already got the lot."

Tonkin stares into the tight, pinched little face of his adversary, and recognises a kindred spirit. Another follower of the rules of the street, which can be summed up in one word: survive.

"Look," he says, "S'pose you give me ..." he searches round the room for something, "them fire-irons," he says, his eyes lighting upon them.

"And if I do, how're we going to keep the fire going?"

"Oh, you'll fink of summat," Tonkin waves an arm airily.

He opens The Ledger.

"So, let's say – them fire-irons in lieu of a week's rent."

The girl rolls her eyes.

"I ain't going until I gets paid."

There is a pause. The girl stares at him. Then at the fire-irons.

"I'm a-waiting," Tonkin says, tapping his foot and raising a small cloud of dust.

"Just the poker then," the girl says finally. "Got to be worth a bit ... solid iron. My dad made it, when he was blacksmithing."

Tonkin nods. "Deal."

He helps himself to the poker. At the back of his mind, he is already working out the next stage of the trade: he will sell the poker to an ironmonger he knows, for the best price he can get. It will be more than the paltry sum he is here to squeeze out of the half-starved family.

He will give the rent money to Crevice, and pocket the profit. Fair's fair. The only wages he gets off his skinflint of a boss is the rough end of his tongue and the occasional blow.

"Pleasure doing business wiv yer," he says.

He heads for the door, shoving the younger children roughly out of the way.

"And don't forget, next lot o' rent's due in a week's time. Or I'll be back," he adds for good measure, as he slams the door behind him.

****

Meanwhile the re-entry of Lobelia and Hyacinth Clout back into respectable Christian society is proceeding apace. Here they sit in the dark oppressive parlour of the vicarage, with its skimpy carpet, faded wallpaper, and stern pictures of former clerical incumbents. They are attending the monthly meeting of the Ladies' Committee for the Charitable Relief of the Poor and Indigent of the Parish.

This was Mama's favourite committee. Indeed, before her final illness, she used to chair it. In her absence, and during that final illness, the chair was taken over by Bethica Bittersplit, but she has now relinquished the seat at the head of the table to Lobelia.

There is something vaguely familiar about Bethica today, Hyacinth thinks. She studies her covertly as she tries to work it out. Then she realises: it is the rather ugly brown woollen jacket Bethica is wearing. It used to belong to Mama. Hyacinth remembers packing it up along with the rest of her clothes for the Missionary barrel. It would appear that the missionaries did not require it.

So that is two disconcerting things, Hyacinth thinks, fiddling with her pencil. Bethica clad in Mama's jacket, and Lobelia sitting in Mama's chair. She catches Bethica's eye and receives a superior little smirk. She decides to ignore it and concentrate upon her sister instead.

And really, it is most remarkable – her sister's jowly, petulant expression and sharp, scolding voice recall the many committee meetings she has attended with her late and not much-lamented Mama.

"Hyacinth!" The querulous voice of her sister breaks into her reverie. "I have asked you twice to pass me the list of applicants. What is the matter with you this afternoon?"

Hyacinth fumbles for the applicant folder, drops it on the floor, bends down to retrieve it, knocks her bonnet askew.

"Oh bother!" she exclaims.

There is a shocked indrawing of breath from the assembled ladies. Lobelia's eyebrows shoot up almost to her hairline. She gives her sister Mama's Look. Suddenly Hyacinth is twelve years old again, standing outside the parlour door awaiting a scolding. Red-faced, she mutters an apology and sinks into her seat.

Lobelia opens the book and begins to read out the list. It is a very long list. So many poor and needy have applied for parish relief. As each case is read out, it is examined by the ladies, and its merits and demerits minutely dissected.

Time passes. Eventually, after much charitable relief has been discussed but little dispensed, there is a knock at the door. The Reverend Ezra Bittersplit glides in and is invited by Lobelia to close the meeting with prayer. As soon as the 'Amen' has echoed round the gathering, Lobelia and Bethica go into an earnest huddle in a corner. Hyacinth rises, and with an apologetic smile, hastens out of the room. She will have to answer for her untoward exodus later, but the sense of oppression she has felt during the meeting, which increased incrementally with the appearance of Bethica's father, is almost overwhelming. She makes her way to the churchyard and settles herself comfortably on her favourite bench in a corner under one of the yew trees.

Hyacinth leans back. The air is soft, and a little breeze fans her face. How pleasant it is to be on her own. She spends so little time on her own. She thinks back over the day. It has been a long day, piled on top of other long days. Hyacinth closes her eyes and lets the clouds of tiredness take her.

She is awoken abruptly by the crisp sound of footsteps on the gravel path. Opening her eyes, she sees Reverend Bittersplit stalking purposefully towards the church. A feeling of revulsion washes over her. Over the past year, since Mama died, she has come to realise that she simply cannot bear him.

The soft snaky voice hissing Bible verses at her. The big yellow vulpine teeth. The flecks of spittle that gather at the corners of his mouth when he towers in the pulpit every Sunday, berating the hapless congregation for their manifold and various sins and wickednesses.

Hyacinth ducks down behind the seat and folds herself up as small as she can. Peering covertly between the wooden slats, she watches until his black figure enters the porch. As soon as she hears the church door slam shut, she is on her feet and flying along the path towards the lych-gate, until, breathless and panting, she arrives on the other side. Here, as luck would have it, she encounters her stern-faced sister making her way home from the vicarage.

"Hyacinth?" Lobelia exclaims. "Where have you been? I was waiting for you in the hallway."

Hyacinth's heart is hammering in her chest, but she recollects herself enough to tell her sister that she has been visiting Mama's grave.

Lobelia's lips pinch tight shut.

"I just wanted to spend a few moments alone with her," Hyacinth lies.

"I see," Lobelia says tartly.

She hands over the heavy cloth bag containing the committee books. "Meanwhile I have had to carry these all the way. Despite my fragile condition."

It is an unspoken and accepted fact that Lobelia's health is and always has been precarious, although no medical authority has ever pronounced upon it. As Mama was, so Lobelia is. Meekly, Hyacinth shoulders the heavy dual burdens of bag and responsibility, and the two sisters make their way home in silence.

****

Meanwhile Emily Benet, having buried her best friend in the municipal cemetery, is also making her way home in silence. A pile of sewing awaits her at her place of work. Mrs Crevice has only allowed her to take time off on the understanding that she returns and makes it up by fulfilling her allotted tasks. Emily reckons she is unlikely to see her bed until after midnight.

She crosses the busy street, trying to recall how many candles remain in her drawer. She hears the boy who sells papers on the corner calling the early evening headlines. It sounds like the usual background noise – just one shrill voice amongst the cacophony that crowd daily into her ear. So at first, she does not really hear what he is saying. But then she does.

Time stands still.

Emily reaches into her underskirt pocket, where she has secreted a couple of coins. She had been going to buy herself something to eat, as she has missed the midday coffee and bread provided by the store. She knows now that she will not be hungry. She gives the boy fivepence, and takes a copy of the paper. The headline reads:

Slasher Strikes Again! Body of Second Victim Found!

The picture underneath shows a tall top-hatted man in a frock coat, large knife in one raised hand. He towers over a young woman who staggers back, her mouth opening in a silent scream. She looks nothing like Violet, apart from the fair hair, but suddenly Emily cannot breathe.

The noises of the street blur into one rhythmic sound that beats in her ear like a warning drum. She feels afraid, as she has never felt before. And cold, even though the sun is shining and the air is warm on her face.

Emily reaches her building and pounds up the stairs, pausing on the landing to catch her breath. She unlocks her door and throws herself onto the bed, clutching the newspaper to her bosom, as if it were precious and beloved.

Time passes, but Emily does not notice. She is lost in memories of happier days, feeling the footprints on her heart of laughing friendship and shared girlish dreams. She is finally roused by the sound of timid but persistent knocking at the door.

She rises. On the other side of the door she finds Little Fan – the latest recruit to the sewing room. She is the twelve-year-old sister of Annie Smith, one of the sharp-tongued pattern-cutters. Now she stands on the landing in the gathering twilight, wringing her hands, her face one big worry.

"Oh, there you are Miss! Mrs Crevice sended me. She says you has to come now!" she exclaims in one unbroken breath.

Emily feels her spirits plummet. She had quite forgotten her obligations to her employer. She reaches for her overall, sliding her arms through the holes and tying the side-ties. Little Fan shuffles her feet.

"Mrs Crevice is very vexed," she remarks, as Emily wraps her mantle around herself. "She says that Mrs Thorpe will be arrivin' for a fitting of her new black silk dress first thing tomorrow, and there ain't nobody but you can do the buttonholes as neat."

Emily forces a smile.

"Don't worry Little Fan. You found me, and now I am coming," she says. She picks up the newspaper. "Do you know what this is?"

" It's a noospaper innit. I can't read it though. Never learned."

Emily runs her finger under the headline.

"Another girl has been killed. Not two minutes away from here. The newspaper says she lived with her elderly crippled mother. They made trimming lace together. She only stepped out to get a breath of fresh air and deliver the latest order to a shop. It is a terrible thing to happen. The poor old mother has been taken to the workhouse."

Little Fan's eyes widen.

"We had all better take care," Emily says. "I have been thinking about it and I am going to speak to the others in the sewing-room. We must not go about on our own after dark. Not until the police have caught the killer and locked him up in prison."

They make their way down the creaky unlit stairs until they reach street level. Emily tucks Little Fan's arm under hers.

"You stay close to me," she says. "That way we'll both be safe."

Outside, day people are ceding the streets to night people – though given the area of the city, there is very little difference between the two. Nobody bothers them as they slip through the crowd. Their drab clothes indicate they have nothing to steal, their unpainted faces that they have nothing to sell.

Inside the basement workroom, the lighting is barely brighter than on the street. The dressmakers are bent over their sewing. Emily glances around but sees no Mrs Crevice looming in the gloom.

"She ain't here," Annie Smith says tartly.

Her eyes run over Emily's face and there is precious little sympathy in them. "Ain't going to miss her nice hot supper. She's put me in charge till she comes back, and she's left your work out for you. Buttons are on the table."

She gestures towards a sumptuous black silk dress hung on a rail. "You better get on," Annie Smith continues, "We're working our fingers to the bone. Sooner you get done, sooner we all finish for the night."

Emily lifts down the dress and spreads it face-down on the table. She threads up a needle with black thread and finds the first cut slit. It is like sewing buttonholes in the night sky. Her eyes quickly feel as if there were rings of fire behind them.

This morning she followed the cheap coffin containing the body of her best and only friend in the world to its final resting place in a common grave. Now she is here, straining her eyes to finish a dress for some rich society woman who has probably not known a day's suffering or loss in her whole life. She feels a pain in the place where only tears come from. But she must not cry; it will stain the silk.

****

There are also no tears being shed chez maison Crevice, where supper is being consumed. A nice plate of hot mutton chops and baked potato, washed down with a pint of porter, is rapidly making its way down the wizened throat of Morbid Crevice.

Mrs Crevice has had to fetch these delicate ingredients from the local cook shop and the Lamb & Sailor public house, as the small poky terraced property does not contain cooking facilities. Now she sits across the table, watching her lord and master eat. She does not participate in the feast, preferring less rich fare. But each to their own, and men need meat at the end of the working day.

Morbid Crevice works a piece of gristle out from between his yellow teeth and spits it onto the plate.

"You wanna have words with that butcher," he snaps. "Half of this is gristle and bone."

Mrs Crevice's thin lips fold in on themselves. She has had words with the butcher, the baker, the candlestick maker. It makes no difference. Even if she were supplied with the finest comestibles in the land, her picky husband would still find something to complain about. She decides to change the subject.

"I 'ad to give one of them gels a half-day to attend a funeral," she says.

"Why? T'isn't as if the dead'll care. And I thought you was busy."

"We are. But I 'ad my orders from management."

Morbid Crevice snorts derisively.

"Well, I 'ope you're going to make her work back the time," he says. "There's too much idleness going on with young people nowadays. Take that boy Tonkin – I sent him on an errand, should've only took him an hour, but he was gone most of the morning. Got a good beating when he came back though. That'll teach him."

"They won't let us beat the gels," Mrs Crevice observes, pulling a face.

"More's the pity. Nothing like a good whacking to show who's boss. And who ain't."

He slurps the last of the porter and pushes back from the table.

"Here, you can clear away now. I'm off out. Got to see a man about a bit of business."

Mrs Crevice piles up the plates, placing some leftover scraps on a separate plate which she will save for the boy's breakfast. In the distance, a church clock chimes the hour. Her eyes narrow. Just time to swill the pots, then she must hurry back to check on those lazy girls. Maybe she cannot beat them, but she has other ways of making their lives miserable. Oh yes.

Night wears on, until the hour arrives when the lingerers and malingerers, the whores in the doorways, the flâneurs on the footpaths have all left the gaslit fairyland of the bewitching streets. It is quiet. So quiet, that when something crashes against the window of Morbid Crevice's shop, the sound thunders like cannon fire, startling Tonkin awake from a beautiful dream of hot sausages and gravy.

Scrambling to his feet, the boy trips and falls his way to the shuttered window. He hears laboured breathing, interspersed with low groans. Tonkin cautiously applies an eye to a crack in the shutter.

The dark figure of a man is standing outside. He shakes and sways, as if driven by some great internal force. Sodding drunk, Tonkin thinks. Crashing around in the middle of the night, waking up honest folk.

He is just about to return to his pallet of rags when the groans cease, to be replaced by a sobbing that turns swiftly to a wailing that is more animal than human. In the sound there is agony, dark tortured places and nameless terrors. The hairs on the back of Tonkin's neck stand on end. He has never heard anything like it.

Then, to his horror, the man turns towards him and starts beating his head against the shutters. It is too much for Tonkin, who legs it back to his bed, pulling the ragged coverlet over his head so that he cannot see the agonised expression, and pressing his hands against his ears to block out the dreadful noise. *Christ allbloodymighty*, he mutters, *I wouldn't like to be thinking wot you're thinking.*

****

Stars and stillness give way to a pale-primrose dawn. It tiptoes on soft rosy feet over the still sleeping city, pausing momentarily on its journey at the lodging house of Mrs Lucinda Witchard, widow of the late Enoch Witchard, piano factory owner. Here, the Foundling, who has been up before the dawn laying fires, is now busy laying the table with the cheap cloudy cutlery for the lodgers' breakfasts.

The air is redolent with the smell of fatty bacon and burning bread as Mrs Witchard exercises her culinary skills in the poky basement kitchen. On the first and second floors, the lodgers are preparing for the working day ahead, and steeling themselves for the first ordeal, shortly to take place in the poky dining room.

Up on the third floor, however, Mrs Witchard's new lodger has other things than breakfast on his mind. He has awoken with a confused recollection of events the night before, thinking he can smell death and bloodshed on the sheets.

A glance in the cracked looking-glass reveals that whatever happened last night, he cannot go into his place of work today. There would be questions, to which he has no satisfactory answers. Also, he does not want to see the glass specimen jars of hare lips, monstrous foetuses, haemorrhoids, hernias and oddly-shaped genitals.

He has cleaned off as much of the blood as he can with a cloth, which he has burned in the grate. The smell of food nauseates him. The prospect of facing his fellow lodgers, let alone his fellow man, appals him. He glances at the clock on the mantelpiece. It is time to seek solace in the only way he knows.

Reaching for and uncorking the small bottle, he dips in an empty syringe, withdrawing it full of reddish-brown liquid. He is not looking for a means to escape the past, he reminds himself, as he tightens a leather strap around his upper arm. That obsessive want of something was there before she appeared.

He inserts the needle into the vein that winds like a blue snake under his skin. He has wonderful thick veins. He remembers someone telling him that. The metal slides through the skin. He injects the drug into his bloodstream. His eyelids half-close and his mouth half-opens. He has that feeling he experiences from time to time that everything is floating, and nothing could happen to him. His head falls back. Oblivion and darkness take him.

****

In 1861 the Victorian General Postal Service was run like a well-oiled machine. From its stately porticoed headquarters in St Martin's-le-Grand, urgent letters, packages, missives of love and newspapers were sorted, bagged and dispatched by train all over the country.

Closer to home, hourly deliveries ensured that from 7.30 in the morning to 6.30 at night letters fell like showers of ladybirds through city letterboxes. As well as letters and parcels, the postal service carried more esoteric items such as cakes, leeches, mosses and manure.

And now, a scarlet-coated postman is stopping outside the Islington town house which is home to Lobelia and Hyacinth Clout. In his hand, he carries a letter. It does not appear to have the customary black border, so it is clearly not a Mama-related missive. Could it be a letter of love? Clearly it is not a box of leeches.

Inside the house, Hyacinth, wearing a clean apron and a pair of household gloves, is busily dusting the parlour furniture. Later, she and her sister are to attend a meeting at the church hall of the Overseas Missionary Society for the Conversion of the African Heathen. The celebrated female philanthropist Mrs Eustacia Mullygrub is to speak. Lobelia is in a state of nervous collapse at the prospect, and has taken to her bed.

The clang of the letterbox brings Hyacinth into the hallway. She seizes the letter, peruses the superscript. Oh, miracle of miracles! It is addressed to her! She feels her heart start beating like a bird in a whalebone cage.

"Was that the postman?" comes a plaintive voice from above.

Hyacinth clutches her letter to her bosom.

"Yes, but it was nothing important. Just another of those advertisements."

"Not another one? Why must we be bothered with this rubbish? There should be a law about it. Such a waste of time and paper."

"Indeed," Hyacinth's eager fingers are already working their way into the envelope. "I shall put it on the kitchen fire."

"That is the best place for it. I think I should like a cup of weak tea and an arrowroot biscuit now," the temporary invalid cries.

But her words fall on deaf ears. For Hyacinth is already back in the morning room, perusing the contents of her letter.

Dear London Lady (the letter begins),

I reply to your letter, which has been passed on to me by the editor of the newspaper. I have read it with the most respectful attention. In placing my own letter in the newspaper, I hoped that nobody would answer through impertinent curiosity, but would regard the sentiments expressed worthy of serious consideration. Such seems to be the response of your letter, and I am therefore prepared to engage further in correspondence with you.

Let me therefore enlarge a little on my position. I am in my early forties, but hale and hearty notwithstanding. I have one daughter – a precious ewe lamb, who has lacked the tender ministrations of a mother's care for many years since the death of my beloved wife.

At present, I rent a substantial property in the Muswell Hill area, but may in the future purchase my own house where, should I find a respectable and sympathising companion willing to confide her happiness in one who is, I believe, qualified in every way to render the matrimonial state conducive to her well-being, I would be happy to settle down.

Before meeting and conversing with you, I should be pleased to receive your response to my letter. My caution in thus proceeding arises purely from the Christian duty I have for my little one, whose delicate nature and temperament must be shielded from the rough ways of the world. If you choose to reply, please be assured that my honour and secrecy may be relied upon.

Yours sincerely,
A Lonely Widower

Hyacinth reads the letter through several times. She has never received a letter from a man before, let alone a man she has never met, and she has absolutely no idea if this is how men write to women. She is also not sure how to respond. Indeed, she is not sure whether she ought to respond, whether it might not be better to forget the whole thing.

She is still puzzling over this when she hears footsteps on the stairs. Hastily folding up the letter, she stuffs it in her apron pocket just as her sister pushes open the morning room door.

"Did you not hear me?" Lobelia demands querulously. "I am parched and weary. I would have thought making a cup of tea was not beyond your capabilities."

"I have been busy cleaning the room," Hyacinth replies.

Lobelia eyes the duster in her sister's hand. Then she moves to the mantelpiece and slowly and deliberately runs her finger along the marble top.

"I haven't dusted the mantelpiece yet," Hyacinth says defensively.

"Slapdash and slipshod. Poor Mama, how she prided herself on her standards of cleanliness. How sad she would be to see the decline into slovenliness wrought since her parting from us."

"You could always help," Hyacinth says pointedly. "Or we might employ a maid. Part-time. I can't be expected to do everything on my own all the time."

There is a shocked silence.

"I wonder you can stand there and accuse me of negligence," Lobelia says indignantly, a bright spot of anger burning in each flaccid cheek. "Who nursed poor suffering Mama day and night? Who was her constant companion both in life and at the end of her life?"

"Only because she preferred you to me."

"Indeed, she did," Lobelia hisses. "And why was that, do you think? Why did she always refuse to have you anywhere near her?"

Hyacinth lowers her eyes, bites her lip.

Lobelia's eyes sweep round the room, this being the nearest she ever comes to domestic work.

"This is my house now. Mama left it to me in her Will. So, finish the cleaning. And when you have done, I should like a cup of tea and two arrowroot biscuits brought up to me on a tray. If it is not *too* much trouble?"

She flounces out, closing the door firmly behind her. Hyacinth retrieves the letter from her pocket and peruses the contents once more. 'Early forties' doesn't sound too bad. Especially if the gentleman is in good health – she has had quite enough of invalids. And sisters. And he has a child. She is fond of children. She likes teaching the little ones in Sunday School. From the tone of the letter, he sounds a respectable man. She decides she will reply after all.

Hyacinth completes her cleaning tasks in record time – skimps might be a better description, but let us not quibble. She then descends to the basement kitchen, where she prepares tea for Lobelia. While she waits for the water to boil, she mentally sketches out her response to *A Lonely Widower*.

Placing the tea and arrowroot biscuits onto a tray, she carries them upstairs to her suffering sister's bedroom – formerly Mama's room, which has now been transformed by the twin miracles of paper and paint. Entering the room, Hyacinth is struck once again by how light and pleasant it is in its new guise.

The windows face south, so that the room is filled with light, and the view over the small garden is delightful. It is just the sort of room she would choose for herself. Except that she has had no choice, and thus remains in the bedroom of their childhood, still with the nursery bars across the window.

"There you are at last," Lobelia says, raising herself up on the pillows.

"If you are indisposed, perhaps I should take a note round to the vicarage," Hyacinth suggests, placing the tray beside her.

Lobelia picks up one of the biscuits and demolishes it in two swift bites.

"You will do no such thing. It is not every day that we are honoured by the visit of such a celebrated philanthropist. I am sure I shall feel better shortly."

She regards Hyacinth disapprovingly.

"Do you not have tasks to continue?"

Hyacinth gets the message and leaves. But she does not continue her tasks. Instead she goes straight back to the morning room and opens the writing desk. She selects a piece of writing paper, frowns, stares into the distance for a few seconds, then dips her pen into the ink and writes:

Dear Lonely Widower,

I was pleased to receive your letter. I should like to reassure you that having read it, I regard your sentiments as worthy of serious consideration. I understand your caution regarding your daughter. Please be assured that I am extremely fond of children.

I have lived a very secluded and quiet life for several years, as I have been looking after my Mama, whom I nursed during her sad decline and final illness. Her death has prompted me to review my life and circumstances and to think about my future, which is why I decided to respond to your advertisement.

Yours sincerely,
London Lady

Hyacinth seals the envelope and addresses it to the newspaper. Then, feeling as if she is a character in one of the epistolary novels she borrows occasionally from the library, she slips furtively out of the house to post it before Lobelia gets up.

****

Afternoon arrives, bringing to the church Mrs Eustacia Mullygrub. She is accompanied by Miss Portia Mullygrub, eldest daughter and amanuensis. Together, they enter the church hall, where Mrs Mullygrub, a large woman wearing a variety of odd garments, a pair of spectacles on a silver chain, and an uncompromising hat, is conducted to the front of the hall and ensconced on the raised platform at the front of the church hall. From here she surveys her audience with a benign and earnest expression.

Miss Portia Mullygrub, who is in her early twenties, hovers in the foyer, greeting visitors as they come through the door and handing out tracts and pamphlets. The meeting is almost ready to begin when Hyacinth and Lobelia (who has staged a magnificent rally), arrive in the porch.

Graciously accepting a tract with a gloved hand but no eye contact, Lobelia sails down the centre aisle, acknowledging various church committee ladies with a graceful nod. Hyacinth bobs in her wake. They reach the front of the hall. There is a single unoccupied seat in the front row. It has clearly been saved by Bethica Bittersplit, who occupies the seat next door and whose sallow features light up when she spots Lobelia approaching.

Without giving her sister a second glance, Lobelia plonks herself down and fixes her eyes raptly upon the stage, where Reverend Bittersplit now rises and clears his throat. A hush falls on the assembled company. Hyacinth glances frantically round. There are no vacant seats anywhere. She has been left the last woman standing.

Humiliated, her cheeks aflame, she returns to the rear of the hall where Portia Mullygrub waits to attend upon any latecomers. It is clear from the expression on the young woman's face that she has witnessed Hyacinth's discomfiture.

"There are no more seats," Hyacinth says, by way of explanation.

Portia nods. Then, unexpectedly, she asks, "Do you really want one?"

Hyacinth's eyebrows lift in astonishment. She stares at Portia, noticing that her hair is carelessly bundled into a net, her bonnet lacks any form of trimming, and her dress has an aura of missionary barrel about it, being a little too tight and a lot too unfashionable.

"I have heard Ma's talk so many times, I could recite it in my sleep," Portia says. "If you like, I could recite it to you. Word for word. Shall I?"

There is something about the way she says this, and the tone of voice she uses, that suggests she is not saying it in a good way. The two young women eye each other speculatively.

"Do you always accompany your mother to these events?" Hyacinth asks.

"Mostly. Sometimes I stay at home. Do you always accompany yours?"

"Oh, that lady I was with is my sister. My Mama died last year."

Portia laughs bitterly.

"Well, Ma isn't going to die. Not for ever as far as I can see. Not while she has me to mind the little ones and write her letters and get Pa's supper ready for when he comes in. And yes, Miss, don't think I haven't seen you looking at my bonnet. I know exactly what you are thinking. It's a disgrace. And my dress is a disgrace too. And my shoes are a disgrace."

"Oh ... no ... please," Hyacinth stammers. "I was thinking nothing of the kind."

"Well then, you should've been. Because it is. And so am I."

And to Hyacinth's utter astonishment, the strange young woman suddenly pulls the bonnet off her head and flings it into the lobby.

Hyacinth rushes to retrieve the battered black object, which now has an added layer of dust to add to its lack of ton. She returns it to its owner, who is yanking at her hair as if she is trying to pull it out by the roots.

"I expect you have nice clothes, don't you, Miss? Silk and satin. Nothing out of the missionary barrel for you. Nothing that lets in the wet and the cold. And I expect you dine on chicken and lobster and jellies every day."

"Um ... I think there is tea in the small hall," Hyacinth suggests cautiously. "Would you like some?"

Portia rams the bonnet back onto her head. She half-opens the double doors, cocks her head to one side and listens.

"There's plenty of time. She has barely begun. And then there will be the questions of course. Thank you, a cup of tea would be lovely ... Miss?"

They exchange names, after which Hyacinth leads the way to the small hall, where a big silver urn is hissing gently on the gas ring. She settles the rather wild young lady in a chair. As she goes about making the tea, Hyacinth wonders whether, despite her new companion's strange behaviour, she might possibly have found a kindred spirit.

****

Sunset falls on castle walls, on place gate, on head of state. Stand in the shadow of this street lamp and you can watch it fall on a square four-storeyed building fronting the road. This is the Strand Union Workhouse in Cleveland Street, a place where the down and desperate, the poor and perishing are forced – by life, by fate, by circumstances, but never by their own choosing – to seek shelter.

A small queue is forming outside the gate, waiting for admission to the casual wards. Look closer. Amongst the shuffling, coughing, stoop-shouldered men and the cowering, weeping, white-faced women hiding their misery and their shame behind ragged shawls, you will see some familiar faces.

A young girl, her face pinched and raw, clutches the hands of two filthy children who stare up at her with bewildered expressions. A baby's face peeps out from a grubby blanket tied to her back. Another child clings to her dress and sobs.

Close by, an unshaven man in a greasy jacket supports a woman carrying a bundle. This is the Clapham family. Former tenants of number 4 Paradise Place, but now, like Milton's Adam and Eve, turned out of Paradise to fend for themselves in the cold hard world.

Eventually the gate is opened and the poor houseless wretches are bidden roughly to enter. They follow the porter across a rough paved yard, till they reach a two-storeyed building whose underground entrance is lit by a single window.

The family enter, lining up in front of a high wooden desk where the porter opens the Admissions book.

"Names?"

The man tells him.

"What are you?"

"Blacksmith, sometimes working casual on the docks," comes the reply.

"Where did you sleep last night?"

"Night Shelter at Marylebone."

The porter indicates a basket next to the desk. It is full of roughly-torn pieces of coarse bread.

"Take some," he says, as he unhitches a bunch of keys from the wall.

"Follow me."

The family are led through a series of dark passages, then across a dismal yard to a bare unlit room. Cold from stone flags seeps into their thin shoes.

"Woman and children in there," the porter says, pointing at a closed door.

The woman clings desperately to the man's arm.

"Come on, old gel," the man says, "it won't be for long. I'll go out and find work tomorrow, and we'll soon be on our feet again." But the hunch of his shoulders and the hopelessness in his voice belie his cheerful words.

The girl tugs at her skirt.

"C'mon Ma," she says. "Best not to linger, eh?"

The man gives the young girl a grateful look. She stares back, her eyes hard like stones. She isn't fooled. She knows that it is the end of the road for her family. She knows that her little brothers and sisters will be sent elsewhere; that her father will sink even further into drink, and her mother into despair. That is what always happens.

What she doesn't know is how she is going to get revenge on those who did this to them. Not yet. But she will.

****

The disappearance of Annie Smith from the pattern-cutting table next morning is first attributed to a beating from the man she lives with, who is known to be handy with his fists, then to a superfluity of the cheap gin that she likes to drink, known colloquially as Blue Ruin.

By nine o'clock, when Annie has still failed to put in an appearance, and no message has been delivered to explain her absence, Mrs Crevice's patience finally snaps.

"You, Miss Benet," she says, pointing at Emily, who is stitching lace onto a bodice, "Put down your work. I have an errand for you to run."

Obediently, Emily gets up and crosses the room, aware of the numerous pairs of watching eyes and listening ears that follow her progress.

Mrs Crevice hands her an envelope.

"Here is a note for Miss Smith. Take it round to her lodgings at once. It is the third time she has been late for work this month. It will be the last time, though."

Emily hurries from the room, glad for a chance to breathe fresh, or nearest approximate, air. She walks briskly along Regent Street, where parasols gleam and flash in the sunshine, and all is movement and colour. Turning right, she cuts through an alleyway and then another, and a few minutes later reaches the corner of Tottenham Court Road and Oxford Street. This is where Annie and her man rent two rooms above a grocer's shop.

To her surprise, there is a small crowd gathered outside the shop. From the murmuring and sombre demeanour of the crowd, it does not look as if free food is being given out.

"Is anything amiss?" Emily enquires of a group of women.

"Young woman lives above the grocer's over there has only gone and got herself murdered. They found her body first thing this morning."

Emily feels an icy comet's tail of fear run down her spine.

"And it weren't the waste of space she lives with what done it neither," a second woman interjects. "Because he was ratting over Wapping way with a group of men. Got a cast-iron alibi."

"See, the police are bringing her out now."

A blanket-covered body appears in the shop doorway, carried on a stretcher by two uniformed constables. A shawled woman follows them, her shoulders shaking with sobs. Little Fan, her face white, her eyes wide and terrified, clutches at her skirt.

A murmur of sympathy runs around the crowd, rising to a roar of anger as Detective Sergeant Jack Cully and another police officer quit the shop.

"Three gels!" A man shouts. "Three fine gels as did nobody any harm, all done to death! When are you going to catch their killer?"

"Couldn't catch a bloody cold!" the woman next to Emily cries. "Fucken useless, the lot of them! Shame on you all!"

Cully glances in her direction and for a split second his eyes meet Emily's. If he is surprised to see her standing in the crowd, he gives no sign, though she feels her cheeks redden in response. Next minute he is gone.

"Good riddance to bad rubbish!" the woman bawls after him. She spits on the ground.

Muttering, the crowd begins to disperse. Emily stares at the grocer's shop, where a queue of women is already forming to buy provisions. She shocked to the core of her being. First Violet, then the lace-making girl, now Annie. Who will be next?

She takes a few deep breaths to steady her nerves before making her way back to her place of work, where, in a shaking voice she informs Mrs Crevice that Annie will not now, or ever, be coming in to work.

****

Mid-day finds Detective Inspector Stride and Detective Sergeant Cully sharing a booth in Sally's Chop House, a dark, low-ceilinged place off Fleet Street, and Stride's favourite watering-hole.

Two plates of hot mutton chops and potato and two glasses of beer have been placed before them by the eponymous Sally himself, who now hovers discreetly in the background.

His lurking presence is not so much to check if everything is to their satisfaction, but to ensure that they do not linger a moment longer than necessary – because at the end of the day, although detectives don't query the bill, attempt to leave without paying, or steal the cutlery, they give off an unmistakable aura of policemen, which other customers find off-putting.

"Whores," Stride says, poking his potato with a fork. "Whores, I can understand. They pick your pocket, steal your wallet and you end up with a dose of the clap. But dressmakers?" He shakes his head. "What on earth is going on? Explain it to me if you can, Jack, because Christ knows, I'm whistling in the dark here. And remember what Robertson told us – he tried to cut their hearts out. All three of them. What kind of a monster are we looking for?"

Cully stares gloomily into his beer. The look on Emily Benet's face when she saw him, the shouted curses of her group of friends, still resonates. He does not like to admit that it has affected him. But it has. He pushes back his plate.

"All the murders took place in the same area," he says. "We know that a lot of dressmakers and home workers live there. It's close to the big department stores. Maybe it is just coincidence."

"And they work long hours, don't they," Stride adds thoughtfully. "Which means that they're out on the streets late. Coming and going, delivering orders. Not as streetwise as the whores, and not as likely to have a pimp or a mate to kick up a fuss.

"So, what is our man doing? Does he live in the area? Is he visiting a whore or a public house? There's something very unusual about his behaviour. I don't understand it. And I don't trust things I don't understand."

Stride forks in a final mouthful of potato.

"Right Jack, let's get going. I want to talk to the young woman's workmates. Let's see if they remember anything or saw anyone acting strangely last night."

****

Precious little dinner has been eaten in the sewing-room at Marshall & Snellgrove. The news of Annie Smith's horrific murder casts a pall of gloom. Not that she was particularly popular, but her death has diminished everybody.

The platter of bread and butter generously supplied by the management for the refreshment of the workers lies untouched on the side. Only the mugs of coffee have been gratefully accepted.

When Stride and Cully arrive at the department store, they find a group of girls standing around in the back alleyway, cradling their mugs. Mrs Crevice, in a rare gesture of humanity, has allowed those who wish to go outside for some fresh air to do so (briefly), in the hope that it will enervate them for the long afternoon ahead.

Among the group is Emily Benet, who colours up and lowers her eyes as the two detectives approach. Stride explains their presence, then asks them whether they have anything to tell the two detectives that might forward the investigation.

"You should call in at the Mother's Arms," one girl says. "That's where Annie and her man used to drink."

Stride makes a note.

"Ask at Mrs Tightly's in Golden Square," a second girl suggests. "She'd know if there were any strange men hanging around. Or one of her ... lodgers might have seen something." A quick knowing smile runs round the little group.

"And what about all of you?" Stride asks. "Has anyone been followed home? Or seen a stranger lurking on a street corner?"

Heads are shaken. Nobody has seen anything out of the ordinary. Stride and Cully search the young women's faces for signs of evasion. Nothing but the truth is reflected back.

"You must take very great care when you are out at night," Cully says earnestly. "Until we have caught this man, nobody is safe."

"Oh, we are already doing that, Mr Detective," the first girl says.

She slips her hand under her overalls and produces a pair of fearsome cutting-out shears.

"All the girls here will carry them now – it was Emily's idea."

Stride purses his mouth.

"After all, Mr Other Detective," she continues innocently, "you never know when you might be called upon to cut out a pattern, do you?"

Cully stifles a smile. Stride is just opening his mouth to make a remark about the danger of carrying sharp objects, even domestically-orientated ones like dressmaking scissors, when Mrs Crevice appears.

"Back to work, girls," she says briskly, clapping her hands.

The young women roll their eyes and follow her into the sewing-room. Stride signals to Cully that they are on their way.

Emily Benet lingers in the alley. She turns to face Cully.

"Earlier on ... I shouldn't like you to think I was ..." her voice trails off into embarrassed silence.

"No ... no, I didn't think anything by it."

She looks relieved.

"I did not know those women; I was only there because Annie had not come in and I was sent to find out why."

"Yes ... of course, I see."

Her brown eyes regard him steadily.

"I have every confidence in the police," she says. "If I can help you in any way to catch this evil person, then I will. My only friend perished at his hands."

"The best way you can help me is by staying safe," Cully says gently. "All of you," he adds hastily.

The two of them exchange a long look. Studying each other's faces. Reading behind the expressions. Unspoken words pass between them.

"Nevertheless," she says, lifting her chin, "I shall continue to keep my eyes and ears open. And if I discover anything, I shall let you know."

"And I shall be grateful for any information you can pass on," he says.

They stare at each other for a bit longer.

"Well, I must go," Jack Cully says at length.

They exchange shy smiles. Then Cully rejoins Stride, who is awaiting his arrival at the top of the alley with barely contained impatience.

****

There are very few brothels in 1861 London. There are, however, over five hundred *"houses where the proprietors overtly devote their establishments to the lodging and sometimes boarding of prostitutes only."* This statistic is applicable to just the Metropolitan area.

Mrs Desiderata Tightly's Rooms for Professional and Visiting Ladies is one such establishment. Set back from the main thoroughfare and accessed by a discreet side-passage, it favours the 'harmony by contrast' style of decorating. The parlour, which Stride and Cully have just entered, has bright yellow papered walls with violet border papers. There is a lot of dark wooden furniture, ornate mirrors and swagged striped drapes.

Mrs Tightly, who has risen from a gilt-legged crimson velvet chaise longue, seems to apply the same decorative rules to herself, having a thickly painted white face and a ringletted black wig.

"Gent'l'men," she says raspily, smoothing down a slightly soiled salmon-pink silk dress. "How can I be of assistance to two fine men like yerselves?"

Stride hands her his card. Mrs Tightly's carmined lips move slowly as she reads.

"I should like to talk to some of your ... lady lodgers," Stride says when sufficient reading time has passed.

Mrs Tightly studies him thoughtfully.

"Would yer now. Well, talkin' don't come cheap."

"Neither does murder," Stride cuts in.

Mrs Tightly's painted black eyebrows shoot up.

"Three young women have lost their lives not a stone's throw from your door," Stride tells her.

"So I heard. Not anybody living under my roof though."

"Not yet."

Mrs Tightly's small eyes narrow. "My lodgers are all respectable, I'll have you know. Highly respectable. They come with boney fido references."

There is a light knock at the parlour door, and a very brightly-bonnetted head is stuck round.

"Oi, Mrs T – 'ave you got any of them ... oh, sorry, didn't know you had com'p'ny."

Mrs Tightly beckons to the head's owner.

"This is Estelle, one of the young ladies wot lives with me. Estelle comes all the way from Paree."

Estelle slides into the room. Her dress is a couple of sizes too tight and a lot too revealing. She eyes the two detectives.

"I told yer Mrs T, I ain't doing threesomes," she mutters, her accent resonating of Poplar rather than Paris. "I can do the gents one at a time if yer wants."

"Well, I ain't askin' yer to do neither. These gents are from the police."

Estelle's face instantly closes like a pair of shutters.

"I wasn't there and if he says I woz, he's fucken lying in his sodding teef."

"Where weren't you?" Cully asks innocently, but Estelle is too smart to be caught out by that.

"I'm a respectable working girl, I am."

As this is a definition of 'respectable' which goes way beyond the normal understanding of the word, neither detective responds.

"The p'lice wants to know about them girls – the ones that was murdered," Mrs Tightly says.

Estelle shrugs. This is a risky movement, given the close-fitting nature of her attire.

"Wot you want ter know?"

"Have you seen anybody behaving oddly? Any strangers?" Stride asks.

Estelle gives a contemptuous laugh.

"Listen, Mr Whatever-Your-Name-Is, round here there ain't nothing BUT strangers. And as for behaving oddly, I could tell you things as would make your hair stand on end. No, I ain't seen nothing like what you wants to know. And if I did," she pauses, "I'd not go sticking my nose into someone else's business. Live and let live."

"Except that these innocent young women aren't living anymore," Cully puts in quietly.

Estelle turns to him.

"I heard as how they was all in the dressmaking business."

He nods.

"So not my fucken problem, is it?"

Stride sighs wearily.

"Are any more of your ... lodgers at home?" he asks.

Mrs Tightly shakes her head. The black ringlets bounce.

"If you or any of the ... lodgers ... see a man following a woman in the street, or dragging one into an alley, let me know," Stride indicates the card in her hand. "If you hear anybody bragging, boasting, mentioning a blade – pillow talk, whatever, let me know."

Mrs Tightly's expression could be interpreted in various ways. Stride chooses to view it as co-operative.

"That's all I wanted to say. We'll bid you both good afternoon, ladies," he says, putting on his hat.

As they leave, they hear the sound of a card being torn into two.

****

Meanwhile, in the basement kitchen in the semi-detached villa on the outskirts of New Camden Town, Mrs Lucinda Witchard, widow of the late Enoch Witchard, piano factory owner, is preparing supper.

It is stew night. Upon the greasy wooden table lies a heap of what might at one time have been parts of a recognisable animal, but are now a jumble of bruised flesh and whitish fat. Under the table sits Griselda, Mrs Witchard's fat cat, licking her paws, having just been given, and feasted upon, the best bits.

From the cold flagged scullery just off the kitchen, comes a scraping sound. The Foundling is acting as vegetable sous-chef. A wilting cabbage and some dry carrots will make up the remainder of the stew, and await her ministrations after she has dealt with the potatoes.

Mrs Witchard sets a pot of water on the hob to boil.

"Hurry up with those spuds, girl," she orders. The Foundling, whose hands are numb and blue with cold, scrapes even faster.

Upstairs on the third floor, Mrs Witchard's lodger sits in a bentwood chair and studies the dentition of the mastodon. Soon he has an exam in this very important subject, followed by another in botany, both subjects considered vital to his future career.

Faint odours of unpleasant cooking emanate from downstairs. They remind him that he has not eaten all day. He will need to get a meal inside him, even if it is only the vile slop he gets served here, before he meets up with the others. Drinking on an empty stomach is not advisable. Last time he tried, he ended up spewing the entire liquid contents of the evening into a gutter. Quite apart from the disgrace, it was a complete waste of money.

He closes the textbook and leans back. Tonight, he is going to go out and get very drunk, and everything will be normal and nobody will notice anything. It always surprises him, the way he can move through the night streets unnoticed, as if he is wearing a cloak of invisibility. By rights, he should have a black aura, or a chill – maybe even the stench of decay – radiating off him.

****

The Mother's Arms ably fills the description of 'local watering hole'. It is off the beaten track, being reached by a back lane, it has a scruffy, run-down appearance, and the landlord (allegedly) waters the beer.

Tonight, the regular clientele is augmented by an extra two: Detective Inspector Stride and Detective Sergeant Cully. Their presence is creating tension amongst the regulars, who sit hunched at their tables, noses buried in their drinks.

Despite wearing ordinary clothes and originating from the same class as many of the clientele, there is an indefinable air of difference about the two newcomers, and the male drinkers (it is largely men at this time of night) sense it. There is a space around the table where Stride and Cully are sitting. You cannot physically see it, but everybody knows it is there.

The atmosphere is such that Stride and Cully are reduced to speaking in low whispers, as every time they open their mouths the rest of the drinkers fall silent and appear to be leaning in to hear what is being said.

"Spoke to the landlord earlier," Stride murmurs, his eyes flicking to the powerfully-built man behind the bar, who eyes him back hostilely. "Usual response."

"Seen nothing, knows nothing, saying nothing?"

Stride nods gloomily.

"The newspapers are having a field day. Did you see the evening headlines? *'Slasher Strikes Again'*. I hate it when they start giving the bastards a nickname. Just makes them seem more important."

Cully takes a sup from his glass.

Stride pulls a crumpled edition of *The Inquirer* from his back pocket, flattens it and reads aloud: *'The murderer must be a perfect savage to inflict such dreadful mutilation on three defenceless women in such a way!'*

He pauses, looks around. Meets people's eyes briefly before they glance off awkwardly. He makes a big deal about folding the paper, then rises to his feet.

"Well, no point hanging around any longer."

He picks up his half-full glass and goes to the bar.

"And this beer tastes watered."

He heads for the door.

"We can only hope no more innocent young women fall victim tonight," he says meaningfully over his shoulder.

At which point the door is flung open from the outside and a group of very drunk young men topple into the bar. Laughing and waving cigars, they barge Stride and Cully out of the way, shouting to the landlord to set up the drinks. It is clear from his response that they are no strangers to the hostelry.

A second later, another reveller staggers through the door. He stands on the threshold, swaying, his eyes dark and unfocussed, his face corpse-white in the flickering uncertain lamplight. He seems barely aware of his surroundings.

His companions roar with laughter and grab hold of his arms, hauling him to the bar. Two hold him fast while a third pours drink down his helpless throat. Everybody starts counting down as coughing and spluttering, the man retches and spews.

Stride observes their antics sourly.

"Come on Jack, we're not going to find our man in here."

Muttering "Bloody students," he thrusts open the door and walks out into the dark, unlit lane. A few seconds later, Cully joins him.

****

It is a fine sunny Spring day and here is Portia Mullygrub, daughter of the celebrated female philanthropist Mrs Eustacia Mullygrub, out enjoying it. Or rather, here is Portia marching briskly along the street with a determined expression and a full perambulator.

Street vendors, pedestrians and sandwich-board men step aside at her purposeful approach. Itinerant musicians fall silent. Small child-beggars regard her open-mouthed as she sweeps by, chin in the air. Every now and then the perambulator's wheels hit a bump, causing the occupants to utter squeaks of protest.

They are ignored.

Across the road she goes, and enters St James's Park. Leaves rustle greenly above her head. Flowers lift their petalled faces to the sunshine. Cows and sheep graze upon the lush grass. It is an idyllic scene.

Portia and perambulator approach a bench by the lake. Someone is already sitting on it. They glance round at her approach. Portia applies the brake, lifts out the small Mullygrubs and places them upon the grass, where, uttering shrill cries of delight, they set off in pursuit of the hapless ducks.

"Well, here we are," she says, by way of greeting, to the occupant of the bench. "How green everything is. I dare say you are glad to escape from all the clever things you do, like mathematics, and embroidering firescreens, and speaking French, and playing the pianoforte."

She bites one of her bonnet strings.

"It must be wonderful to be educated. I can't do any of those clever things, of course. I can only write letters for Ma and keep house. I wonder you are not ashamed to be seen in public with me, I do really."

Hyacinth Clout (for it is indeed she) is about to respond when there is a splash. A small Mullygrub has fallen in the lake. They both jump up and rescue it. When order is restored, and the miscreant has been sat in a sunny patch to dry, they resume their seats.

"Ma is attending a meeting of the Society for Returning Young Women to Their Friends in the Country, so I expect there will be a lot of letter-writing to do when she returns," Portia remarks gloomily.

She begins feasting upon a new part of her bonnet string.

"Sometimes I think I shall never enjoy a normal life," she continues, and Hyacinth, who has so far been unable to get a word in edgeways, sees tears in her eyes. "And all I want is to have a nice home and a nice husband to share it with. But it is clear that is never going to happen in the near future. Or even in the far distant future either."

"Perhaps you will get married one day," Hyacinth ventures.

"I don't see how. I have been engaged for two years now, but what with the letters, and Pa, and the house to run, and the meals to get, and the children to mind, I cannot see how it is to be brought about."

"You are engaged?"

Portia sighs.

"I am, Miss Clout. His name is Trafalgar Moggs and if you were to meet him, you would think him the nicest man in the world. I'm sure I do. He is office manager for King & Co." She leans forward confidentially. "The business is actually owned by a young woman who inherited it, but Traffy runs it for her."

Hyacinth's eyes widen.

"A woman in business? How can that be?"

"Her uncle left it to her in his Will," Portia tells her. "Traffy has been instructing her in the ways of business. He says that if a Queen can run a country, why can't a woman run a company?"

"That is ... very modern."

"I think so, and it is exactly how he is."

She stares moodily across the lake.

"He has been so patient and kind and has waited so long. And I do want to make him happy."

"I hope with all my heart that you will be able to marry him soon," Hyacinth says.

Portia gives her a rare smile, showing how pretty she is.

"Thank you, Miss Clout. That means a great deal."

They sit in silence for a while admiring the view. Then Portia ties up her bonnet strings and rounds up the small Mullygrubs who have scattered across the park in search of adventure and excitement.

"We must go," she says. "I have left Cordelia at home in charge of the bigger ones, but she is not to be relied upon."

Hyacinth accompanies her to the park gates.

"Wouldn't you all like to come and have some tea and cakes?" she asks. "You have a long walk ahead of you."

For a moment, Portia seems tempted. Then she shakes her head.

"The children are covered with mud and grass and not fit to be seen in a public tea-room."

She grasps the handles of the perambulator firmly.

"It was kind of you to suggest it though. Perhaps some other time?"

"That would please me very much."

Portia Mullygrub sets off briskly. The word *"Cakes?"* comes floating back, uttered in a hopeful childish treble, followed a few seconds later by a dismal wail.

****

No cakes are being consumed by Detective Inspector Stride or by Jack Cully either. However, consumption of a sort is happening, in that Detective Inspector Stride is currently being consumed by rage.

A pile of letters has arrived in the lunchtime post all addressed to the detective division. Having opened them and laid them out on his desk, he is now staring at them in total disbelief.

"What the ....!" he splutters.

"It is very strange," Cully agrees.

Stride picks up one letter, written in red ink:

Dear Detectives
I had to laugh when I heard you was looking for me. You won't find me anywhere. I am not to be caught by the likes of you. Them whores had it coming. There will be more deaths before I am done, see if there ain't.
your 'fiend' (Ha Ha)
The Slasher

"Who on earth writes this stuff?" Stride demands, throwing the letter down and gesturing towards the others.

"I thought the letter pretending to come from his mother was rather amusing in parts," Cully remarks.

Stride quells him with a stony glare.

"THIS," he says angrily, stabbing a finger at his desk, "is ALL the fault of our beloved newspaper brethren. They gave him a name. They made him out to be some sort of celebrity. Now WE have to deal with the lunacy of a small section of the populace who think it is FUNNY to write crackpot letters to the police and waste our time."

Stride sweeps the letters off his desk in a dramatic gesture.

"Rubbish!" he exclaims. "Total and absolute RUBBISH!"

He reaches for his hat.

"Right Jack, I have had enough. We are going over to the offices of *The Inquirer* and we're going to put a stop to this nonsense once and for all."

"I thought you said you'd never talk to the press," Cully murmurs, but his words fall upon empty air.

****

Printing House Square, the location of Stride's nemesis, is reached via Ludgate Hill, where the shops are large, and stock silks and tempting Indian shawls. Halfway up the hill is a small gateway leading to a labyrinth of narrow, ill-paved streets that, at this time of day teem with stray dogs and gossiping women. Children monopolise every available strip of pavement with their hopscotch, thread-the-needle, shove-halfpenny and tipcat.

The air smells of second-hand fish, coal-dust, potato sacks, fruit, vegetables, the adjacent gasworks, and chemicals from nearby Apothecaries' Hall. Stride and Cully keep walking until they reach the square, with its quiet dingy-looking houses and clump of green trees. This is where the brain-pan of modern journalism has its headquarters.

The Inquirer is a hive of activity when the two detectives arrive. The lunchtime presses are busy, the air thrumming to the sound of giant rollers and the rhythm of complicated machinery. A porter takes Stride's card. A messenger leads the way into the interior of the building, where Stride demands brusquely to see the editor.

The editor, he is told by a spotty youth who looks as if he has just escaped from behind a school desk, is in an important meeting and cannot be disturbed. Stride's expression darkens. He plonks himself down on a bench and announces loudly that he will wait. Here. However long it takes. The youth sucks his lower lip, then scurries off into the bowels of the building.

A short while later he reappears, followed by a portly middle-aged man with a broad face and an energetic countenance. He is dressed in the finest broadcloth, with a spotless white linen shirt. A gold watch and chain, studs and spectacles complete the outfit. This is the editor. The King at the centre of his Court.

"Now then," says the vision, advancing upon them like a ship in full sail. "What's to do?"

Stride waves the bundle of letters.

"These," he says. "Received at Scotland Yard today. All pretending to come from 'The Slasher'. I presume you know who 'The Slasher' is? Since he seems to have derived his title from one of your journalists."

The editor peruses the letters thoughtfully.

"Jim," he says, beckoning to the youth. "Fetch Mr Dandy, would you? I think he's writing copy in the press room."

Jim darts off.

"Now, if you'll excuse me, gentlemen," the editor says, "Parliamentary business calls. I have an MP in my office waiting to go over his speech with me. Richard is your man on this matter. Bid you good day."

Stride mutters something. There is a pause. Then the youth comes back accompanied by the familiar and much-loathed Dandy Dick. The latter's face lights up at the sight of the two men.

"Why if it isn't the great Detective Inspector Leo Stride, Scotland Yard's finest," he crows. "Come to give us a scoop, have you? ***How I used the Police Benevolent Fund for nefarious purposes***? Haw haw."

Cully can almost hear Stride's teeth gritting.

"No," he snaps, "I have NOT."

He waves the letters under Dandy Dick's nose.

"See these? I wouldn't put it past you to have written these yourself! Here, read what 'The Slasher' – as you call him – has to say."

Dandy Dick takes the letters and gives them a contemptuous look.

"If I had written them, I'd've made a better fist of it," he sneers. "We've had letters from people claiming to be 'The Slasher' too. We get letters like those every day. Whenever there's a juicy murder, or a theft, The Man in the Street decides to put pen to paper admitting 'they done it'. We generally file them in the bin. Which is what I'd recommend you do, detective inspector."

Dandy Dick assumes an innocent expression.

"Is that all? Can I get on? Because if I don't file my story in the next half-hour, it won't make the early evening edition."

"No, it isn't all. I want your paper, and the rest of your foul reporter friends, to stop calling this man The Slasher," Stride says grimly. "You're making him out to be some sort of celebrity."

Dandy Dick thrusts his thumbs into his brightly striped waistcoat and grins maddeningly.

"No can do, I'm afraid, squire. Celebrity sells papers. And that's my job. Besides, it's too late: the name's already out there. And it seems to have stuck. Good luck detectives both, I hope you catch the villain .... eventually. If you do ... IF ... let me know and I'll get it on the front page. Maybe with a nice picture of you both."

And laughing merrily, Dandy Dick saunters off, leaving Stride to fume impotently with rage.

"See, Jack," he growls as they head back to the Yard, "Didn't I tell you never to speak to the Press?"

Jack Cully forbears to point out that not only did he tell him, and now has told him he told him, but he has just gone and broken his own advice. Sometimes silence is both golden and self-preservatory.

****

On their return, Stride and Cully spend some time collating various interview reports from local officers while trying to see an emerging pattern that is refusing to emerge. They are eventually interrupted by the desk constable who brings in a letter. This one, however, is not from another fake Slasher, but from someone claiming to know the identity of the real murderer.

Stride scans the scrawled missive, his eyes widening in disbelief as they travel down the page. Reaching the end, he passes the letter to Cully.

"Read this, Jack. According to our unnamed correspondent, if we are prepared to part with fifty guineas, he – I'm guessing it is a 'he' – will whisper the name, and we can then go our separate ways without another word."

Cully reads. Frowns.

"A box number? Strange."

"Guess which newspaper it's been sent from?"

"Ah. You think that it is related to our visit earlier?"

"I'm absolutely certain it is. We're being set up. The moment we respond, there'll be headlines in all the papers. *'Detectives offering monetary bribes as incentives for information'*. I'll be hauled up in front of the Home Secretary."

Stride's expression darkens.

"No, Mr Dandy Dick, we do not pay for information. What we might do, though, is slap you in handcuffs, preferably with all your colleagues watching, then accompany you to the station and lock you up overnight, after which we might accuse you of wasting police time. Did you notice anything about Mr Dandy's fingers this morning?"

Cully shakes his head.

"Primary rule of detection, Jack. Eyes first, second and third. I noticed they were stained with purple ink. There was a spot of purple ink on his waistcoat too," Stride says triumphantly.

"Same colour as the ink in the letter. So, what are you going to do?"

"Nothing, Jack. Nothing at all. For the time being. I shall file this away. And next time our Mr Dandy, in his role as speaking for *The Man in the Street,* chooses to write one of his scathing articles about the police or about me in his tawdry rag of a paper, I shall expose him for the rogue and scoundrel that he is."

He folds up the letter with an air of satisfaction and slips it into his desk drawer.

"Excellent. A good morning's work. I think I may celebrate this turn of events with a nice mutton chop and a glass of ale to wash it down. Would you care to accompany me to Sally's?"

****

Letters are also the focus of attention at the Islington town house of Lobelia and Hyacinth Clout, where earlier in the day Hyacinth returned from her outing to St James's Park to a light luncheon and a heavy scolding.

Her absence has meant that Lobelia has had to take charge of the meal – even though Hyacinth left a pot of soup on the stove and a loaf of bread and pat of new butter on the bread board.

Now the two sisters are seated opposite each other at the dining-room table.

"I do not think Mama would approve of your gadding about," Lobelia remarks.

"I was not gadding, I was meeting Miss Mullygrub, as I explained to you earlier," Hyacinth replies, wielding the bread-knife with a rather determined air. "I hardly think Mama would mind. After all, her mother has addressed the church upon charitable matters."

Lobelia sips soup from the side of her spoon.

"And anyway, I think it is a good thing to make new friends and acquaintances," Hyacinth continues.

Lobelia sets down her spoon with an air of deliberation. She folds her arms and regards her sister accusingly. Hyacinth feels her heart quail. She recognises The Look. Something unpleasant is about to be visited upon her.

"Mama was always very particular about social contacts," Lobelia says tartly. "She believed it was better to stick to one's own circle of acquaintances. That way, no unfortunate 'mistakes' could be made. People are frequently not what they seem, Hyacinth. You are too naive to understand that. Would your determination to disobey her wishes apply to epistolary acquaintances also?"

Hyacinth looks at her, puzzled.

Lobelia reaches into her pocket and pulls out a white envelope which she waves triumphantly in the air.

"A letter arrived for you this morning. It is not in a hand that I recognise."

Hyacinth jumps up and snatches the letter from her grasp. She checks the seal – it is unbroken.

"Who is writing to you, Hyacinth? Why have you not told me about it?"

"Because," Hyacinth says stoutly, "it is none of your business."

Her brain is in a ferment. She recognises the handwriting – it is that of the editor of the newspaper. Therefore, within the envelope must be a letter from Lonely Widower.

Lobelia eyes her coldly.

"It is indeed my business. Since Mama's death, everything in this house – which means you also – has passed into my charge. So, I repeat, who has written that letter?"

"It is from Mudie's Circulating Library," Hyacinth lies, the words issuing with a speed and fluency that surprise even her. "I requested a new book. Mr George Eliot's *Adam Bede*. It is, I gather, a very moral tale. The letter is undoubtedly from one of the staff advising me that it has arrived."

"Humph," Lobelia snorts. "I am not sure Mama would approve of all this novel-reading either. The Bible and Fordyce's Sermons are more suitable to a Christian young woman than novels, even if they are written by a male author."

"But I do read my Bible every night before retiring," Hyacinth says.

She spoons up the last of her soup.

"I have finished my luncheon, so I think I shall go up to my room. There are some drawers that need rearranging. I shall clear the table later."

Ignoring Lobelia's frown, Hyacinth pushes back her chair and scurries out. She will have to borrow a copy of *Adam Bede* (which she actually read before Christmas) and leave it prominently displayed somewhere in the house, so that her sister will believe she was telling the truth. But that is for later. Now she closes her bedroom door and with trembling fingers, opens the envelope.

Dear London Lady (she reads),

I was very pleased to receive and read your reply to my letter. After perusing the contents, I now wonder whether the time has come for us to meet. If this is agreeable to you, please let me know.

There are many pleasant and discreet small tea-rooms situated around London, where a light repast may be purchased by respectable individuals of both sexes without fear of bringing down any social opprobrium upon their heads.

If you are agreeable to meeting in this way, please send a response indicating your willingness. I shall then suggest a suitable venue.

Yours sincerely
Lonely Widower

Hyacinth breathes in sharply. So finally, she is to meet her unknown correspondent. Or could meet with him, if she chooses. She feels as if she stands at the threshold of her safe predictable world. One step – and she might enter a different world altogether. A world where marriage and a new life await.

Hyacinth rereads the letter carefully. She reminds herself that Portia Mullygrub, a young woman of a similar age, and not that much prettier, is engaged to be married. If Portia can be, then why cannot she?

Downstairs, the dining room door slams. A sure sign that Lobelia is in one of her moods. She hears heavy footsteps mount the stairs and quickly stuffs the letter under her pillow. As soon as she is quite sure her sister has retired to her room for the afternoon, she decides that she will sneak downstairs and pen her response to Lonely Widower. The dishes will just have to wait.

****

There is not a lot of waiting inside the dark and dusty dolly shop owned by Morbid Crevice. Indeed, business couldn't be brisker if it tried. This is because today is Friday, when rent is due. All day a steady stream of tenants has arrived at the counter with money or excuses. The former has been accepted, the latter have not.

Also entering the shop are people with items to pawn, it being the weekend, when food and fuel become slightly more necessitous than during the working week. And finally, those who pawned their Sunday clothes on the previous Monday arrive to reclaim them for the approaching Sunday. After which they will pawn them once again.

Such is the world of Morbid Crevice and Tonkin. All day long they have been grasping and squeezing and threatening and cajoling. Now it is the end of the day's trading, the ledger is closed, and the money is counted, bagged and locked away in the big iron safe.

"It has been a good day," Crevice says, boxing Tonkin's ears in celebration.

The apprentice scowls. He has been chivvied and shouted at all day. He has not been fed, and the warm coat he has been using as a blanket to cover himself at night has been redeemed and taken away by its owner.

"Put up the shutters, boy," Crevice commands.

Tonkin lifts the heavy wooden shutters and begins to slot them into place. He is so focused upon his rumbling stomach and his rebellious spirit that he does not notice the girl on the opposite pavement. Half in lamplight, half in shadow, she stands and watches the shop intently, like a cat outside a mouse hole.

But even if he did notice her, Tonkin wouldn't recognise her any more. Life in the Workhouse, even the short life she has endured, has exacted its pitiless toll, etching lines into her youthful face, paring away flesh to barely-covered bone.

The girl's eyes are daggers in the dark as she stares at the darkened, shuttered shop. Then, as Morbid Crevice appears from round the back, she spits on the ground and shakes her fist at him, before slipping into shadow and disappearing from sight.

****

London by night is a place of secrets and fantasy, where gas-lamps flicker like corpse-candles. Phantoms arrayed in satin and lace flit upon the sight, a gothic scene of lost souls. Mrs Witchard's lodger is hurrying back to his room. He has sought her all night, but this time he has had no luck. Sometimes he thought he caught a glimpse of her and his heart leaped, but when he drew closer, it turned out to be someone else. Somebody he did not recognise at all.

Once, sickened with longing and despair, he went into a bar, sat at a table with a drink. Nobody noticed him. Nobody wished him any harm. Sometimes that was not enough. A clock chimes midnight. A gust of wind catches the lamps; shadows dance across the pavement.

He quickens his pace, wondering whether the sleepers whose houses he passes shiver in their warm beds. Do they feel a chill entering at bone-marrow level, like a door unlocking itself on a cold night and suddenly blowing wide open?

Where does it come from, this evil that follows him, dogging his footsteps like a black cancer, like a thousand years of darkness formed in the depths of the earth? He wants to run from it, to trample it down. But he cannot. He is the monster. The monster is him. There is no longer any separation.

****

Death is unfortunate. Always. But not always for everyone. It is early morning, and the gas lamps have been extinguished. A clattering on the setted stones heralds a solitary cart, pulled by a solitary horse, driven by a solitary man wearing a long dark overcoat and a hat pulled well down over his forehead.

The cart stops at the back entrance of a large building in Gower Street. The driver descends and knocks. Eventually, the door is opened by a porter.

"Another one for you," the carter says laconically.

The porter's hands are thrust deep in his trousers pockets. He stares at the cart.

"Man or woman?" he asks.

"Old woman. Starved to death in the Workhouse."

The porter nods. The two men unload the cart of its tragic burden. Money changes hands. The carter whips up the horse. The relic of humanity, who in death barely weighs anything, is placed upon a table in the centre of a high-ceilinged, circular room. Round the sides runs a wooden gallery with wooden benches.

There are over a thousand medical students in London in the 1860s, and part of their anatomical education consists of dissecting corpses. Each student requires three bodies during the sixteen-month training. Two are for learning anatomy, the third for practising operating techniques.

As soon as it is light, the students attending this medical school will stream into the dissecting room and await the division of the body. Those given the torso will comment upon the way the bones protrude and are barely covered by the yellowy-white skin, so that each bone and its peculiarities can be clearly seen.

Those allocated the limbs will observe the lack of musculature and the tightly-stretched skin, together with the bent and twisted fingers. The rope-like veins on the backs of her hands, and the particular callousing of the first two fingers of the right hand, will be remarked upon, but no association will be made with the deceased's former life in an attic in Carnaby Street, or her profession as a lacemaker, or the recent tragic death of her daughter. For as far as the students are concerned, those are of no interest whatsoever.

****

Death has also brought good fortune to young dressmaker Emily Benet, in the form of an unexpected promotion. Mrs Crevice has raised her status from second hand to deputy superintendent. It is a popular move. Annie Smith, the former occupant of the post, was an abrasive character, never afraid to speak her mind or throw her weight around. Emily's quiet but determined personality has won her many friends and admirers amongst her co-workers. She is seen as fair and reasonable. And the sad loss of her best friend strikes a chord with all the girls. There is nothing like a tragic story to win people over.

Today, as part of her new-found elevation, she is starting off a new girl who has come in as an improver – having mastered the drudgery of the trade as an apprentice. Emily takes her over to the pattern-cutting table, where a roll of expensive crimson watered silk awaits.

"Innit beautiful," the girl sighs, brushing the material reverently with a forefinger.

"It is to be made up into a day dress," Emily tells her. "The pattern girls will lay on the papers and cut it out. Then you can chalk it and baste the bodice seams."

"It must be luvverly to be able to afford beautiful dresses," the girl says. "I never had more than one dress, and this is it what I'm wearing."

Emily consults the client book.

"Well, this dress is for a Mrs Lilith Marks, from Hampstead."

"Another rich bitch," one of the dressmakers adds, to be quelled by a quick warning shake of Emily's head, coupled with a significant sideways glance at the new girl.

"Well they are," the complainant persists. "I hate the Season. March to July, it's nothing but slave, slave, slave. They order their dresses the day before they're going out, and we have to slog away till gone midnight making them. Hampstead. I bet this Mrs Marks has never lifted a finger all her life. Rich husband to pay for her clothes. Servants to wait on her hand and foot, I don't doubt."

"Maybe so," Emily says equably. "But that doesn't mean we shouldn't make her a lovely dress. And whatever her life may be like, I'm sure she can't sew pleats and tucks as fine and neat as yours, Caro. Nobody can, can they?"

"Hmph," Caro says, but a small satisfied smile lurks at the corner of her mouth.

Emily turns back to the new girl.

"Mrs Crevice is up in the showroom at the moment, so why don't you go and watch the silk being cut up."

The girl nods, and heads for the cutting-out table, where the silk has just started to be rolled out.

Emily lowers her voice, "She's arrived from the provinces," she says to the truculent Caro. "Maybe we should watch our tongues."

"If you say so, Em," Caro shrugs, her needle flying in and out of her work. "Have you told her about The Slasher?"

Emily pulls a face.

"I will do. Soon as she's settled in."

"They ain't caught him yet," Caro says. "How many more of us is he going to kill before they do?"

"None of us," Emily says firmly. "Because we are taking care on the streets at night and looking out for one another."

"Why us though?" Caro's neighbour queries. "I mean, what have we done?"

Emily shakes her head with a sigh.

"I am not sure. But then I don't understand how anybody could have such hatred in their hearts in the first place."

"That's because you are a good person," Caro declares stoutly. "And I'm not the only one to think so, eh girls?" she adds slyly.

Emily colours up.

"A certain member of the detective police seems to agree with me, don't he, girls?"

There is a ripple of laughter, but it is friendly and well-meant.

"How many times has he called to walk you home? Wish I had someone like that to keep an eye on me," Caro's neighbour sighs. "Every time I leave my lodgings, I feel my heart quaking inside."

"I'm sure Detective Sergeant Cully is looking out for all our welfares," Emily says, but her blushing cheeks tell another story.

"Well, good luck to you, Em," Caro says. "None of us here would begrudge you a nice man. Not after what you've been through with your friend."

Emily lays her finger to her lips as the sewing room door opens and Mrs Crevice appears. Her eyes rake the room, seeking something to criticise. Finding nothing, she beckons Emily to her.

"Miss Benet, I find we have more orders for new ball gowns than can be fulfilled in normal working hours. I shall need you to organise some home workers for me."

Emily's heart sinks. Home working is generally hated, not just for the pittance paid, but for the encroachment into the young women's free time. Threepence an hour barely covers the cost of candles, and the extra workload leaves precious little time to get to the shops and buy food, let alone eat it.

"I need hardly mention," Mrs Crevice sniffs, "that given your new position, I shall expect you to set the example."

Emily bows her head. "I shall see what I can organise."

She picks up the order book and turns to the back page, where the names and addresses of the sewing-room employees are kept. Reminding herself that it will only be for a couple of months, she begins to work through the list, selecting those she hopes will take on extra sewing.

Not for the first time, Emily Benet thinks about her future and wonders whether she will ever stop plying her needle to make dresses for rich women who, as Caro suggested, never have to lift a finger. She remembers the dream she and Violet shared of having their own business one day.

Now the dream has gone, and there is nothing to replace it. She feels a sadness so profound that for a moment it threatens to overcome her. Then one of the pattern-cutters calls to her. Taking a deep breath, Emily straightens her shoulders and hurries over to see what is amiss.

****

Later that day, we find Hyacinth Clout walking determinedly towards an impressive building in New Oxford Street. The building, with its classical façade, is Mudie's Circulating Library, where, for an annual subscription of a guinea, members of the public may borrow the latest novel, poetry book, religious tract or scientific work.

Hyacinth enters the Temple of the Muses, as its founder Charles Edward Mudie liked to refer to it, and approaches one of the semicircular desks where books are exchanged and borrowed. The interior of the library has been deliberately designed to resemble the famous round Reading Room at the British Museum.

Hyacinth hands in her request. The assistant checks the shelves of volumes, then informs her that regrettably, *Adam Bede* is not currently available for loan as it is on loan to another borrower. Hyacinth's spirits sag slightly. The thing about a good lie is that it should always contain a modicum of truth.

She selects *The Mill on the Floss* instead and is just turning to leave, when she spots a familiar figure stalking purposefully towards the desk. It is Reverend Ezra Bittersplit. Oh horror! He carries a large volume under his arm – Hyacinth just knows it will contain dry boring sermons and commentaries. She tries to flee, but it is as if an invisible spotlight has fallen upon her. The Reverend spies her at once.

"Ah, Hyacinth," he says, giving her a disapproving look. "I see Satan finds work for idle hands ... Proverbs 23, verse 15."

Hyacinth hasn't got a clue what he is talking about. Fortunately, she does not have to wait long for enlightenment.

"Is not your sister attending a committee meeting of the London Truss Society for the Relief of the Hurt and Ruptured Poor this afternoon? I believe she is. But you, it seems are not attending. Instead here you are gadding about London."

Hyacinth bites back the overwhelming inclination to accuse him of the identical crime. Instead she takes a couple of steps back to create some distance between them. As always, Reverend Ezra is standing far too close for comfort. And his breath smells.

"Ah, and I see you have borrowed a book," he continues, "I hope that it is not some trashy modern novel. I believe you have heard my sermon on the subject of reading fiction and its unfortunate effects upon the female mind? What is the book you carry in your hand, pray?"

"It is called *The Mill on the Floss*," Hyacinth says. "It is by Mr George Eliot. It is a geographical book about rivers and ... mills."

Reverend Ezra shakes his head.

"Far, far better that it was a commentary on the best book of all: the Bible. In the Bible lies everything you, as a young woman, need to know. Matthew 6, verse 27."

"Oh, is that the time?" Hyacinth exclaims, glancing up at the clock on the wall. "I must go."

And she hurries away before he has time to make more deleterious remarks or quote more verses of scripture at her.

Horrible man, Hyacinth thinks, as she crosses the road. *His teeth are all yellow and crooked. And he spits when he talks.* She walks quickly towards Tottenham Court Road, where she intends catching an omnibus. Just on the corner, however, she comes across a cake shop, its windows filled with luscious buns, almond cakes and rout drops, all temptingly displayed upon a series of tiered stands.

Hyacinth pauses, her mouth drooling as she surveys the good things on offer. A momentary hesitation, then she enters the shop, the ting of the bell bringing the white-aproned baker from an inner recess.

She selects two ginger buns, a slice of cherry cake and a small cornucopia, which is filled with fresh whipped cream before being placed in a paper cone.

Hyacinth pays for her cakes and continues her walk. A feeling of reckless joy is surging up inside her. She is eating in the street – something Mama has always strictly forbidden. She is licking whipped cream off her ungloved fingers as if she were a common person, and she is consuming cakes bought in a shop.

And to cap it all, she has a brand-new novel in her bag. If the road to Hell is paved with fiction and baked goods, she is well on her way.

****

At the same time as Hyacinth is making her way home, a thin young man with a pale bony face, a pale bony nose and pale straw-coloured hair is making his way through a populous and poor neighbourhood just off Holborn.

He is carrying a small bunch of violets, recently purchased from a small violet seller and looks to all the world as if he is going a-wooing. Which indeed he is. The young man enters a street of broken paving stones, runny gutters, and houses that seem to absorb the light and reflect back only sooty gloom.

He pauses in front of one house that is even more run-down than its neighbours. A milk can hangs on the area railings, and a few pots of flowers wilt on the sill.

He knocks at the door. After a considerable wait, the door is opened by Portia Mullygrub, her hair even more tumbled. Her dress appears to be held together in places by pins. On her feet, she wears a pair of satin slippers, very down at heel.

"Oh, dear me, it's you!" she says.

The young man greets her affectionately.

"Where is Clinker?" he asks.

"Don't ask!" Portia groans. "She walked out this morning. Said she wasn't going to stay and be made a slave of. And who can blame her? And now Ma has gone off to a meeting of the Society for the Rescue of Boys Not Yet Convicted of Any Criminal Offence, even though I told her it was your half-day and we were going for a walk."

She grabs the sides of her hair and yanks it with both hands. From inside the house a long wailing cry uncoils itself.

"Oh no!" she exclaims. "The baby has fallen in the scuttle again!"

The young man follows Portia along a dusty hallway strewn with toys and waste paper. The wailing increases in volume as they enter the parlour, where a variety of small Mullygrubs are clustered around a coal-streaked baby.

A girl of some twelve years, who bears a distinct resemblance to her older sister in both expression and state of dress, is trying to remove the worst of the coal dust with the edge of her pinafore.

Portia yanks her hair a bit more, then scoops up the baby and bears it off to the kitchen for further ablutions. Meanwhile the young man is greeted rapturously by the small Mullygrubs, who demand that he play with them, and it is not long before a jolly game of puss-in-the-corner is taking place, in which

Portia and the newly-cleaned baby join upon their return.

Eventually Portia asks Cordelia, the twelve-year-old, to go and make some tea, which she is only too pleased to do. Barely has it been poured, however, when the front door blows open and the celebrated female philanthropist Mrs Eustacia Mullygrub hurries in. She is wearing the same formidable hat as last time we encountered her, though this time it is askew and her greying hair is escaping from its pins.

Mrs Mullygrub is carrying a great pile of papers, some of which slip from her grasp and drift to the floor, where they are seized upon by small Mullygrubs, who throw them up into the air with a cry of "Birdies!"

"Ah there you are at last, Portia," she declares, as if she has been impatiently awaiting her daughter's return, rather than the reverse. "Here, take these."

Portia rolls her eyes and places the papers on the already overflowing table. Her mother unlatches her bonnet strings and drops the bonnet onto the sofa. She pays no attention to the young man, nor to the children who appear to be invisible, despite the noise they are making.

"Such a lot of correspondence," she murmurs, sifting through the papers. "We shall probably be busy until nightfall. Where are my spectacles, Portia? Oh, here they are round my neck!"

"Ma, do you not see we have company?" Portia asks despairingly.

Mrs Mullygrub raises her head and peers over the top of the spectacles.

"Oh yes – good afternoon, young man. Are you here about one of the charities?"

"Ma, it is Traffy," Portia says exasperatedly. "Surely you recognise him?"

Her mother nods vaguely. More hairpins fall out.

"Delighted I'm sure. Now Portia, I must tear you away from your guest. We cannot think of our own amusement when there are so many poor and needy right on our doorstep."

A flush rises to Portia's cheeks.

"But Ma I told you: Traffy has a half-day."

"I'm sure he has," Mrs Mullygrub says equably. "And I wish him well in the enjoyment of it. But you do not, for you have letters to write."

Portia gives Trafalgar Moggs a glance of entreaty. He shrugs and shakes his head. Biting her lip, she walks towards the door.

"Well, I'm sure you won't object if I show him out," she says, the words coming thickly through unshed tears.

Without looking up, Mrs Mullygrub waves a condescending hand. She has already seated herself at the table, and is sorting the papers into piles.

"Tell Clinker to make some fresh tea, would you dear," she says. "This cup is stone cold."

Portia leads the way back into the hallway.

"She is impossible!" she bursts out, pulling at her hair.

"She is your mother," Trafalgar Moggs reminds her gently. "Never mind. It is of no account. I will have other half-days."

Portia gives him a despairing glance, and wrenches open the street door. The Ma-crossed lovers exchange their all too brief farewells. Then Portia shuts the door with a bang, after which she spends a few agonised minutes standing in the dusty hallway yanking at her hair until she is abruptly summoned back to the parlour to begin work.

****

It is a far cry from the mean dusty streets of Holborn to the beautiful Cremorne Pleasure Gardens with its trees, lush green lawns, its flower beds, and its fountains and statues. A pastoral retreat from the hustle and bustle of the city.

Here, for the price of a shilling, a family might enjoy a picnic, or watch the marionettes, or just stroll amongst the verdant parkland, breathing in clean air and listening to birdsong.

But it is at night that the Cremorne Pleasure Gardens comes into its own, and it is at night – tonight in fact – that a group of female shop assistants from one of the very upmarket West End department stores has arrived to see the glittering attractions.

Here they come along the illuminated river walk from Chelsea, laughing and chattering, pointing out to each other the orchestra playing in its brightly coloured fretted pagoda, the circular dancing platforms filled with rotating couples, and the discreet supper booths where a gentleman can entertain a lady ... discreetly.

And look – there are people actually making a night-time ascent in a balloon! How awfully exciting! And soon there will be fireworks, and spectacular entertainments. And the assistants won't go home until after midnight, even though they will regret it early next morning, when the alarm goes off in their dormitory high above the shopping floors.

They secure a table under the trees and on the edge of the dancing area, and order a cheap supper and a bottle of cheap champagne, which they share among them. And of course, it isn't long before their chatter and pretty faces and light girlish laughter attract the attention of a group of young bucks out for an evening's entertainment. And before you can say 'May I have the pleasure?' they are swept up onto the dance floor.

All but one. Seated alone at the table in the gaslit fairyland, she stares longingly at her workmates. She would love to join them on the dance floor, to feel a young man's arm encircling her waist, to be spun round to the joyous blaring of the music. But she is lame, has been lame from birth, and so such delights are denied her.

Inevitably, while some continue to polka and galop, a couple of the girls are led away by their partners to stroll down the tunnel of coloured lights leading to the Crystal Grotto, or any one of the gaslit groves, where kisses can be stolen and liberties taken. For manners and morals are left at the gate on a night out at the Cremorne Gardens, and thus it is not until the fireworks start, and all the girls hurry back to their table, that they discover their friend, the lame one, has disappeared.

At first it is assumed that she has picked up a young man – after all, when she is seated you can't tell she has one leg shorter than the other, and her face is as fair as any of theirs. But as the night wears on, and their companion does not return, a sombre mood sets in. And when midnight strikes and there is still no sign of her, it is decided to find a policeman and report her absence.

It will take two days before her body is found, lying in undergrowth in a remote part of the grounds. Upon discovery, a message is immediately dispatched to Scotland Yard, and by the time Detective Inspector Stride and Detective Sergeant Cully arrive at the Cremorne, the gate has been closed and the manager, Mr Simpson, is pacing up and down, awaiting their arrival. He is a small fussy man with a big cigar, an expensive tailored suit and a worried expression.

"Gentlemen, gentlemen, thank goodness you're here!" he exclaims. "This is a most unfortunate incident. Most unfortunate indeed. A murder at the

Cremorne! What a tragedy! Only last year we held a number of floral fêtes, attended by the Queen herself and members of the Royal family. Next week we have invited all the local children of the parish to dance round the Maypole. And now this! It seems the infamous Slasher, the terror of London town, has struck at the very heart of the Cremorne. Our reputation lies in tatters. Tatters!"

Stride brushes him aside.

"Can you show me where the body is located?" he instructs one of the waiting ground-staff, who leads the way along a winding path until a small clearing is reached.

"It's in them bushes, sir," he says, pointing. "I found it, but I ain't touched nothing, other than to see if the pore woman was still alive."

Stride nods curtly. He and Cully bend down, and Stride cautiously parts the branches. The battered and bloodstained face of a young woman stares sightlessly back at them. Her throat has been cut. And it is clear, from the state and disorder of her dress and undergarments, what else has taken place.

Stride stares silently at the body for several minutes. Then he gets out a notebook and writes a description of what she looks like (as best he can tell). He checks the clothes she is wearing and makes a note of them also. Finally, he kneels and gently runs a finger over her left breast. Getting to his feet, he gives Cully a meaningful look, but before he has time to share his thoughts, the manager appears.

"I have been thinking about this whole matter, gentlemen, and I am determined that it must not become public knowledge," he says, gesturing towards the undergrowth where the body lies. "If this got out ... well, it would ruin the reputation of the Cremorne Pleasure Gardens as a recreative and wholesome place.

A little piece of Paradise amidst the hustle and bustle of the city."

Stride smiles grimly. He has lost count of the number of complaints filed against the Cremorne. They generally involve moral improprieties committed by young ladies of a certain type, or drunken lewdity exhibited by young bucks. For as long as Stride can remember, the Chelsea Vestry has been running a determined and very public campaign to get the gardens closed at night.

"I'm afraid it may be too late for that, sir," he says. "The young woman, if she is who I think she is, was out for an evening's entertainment with a group of her workmates. They reported her missing two days ago. They will also have informed their employer and their friends by now, and as soon as the body is formally identified, the news will be all over town."

"But can nothing be done?" the manager cries, wringing his hands despairingly.

"Oh, I shouldn't worry about it sir," Stride says, his face expressionless. "Look upon it as good publicity. A visit by The Slasher? You'll have every man and woman in London queuing up at the gate once the press spreads the story. People can never resist a juicy murder. You'll be packed out day and night."

"Do you really think so?" the manager asks hopefully, his face brightening.

Stride casts him a withering look. When he speaks again his voice is short, clipped down to the edge of rudeness.

"I will arrange for some of my men to carry the body to the morgue," he says. "Now if you'll excuse me sir, I think we'll leave you. People to question. Investigations to carry out. That sort of thing."

He spins on his heel and walks quickly towards the gate. Cully follows. Once they are out of earshot, Stride stops and says quietly,

"Her bodice wasn't cut, Jack. It is not our man, though it is similar."

"A copycat murder?"

"It looks that way. Somebody assaulted this poor woman, and then slit her throat to make us think it was The Slasher. Unfortunately for him, he didn't know what we know: that the real murderer tries to rip out the hearts of his victims. And the real murderer doesn't rape them first."

"The manager thought it was him. And so will the press when they get hold of the story."

"Let them think it," Stride says. "I'm not going public with what we know. It would only encourage more copycats out of the closet. And think of the effect on the victims' families. Or their friends," he adds, giving Cully a raised-eyebrow look. "Do you really want Miss Benet to know exactly how her friend died?"

Cully bites his lip.

"We'll put out a public appeal for witnesses though. The Cremorne is always busy; if the body is that of the missing girl, and I'm pretty sure it is, then someone must have seen her talking to a man before leaving the table and going off with him."

He glances at his watch.

"The big department stores will be open now. Why not cut along and arrange for one of her workmates to do a formal identification. Then ask her to sit down with the police artist and get the picture sent to *The Times*, the *Illustrated London Gazette*, and some of the evening papers. Let's make the press work for us for a change."

"What are you going to do?" Cully asks.

"I," Stride declares, "am going to find a nice strong cup of coffee, to take away the very nasty taste I seem to have got in my mouth."

****

Of course, there are many other ways to pass one's precious leisure time outwith the rather louche charms of the Cremorne. A pleasant Sunday stroll in one of the city's many public parks that thread through central London like a green necklace is always a popular diversion. Especially on a fine Spring afternoon when nature is putting forth her finest display of flowers and blossom, birds are carolling in the leafy branches overhead, and all seems right with the world.

Here is Hyde Park, vernal and inviting. And here, a few days after the discovery of the murdered shop girl, is Detective Sergeant Cully, out of his work suit and dressed in his not-work suit (there is a difference, truly). On his arm is a young lady. Look more closely. Do you recognise her? She wears a neat light wool dress – second-hand, admittedly, but reworked and altered to fit her perfectly.

She also has a smart mantle and her bonnet is newly trimmed. But then, having access to the latest fashion magazines and remnants of good-quality material, and being gifted with nimble fingers, she would be able to remake a dress, add a new lace collar and trim an elegant bonnet with flowers.

Emily Benet (for it is she,) glances about her with delight. She has spent the past week either cooped up in the sewing-room, or stitching away by the light of a guttering candle. For this is the Season, and the rich society ladies are in town and must have their fine ball gowns or afternoon dresses made and delivered as quickly as possible.

They only want to be admired, to be the cynosure of every male or female eye as they sparkle and dance and laugh. They do not care – why should they? – that every tuck, pleat and minute piece of decoration on their stunningly beautiful dresses has been sewn by one of the seventeen thousand skilled dressmakers working all over London, often in cramped or unsanitary conditions, with few breaks for fresh air and food.

But today Emily Benet is not stitching her fingers to the bone. Instead, here she is enjoying the sunshine and the fresh air and the company. So they stroll through the park, the detective and the dressmaker. What are they talking about? What do people falling in love talk about? The weather, the scenery, the flowers, the people around them. Light, artificial safe things. What is important is the conversation taking place elsewhere: the conversation of touch, and smile, and stolen glances.

"Would you like to see the fashionable carriages and riders pass?" Cully asks after a modicum of strolling and admiring has taken place.

"I should like that indeed. I haven't seen it since ..." her voice falters, "for many weeks."

Cully steers her through the throngs of couples and families also out for an airing until they reach the road known as Rotten Row, where the rich and fashionable like to parade and take the air, to be seen and be admired.

"If we stand just here, we shall be able to see perfectly."

While they wait for the procession to make its way over from Regent Street, he tells her about the riots of six years earlier, when protesters against the new law stopping refreshments being sold on Sunday in public parks, and other places of leisure frequented by the working class, stood shoulder to shoulder along the Row with placards, waiting for the rich to pass by.

"It has always been like this," Emily nods wisely. "Rich people must be allowed their pleasures even if we are forbidden ours."

"I was one of the constables on duty," Cully says. "I remember thinking at the time that it was unfair these people could make their servants work on a Sunday, and their Clubs remain open, while working people were denied their few pleasures on their one day off."

Emily Benet turns to face him, her eyes dancing.

"Why Mr Cully, you are a socialist!"

Cully looks at her in amazement.

"You know about socialism?"

Emily Benet's lips curve into a smile.

"Oh, I may be only a weak and feeble woman, but I read newspapers and pamphlets. I see the world around me. And I believe it is unfair that some have so much and others so little. Violet and I always said when we had our own business we would pay everybody the same wages, and make sure they did not work long hours, as we have had to," she pauses. "But of course, that will never happen now."

"It might, some day," Cully says, but Emily merely shakes her head sadly.

The awkward silence is broken by the unmistakable clip-clop of horses' hooves and the jingle of harness. A group of Dragoon Guards from the Knightsbridge Barracks trot by, their scarlet uniforms immaculate, their horses polished to perfection.

They are followed by a procession of open carriages filled with smartly dressed men, and women in the latest copied Paris fashions. The women twirl parasols and gossip. The men stare over the heads of the watching crowds.

Cully, ever on duty even when he isn't meant to be, scans the crowd, watching for pickpockets, while Emily stares hard at the high fashion dresses, admiring their cut and colour, mentally pricing them up and working out how long some of them would take to make.

As soon as the dazzling procession has passed by, Cully suggests they go down to the bandstand and listen to the band playing popular songs. Which they do, and both enjoy greatly. And then it is time to leave the park. Their lovely afternoon has slipped by so fast, each minute like a precious pearl on a string.

Cully walks Emily Benet to her dusty front door. They stand on the step, going through the customary farewell routines. Then she unlocks the door and hurries up the unlit stairs to her room, where she is awaited by a meagre meal and a large pile of sewing.

Meanwhile Jack Cully walks home alone through the gathering twilight, reliving the glorious afternoon in his head, and wishing he had plucked up enough courage to ask her to join him for supper.

****

Meagre indeed is the Sunday supper being served at Mrs Lucinda Witchard's Boarding House for Commercial Gentlemen. The principal components are thin bread and butter, sour watercress, fatty ham and watery tea.

The lodgers gather round the table. They pick and prod the offerings with a sigh, and think of other tables groaning with good things, and a pleasant woman in attendance to heap their plates high and smilingly refill their cups.

The lodger on the third floor seems unconcerned by the poor fare on offer. His mouth moves mechanically as he chews the stale bread. He keeps his head down, focusing instead upon his chipped plate. He takes no part in the conversation, which is mainly about the various occupations pursued by the rest of his fellow-diners.

He wonders what they would think if he described his occupation. Would they like to hear how he prepares dead bodies for dissection, sawing and cutting, separating limb from torso? How he clears up and disposes of the bits and pieces once they have fulfilled their final purpose? How he follows the surgeons on their rounds, standing in the background as they probe festering wounds and drain pus-filled abscesses?

Would they like to hear about the Foul Wards, where women with secondary and tertiary syphilis lie moaning and writhing in agony on sweat-soaked sheets, their noses eaten away, their private parts chancred and rotten with disease? He remembers with a shudder of disgust the first time he entered one of these polluted places, saw the bright blue faces of those who'd let cheap gin be their solace and comfort, smelled the stink of corruption.

Whores. Harlots. Carriers of disease. Polluters of the marriage bed. Unholy. Like she was. Like she did. His gorge rises. His colour suddenly turns to livid white, ominous marks forming about his nose, as if the finger of the devil himself has touched it. He jumps to his feet, knocking over his chair.

"All right there, old man?" one of the lodgers asks. "Looking a bit seedy."

He does not reply. Instead he runs upstairs, takes down his coat from its peg behind the door, and crams his hat on his head. Tonight, he will find her. Wild-eyed, his lips parted, he rushes frantically out of the house as if it were a matter of life and death. Which in a way it is. Although mostly death.

****

London sleeps. At least, the respectable section of it sleeps. The chiming of church clocks, the shouts of the late ones meandering drunkenly homewards, disturb not their slumbers. But in low lodging houses, in dark derelict buildings dating back to before the Great Fire, whole families lie where they can on bare floorboards, prey to the bugs and fleas and vermin that make sleep almost impossible.

The Foundling is finding sleep almost impossible. Hunger does not make a good bedfellow. Leftover crusts and fatty ham rinds from the lodgers' tea are all she has been allowed. She tosses and turns on her basement bed, her growling stomach a constant reminder that she has had virtually nothing to eat all day.

Mrs Witchard takes the attitude that Sunday is a day of rest – which means that she does not prepare any meals (apart from supper,) for the lodgers. Which in turn means no food for the Foundling, who relies on the leftovers and scraps to fill her belly.

Mrs Witchard's day of rest also includes a day of rest from all domestic chores. By inference this includes those who perform them, so the Foundling is turfed out of the house at eight am and only allowed back in to lay up for supper. How she spends the time in between is of no interest whatsoever to her employer.

The other thing currently keeping the Foundling awake is the sensation that somebody is moving around directly over her head. She can hear footsteps, boards creaking. She throws back the ragged coverlet that used to be a curtain, and with catlike tread creeps up the basement stairs to take a look.

There is a light in Mrs Witchard's parlour. She sees the flickering strip of it under the door. The Foundling puts an eye to the keyhole. She can just make out a dark shape hovering by the mantelpiece, where the solid-silver-framed pictures of Mr Witchard (her employer's late husband) and other members of the family are displayed. She hears ragged breathing, a muffled groan. Then she sees a hand reach out and take up one of the pictures.

Next minute the candle is blown out. Footsteps stumble towards the door. The Foundling draws back and crouches down by the stairwell. The door is thrust open. Somebody enters the hallway, and climbs the stairs.

She does not see his face, but she does not need to see it, for she knows at once who it is. Every night the Foundling collects the boots and shoes left by their owners outside their doors and takes them down to the scullery, where she cleans and polishes them before returning them ready to wear to work next day. So, she knows those boots. Probably better than the boots' owner knows them.

The Foundling waits until all is quiet overhead. Then she creeps into the parlour and feels along the mantelpiece. There is a gap where one of the pictures used to be. She moves the others along to fill it. Then she returns to her basement bed and tries to puzzle out what she has just seen. She is still puzzling when the first streaks of dawn gild the sky, and Mrs Witchard thumps downstairs from her comfortable feather bed and kicks her into action.

****

Hyacinth Clout is also in possession of something puzzling. In her case, it is how to come up with a plausible excuse to leave the house for an afternoon. For Hyacinth has finally received a letter from her *Lonely Widower* inviting her to take tea with him.

He has suggested a discreet tea-room in the pleasant and totally respectable environs of Hampstead. He has also suggested a date and time: this afternoon. At three.

Hyacinth is both thrilled and terrified in equal measure. She has spent all morning going through her not-extensive wardrobe trying on this, discarding that, and staring at herself in the cheval glass. It is impossible to guess what this stranger will think of her appearance. First impressions count so much – she has read that in a ladies' magazine. She really wants to make a good first impression.

But now she has to work out a strategy for getting the other side of the front door without her sister knowing why. She has checked the diary Lobelia keeps in the writing desk. There are no committee meetings scheduled. No afternoon calls pencilled in. She is going to have to employ all the qualities of duplicity and mendacity that she never thought she possessed before starting her illicit correspondence with *Lonely Widower*.

Lunch provides her with an initial opportunity to introduce the concept of her absence.

"I notice we are out of several items of food," she observes. "I wanted to make a nice treacle tart for supper, but there is no treacle left in the larder."

Lobelia wipes her mouth with her napkin. She is particularly fond of treacle tart, as Hyacinth knows full well. In fact, Hyacinth strongly suspects, from the speed with which the tart disappears every time she makes it, that her sister has been slipping downstairs at night and helping herself to extra slices. Either that, or the Clouts have a very sweet-toothed mouse.

"Perhaps I should get some more treacle, what do you think?" she suggests. "And some fresh eggs for the custard sauce."

Lobelia eyes her empty plate. She has just enjoyed an excellent luncheon of cold beef and new potatoes, but the thought of treacle tart later is clearly enticing.

Hyacinth clasps her hands together under the table and waits.

"Yes. I think that would be a good idea," Lobelia says finally.

Hyacinth carefully tunes her facial expression to neutral.

"Then I shall slip out when I have tidied up the luncheon things," she says, her heart dancing in her chest with excitement.

And here she is now, dismounting from an omnibus. She is wearing her best cherry and grey striped day dress, enhanced by the judicious insertion of bust improvers – for Hyacinth is rather flat-chested, and current fashion favours a more rounded look. She also has a fringed Indian cone shawl, and a bonnet that is almost but not quite fashionable.

Hyacinth checks her watch: it is a quarter off three o'clock. She slows down – she doesn't want to arrive at the tea room too early; that would not be proper for a young lady in her position. So, she dawdles in the High Street, glancing into shop windows, seeing nothing, until the watch shows three o'clock. Then she crosses the road and makes her way to the Lily Lounge, the rendezvous suggested by *Lonely Widower*.

Hyacinth enters the busy tea room. It is very full of people. Waitresses are rushing to and fro carrying trays. She stands on the threshold, hesitant, uncertain, suddenly wondering whether this was a good idea after all. She is just about to turn tail and flee, when a heavily-bearded gentleman rises from a seat and lifts his gloved hand to his top hat in greeting.

Blushing furiously, she crosses the floor.

"*London Lady*, I presume?" he says, in a pleasant tone of voice.

"Oh. Y-yes, I am," she stutters.

Her interlocutor is wearing a sober grey suit, white high-collared shirt and blue silk necktie fastened with a gold horseshoe pin. He waits politely for her to sit down. Hyacinth lowers herself decorously onto the chair opposite. Suddenly she feels shy, tongue-tied.

Fortunately, a waitress appears at her shoulder.

"Tea, sir and madam?" she murmurs.

"Indeed, tea," *Lonely Widower* says. He glances across the table. "And cakes?"

Hyacinth nods, suddenly too shy to speak.

The waitress repeats the order, then glides away.

Hyacinth steals a glance at her companion. Apart from the beard, which is a little disconcerting in its bushiness, he appears perfectly normal. She does not know what she was expecting, then reminds herself that he is in exactly the same position. She attempts a smile. He smiles back.

"I am delighted meet you in person at last," he says. "I found your letters so full of interest. By the way, my real name is John Smithson."

Hyacinth tells him her name, feeling as if she was sharing some great secret.

"Hyacinth: what a lovely name," John Smithson exclaims. "A lovely name for a lovely young lady, if I may be so bold as to remark."

Hyacinth feels her face flush. No man has ever paid her a compliment before. It is both strange and intoxicating at the same time. And here she is, alone with a man for the first time in her life. The only man she has ever been alone with before this afternoon is Reverend Bittersplit, but he is a clergyman, and so barely registers as a man as far as she is concerned.

Over tea and luscious cakes (Hyacinth notices with approval how delicately and carefully her companion eats), she tells Mr Smithson about the death of Mama, and her current life, keeping and sharing the house with her sister.

"It was very brave of you to write to the newspaper," he remarks when she is done.

"Oh, I just felt so unhappy and alone," Hyacinth confesses. "It was as if my life was empty and meaningless."

He smiles at her across the tea table.

"And do you still feel like that, Miss Clout?" he asks gently, his eyes searching her face.

Hyacinth drops her eyes to her plate and chases the last few crumbs around with a finger.

"I am so glad we have met," he continues. "I felt we had a bond the moment I opened your letter, for I too, have known great unhappiness. When my beloved wife passed away, I also couldn't see the future for the dark clouds of misery that threatened to overwhelm me."

"But you had your child," Hyacinth says.

"Ah. Yes. Indeed. Dear sweet Agnes. Such a treasure and comfort to me in my lonely state."

"How old is she?"

"She is thirteen. On the threshold of womanhood. That was why I decided I needed to find a companion – a special companion – who would be the mother to her that I cannot be. A good woman who could guide her through the snares and pitfalls of this world." He glances earnestly at her. "The sweetness of a mother's love. Who can put a price on such a commodity?"

Hyacinth, whose experience of maternal love has encompassed rather more bitterness and gall than sweetness, does not reply.

He heaves a sigh.

"It has been a most delightful afternoon, but now I must return home. Agnes is still very delicate – the death of her mother has affected her greatly, and I do not want to cause her any more distress."

"Does she know you were meeting me today?" Hyacinth asks.

"Not yet. I wanted to see you, to find out a little more about you. Now that I have met you, and spoken with you, I shall tell her. And next time we meet, maybe I will bring her with me."

"Oh, I should like that very much!" Hyacinth exclaims. "I am particularly fond of children."

"Then let it be so," he smiles. "And now I shall settle the bill and put you in a carriage."

"I am quite happy to catch the omnibus," Hyacinth demurs.

"Indeed, you shall not!" *Lonely Widower* says, waving a finger roguishly at her. "Riding about London in a common omnibus? A lady of your beauty and elegance? I cannot hear of it."

He pays the bill, then ushers Hyacinth out of the tea-room, where a hansom is summoned and she is put inside.

"Until the next time we meet, *London Lady*," he smiles. "A merry meeting, that I hope will take place very soon. Watch out for the letter carrier."

He raises a hand. The cab rattles away.

Hyacinth sinks back rapturously onto the leather banquette. Her head is in a whirl. There is so much to think about. She runs through the afternoon, reliving the thrill of it, blushing as she recalls the compliments, the smiles, the way he listened intently to everything she said, the absence of bible verses.

It is only when the cab drops her at the end of the street that Hyacinth suddenly remembers her original stated purpose in leaving the house, and realises that in all the excitement, she has clean forgotten to buy any treacle for the treacle tart.

****

It has been a busy day at Morbid Crevice's dolly shop. From the moment Tonkin took down the shutters, the same customers who came in on Friday to redeem their belongings for the weekend have reappeared to pawn them again.

A brief lull in proceedings has prompted Crevice to dispatch Tonkin on a quick errand, the instructions accompanied by a box round the ears and the advice that if he chooses to take all bloody day, he might return to find the shop door closed, and he will be out of work, out on his ear, and have to sleep in the gutter.

The departure of Tonkin is followed a short while later by the appearance of a stranger – for Crevice has his regulars and his irregulars, and this man fits into neither category. He enters the shop furtively, his left arm folded protectively over a newspaper-wrapped parcel, and approaches the dusty, finger-smeared counter.

Crevice steps forward, giving the man the leering grimace that passes for customer service.

"Yers, young sir, 'ow may I 'elp you?"

The man eyes him with distaste. He places the parcel on the counter.

"How much will you advance me for this?"

Crevice's fingers fumble the parcel. Inside is an ornate silver frame, empty of its contents. He turns it over, noting the hallmark. Then he flicks it between thumb and forefinger and brings it to his ear. He vaguely recalls having seen someone in the trade doing this, although whether it was to test gold, or silver, or cut crystal, he can't remember. Maybe it was cigars. Whatever it was supposed to be, his ragged clientele is always impressed by such evidences of his expertise.

The man waits impassively, showing no emotions of any kind.

Crevice eyes his customer narrowly. He has a good eye for a bad guy, and he is pretty sure that the item in his hand has not been come by honestly. The very fact that the stranger has washed up here in his emporium is proof of that. There are many bigger, more legit businesses, not a stone's throw from his door, where a customer could get far more money for a solid silver frame.

And yet the man doesn't seem like a wrong 'un. His clothes, clearly need of a little care and attention, look like they are expensive. Or were expensive, once. He certainly speaks better than the usual patrons. Crevice is puzzled, but decides it is none of his business. His business is doing business. He cuts to the chase and names a sum.

The man swallows hard, seems to hesitate, then nods. Crevice digs out his cash box from under the counter, unlocks it and carefully counts out the money. The man thrusts it into an inner pocket and turns to leave.

Just as he reaches the door, Tonkin bursts in, panting. He draws aside to let the man pass, staring hard at him, as he walks out into the teeming street.

"What did he want?" Tonkin asks, when Crevice has welcomed him back into the fold with a blow.

"Why? What's it to you?" Crevice snarls. "You know him - do yer? Friend of yours?"

Tonkin shakes his head. He certainly does not know the man, who is beating a path to the nearest chemist and druggist shop. He has seen him though. Oh yes, he is quite sure about that. Seen him through the shuttered shop window one dark night. But on that occasion, he looked different. Very different indeed.

****

Meanwhile Detective Inspector Stride is poring over a map of the West End, specifically the area around Regent Street and New Oxford Street. On it he has marked the locations where the three murders took place. He has joined the locations up with straight lines. Now he is staring at the triangulation he has created and racking his brains to work out some sort of connecting principle.

It is not the first time in his career that Stride has had to deal with multiple murders. He recalls the Case of Eileen Mannington, a singularly ugly woman who nevertheless managed to attract the attentions of three suitors, and dispatched each of them in quick succession. In that case the murder weapon came in powder form – rat poison mixed in their food.

There was the Case of the Four Students and the Sexton's Umbrella, and the Case of the Bankers' Thumbs, all involving multiple murders committed by one single individual. Not forgetting the Case of the Haunted Hansom.

There is always a pattern. Sometimes it is a cry for help, with the murderer leaving small coded messages as if he is trying to get somebody to stop him. Stride considers the clumsy attempt by this murderer to cut out the heart of each victim. What is he trying to show? What does it signify? A thwarted love affair, perhaps?

Also, there is always a motive – the primary ones being money and sex. But here, Stride's logic runs up against reality. None of the three victims possessed anything of value, and although the murders have been violent and brutal, no sexual assault has taken place.

What is also nagging away at him like a sore tooth is the sudden cessation of activity. Apart from the Cremorne murder, which, as he suspected, was a different case altogether and for which a member of the Guards is currently being held on suspicion, there has been nothing for some time.

In his experience, most men who kill more than once possess a kind of self-destructive passion that ends up by betraying them. This man, however, seems to have the ability to lie low, as if he suspects that someone is on to him.

He clearly hasn't read the newspapers, Stride thinks ruefully. The daily diet of scare stories, accompanied by damning accusations of police incompetence, are enough to give any potential murder the feeling that he will never be captured and can easily escape the hangman's noose.

No, Stride reasons, there must be a pattern. There is always a pattern. Not because the killer plans it, but because all humans are creatures of habit. It is just a case of finding what this particular creature's habits are.

A knock at the door heralds the entrance of Detective Sergeant Cully bearing a cup of black coffee. Stride waves at the spread-out map on his desk.

"Three murders in three separate locations. All within walking distance of one another. What do you make of it, Jack?"

Cully sets the coffee cup down carefully, trying not to put it on top of any important paperwork – no mean feat, given the state of Stride's desk. Then he stares at the map.

"It's four murders now," he says grimly. "The body of a young woman has been discovered in a side alleyway behind a shop off Tottenham Court Road. Murdered last night. I have been at the scene since first light making notes. Throat cut, blows to the head, bodice ripped, injuries to the chest, nothing stolen, body propped up against a wall. Exactly like the others. They've just brought her body into the morgue."

Stride stares down into the cup, as if he can see something nasty lurking its inky depths. He feels a tightness in his chest, a sense of vertigo, as if the world is spinning out of control round him and there is nothing to hold on to.

"Are you alright?" Cully asks.

With a tremendous effort of will, Stride pulls himself together.

"I'll live, Jack. Which is more than can be said for that poor unfortunate young woman,"

He pushes himself to a stand.

"Let's get it over with," he says wearily.

****

"You're keeping me very busy, detective inspector," the police surgeon remarks drily, as Stride and Cully enter the cold, clinical basement room.

"Believe me," Stride growls, "I'm not doing it willingly."

"No indeed, I'm sure you are not. And I presume you would like me to comment upon the latest addition to the sad catalogue of crime once again laid out before me."

"I'd appreciate that. If it would be no trouble, of course."

There is an edge to Stride's tone. It is noted by the surgeon and picked up instantly.

"Well, now ... that of course depends upon your definition of trouble," he remarks, staring into the middle distance. "For the victim, trouble has been, one might say, her middle name. Young, barely out of her teens. Yet clearly acquainted with the moral irregularities and vicissitudes of this wicked world."

Stride raises both his hands in a gesture of defeat.

"Just bloody tell us if she was killed by the same bastard who murdered the other three, would you?"

The surgeon clicks his teeth.

"Your lack of finesse will be the death of you, detective inspector," he says, chuckling at his own cleverness. "Yes, it is clearly the work of the same man. The throat has been cut and there is evidence of the same ritualistic slashes around the heart."

Stride breathes in sharply.

"Thank you."

"It is no trouble, detective inspector. None at all, believe me. Only too happy to aid you in your investigations. It is, after all, what I am paid to do. I just hope that they will soon reach a satisfactory conclusion, before the streets of London begin to resemble a bloodbath."

A couple of meaningful seconds slink by.

"What did you mean about the moral vissy ... vissy...?" Cully asks.

"Vicissitudes, detective sergeant. A word meaning a change of fortune. In this case, shall we say, a straying away from the path of rectitude."

Stride gives him a hard-eyed stare.

"So, you're saying that this one was not a dressmaker?" Cully queries.

"A dressmaker in the euphemistic sense only. This one, as you nominate her, followed a different profession. Without being too coy about it – as we are all men of the world here – the oldest profession in the world."

"She was a prostitute?"

The police surgeon nods.

"Damn and blast it to Hell and back!" Stride exclaims.

The police surgeon raises his eyebrows in rebuke.

Stride mumbles a half-hearted apology, spins abruptly on his heel and stalks out.

They head back towards the main building.

"Our man is not just targeting members of the dressmaking profession," Stride says grimly. "I had thought that was the underlying pattern."

"So, what is the underlying pattern?"

Stride shrugs.

"I don't know, Jack. I can't see any. But there is one. Has to be. And he's right, curse him," he adds, jerking his thumb over his shoulder. "We must catch whoever is responsible for this before he unleashes a veritable bloodbath. And we have very little time and not a lot to go on."

****

"Very little time" could be the leitmotif for that pair of most unfortunate lovers Portia Mullygrub and Trafalgar Moggs. But somehow time's forelock has been grasped, and now there is a wedding to plan, a church to be booked, a dress to be made, a wedding breakfast to be sourced, and guests to be invited. Not to mention the most important task of finding somewhere to rent that is not too expensive for a clerk's salary.

Here is the would-be groom mounting the dusty steps of the Mullygrub house. He knocks upon the door, which is opened by Cordelia, the half-grown sister. She is wearing a smut-stained pinafore and a terrified expression.

"Oh, Mr Moggs, thank heavens you have arrived!" she gasps.

"Why, whatever is the matter?"

"It is Ma and Porty. They have been going at it like knives since daybreak," Cordelia says. "Porty has told Ma she is getting married and Ma don't want her to."

Sure enough, the sound of raised female voices backgrounds her words, punctuated by a chorus of high-pitched and miserable wailing.

Moggs hesitates on the doorstep. Who can blame him?

"Perhaps I should call another time?"

"No, no! Please, you must come in. Maybe they might listen to you." Cordelia pleads.

She takes him by the coat-sleeve and drags him into the hallway.

Moggs follows her to the parlour, where Portia and her mother are facing each other across a table piled high with papers and pamphlets and cups and dirty plates.

Portia's face is bright red, her hair stands out from her head as if it has been recently yanked by a pair of frantic hands. A smoky fire is making its own contribution to the already highly-charged atmosphere.

In a chair in the corner sits Mr Mullygrub, who works by night as a limelighter in the Colosseum and by day as anything that keeps him out of the house, but has sadly not managed to find anything today to secure his absence.

He has taken refuge under a blanket. Small sobbing Mullygrubs are clinging like grim death to his legs, as if terrified that the argument raging about the room might blow them out of the house altogether.

"Ma, Porty, see who is come?" Cordelia says, pushing Moggs into the eye of the storm.

Portia throws her Beloved a frantic and agonised glance.

Mrs Mullygrub, philanthropist and taker-up of good causes, pays him not the slightest attention.

"I say to you again Portia: how can you be so selfish?" she declares. 'You know full well I have all my charitable work to oversee. How am I to ensure that the savages of Boongallonga get their tracts and missionary barrels if you leave me? Let alone the lectures and talks I must undertake over the summer. And then there are all the letters asking for subscriptions. I cannot manage without an amanuensis. No, marriage is quite out of the question and there's no point in discussing it."

"But Ma, Traffy and I love each other," Portia pleads desperately.

"Yes, of course I understand that. You are young, and foolish. You think yourself in love. Maybe you are, but not now. Not when I need you here. And as I have repeated, you are far too young for such an enterprise as marriage."

"I am twenty-two, Ma. And you were married at sixteen, you know you were."

Mrs Mullygrub brushes the statement aside with a wave of her hand.

"Let us not bring my youthful follies into this conversation."

The blanket quivers.

"And we have been engaged such a long time. And now we are decided to marry, and that's an end of it."

She stares defiantly across the table.

"And where, pray, are you intending to live after taking this rash and foolish decision?"

Portia flings Moggs a pleading glance.

"Traffy will find somewhere soon, won't you?"

"I am searching for a suitable place for us to live, Mrs Mullygrub," he says. "It is hard, as the good ones are expensive."

"Aha! So you have not found anywhere," Mrs Mullygrub states. "And until you do, no marriage can take place, can it? So here Portia stays. Where she belongs. And that is an end of it."

And with that, the renowned philanthropist picks up a document, settles her spectacles firmly upon her nose and starts to read. Portia glares at her, then buries her face in her hands. Her shoulders shake.

The small Mullygrubs recommence clinging and wailing. Cordelia wrings her hands. Poor Moggs stares from one to another with an expression of quiet desperation on his face. Then shaking his head sadly, he tiptoes silently away.

****

Across London, Mrs Witchard's lodger, having returned from the chemist and druggist and emptied a syringeful of reddish-brown liquid into his veins upon his return, now begins to stir. He opens his eyes to the sound of church bells, and a taste in his mouth as if he has been running. For a moment, he has no sense of place. The noise outside his window and the bed he lies upon mean nothing.

He blinks, and the world comes back.

There are shapes, patterns of light and dark, motion that corresponds to sounds arriving from outside. They knock at his door with luggage. Tendrils of memory drift through his gathering moments of consciousness. He pages backward, forward, back again, always chasing ghosts.

His nerves are pulled tight by too little sleep, and an oily slick of fear that clings to his skin. He never thought of himself as a good or a bad man. Nothing so simple. He was only ordinary. An ordinary man who just happened to fall for an extraordinary woman.

And now? This wasn't the plan. His plan was better, it made sense. He has no idea what the sense of this is. The world has become frightening, impossible in its thinness. He struggles to raise himself in the frowzy unmade bed, but his head is spinning and he falls back on the pillow. He doesn't want to think about anything. Just sleep. Sleep until eternity.

****

There is no sleep for Police Constable Tom 'Taffy' Evans, whom we last met on duty in a cramped Watch Box guarding the posh purlieus of Russell Square. He has got a new beat in the West End. Some might consider it a step down socially. They would be wrong.

A change is as good as a rest – though in his case it is not, as he is far busier now than ever he was when loitering within a box. There are crowds, there are fashionable shop windows, and fashionable ladies and gentlemen in their shiny carriages.

Street vendors and musicians ply their trade. As do pickpockets and petty criminals. Sandwich-board men stroll up and down advertising things he has never heard of. Every now and then the press of vehicles trying to get into Regent Street from Oxford Street comes to a grinding halt, and there is a lock, which he has to sort out as best he can.

As a consequence of all this, his letters home to his sweetheart Megan, who is in service in Cardiff, have improved considerably both in legibility and in content. Yes, it is fair to say that there is never a dull moment.

One of these anything-but-dull moments is about to arrive right now.

Constable Evans is swinging his truncheon in what he hopes is an assertive fashion, while wondering whether he might scoot quickly around a corner to perform an action that is becoming increasingly urgent as the minutes tick by, when somebody hails him from behind.

Turning, he spies a young woman in a very shiny-bright dress, a little short at the bottom and extremely low at the top. She has a small bonnet perched saucily atop stylish blonde ringlets and a slight swagger to her step, indicating that she is, in the local patois of the area, a lady in waiting. To be more precise, a lady in waiting for Mr Right, or at least Mr Right Amount.

Closer inspection also reveals a slightly wild look about the eyes, somewhere between ravenous and sensual. She has a wide mouth and puffy lips, parted slightly as if starving. The young woman sidles up to Constable Evans and gives him a long hard stare as if making up her mind about something.

"'Ullo p'liceman," she says in a husky voice.

Another interesting aspect of Constable Evans' new beat is dealing with 'ladies of the night'. Sometimes he also has to deal with ladies of the day whom gentlemen have mistaken for ladies of the night. His skills in tact and diplomacy are increasing incrementally as a result.

"Yes, my good woman, how can I help you?" he asks in his lilting Welsh accent.

The young woman looks him up and down *very* slowly, in a way that brings the colour to Constable Evans' honest face.

"Well, now, you're a nice big man, ain't you," she says, with an emphasis on the word 'big' that produces further blushes.

"Um," says Constable Evans.

"I fink we are going to get on like a house on fire," the young woman murmurs seductively, leaning in.

Constable Evans recalls the only time he ever saw a house on fire. There were no survivors.

"Miss ... I have to warn you that I am an Officer of the Law," he says, mentally paging frantically through the Police Handbook. "And if you are propositioning an Officer of the Law while he is engaged in carrying out his official duties, I have to warn you that it is a crime for which you may be arrested and taken to the nearest police station. In handcuffs," he adds for further dramatic effect.

Undeterred, the young woman gives him a cheerful and infectious grin.

"Well, you can't blame a girl for trying to drum up a bit of trade on a slack day, can yer?"

Constable Evans assumes what he hopes will be interpreted as a stern and forbidding expression.

"Now if there is nothing further, I must be about my lawful employment."

"No, wait a bit," the golden-ringletted one says. "There is summat."

He pauses.

"It's Sawney Sue."

"I am sorry?"

"She shares my patch. Well, she did. Ain't seen her around for two days now."

"And this Sawney Sue would be ..."

"Yeah, she would be. Only she ain't now. And I was wondering whether I oughter mention it, like."

She looks at him, head on one side coquettishly.

At this point, it would be all too easy to tell her to *"Move along, my good woman and stop wasting police time."* Indeed, most of his colleagues would have done just that.

But Constable Evans possesses, in embryonic form, that intuition and acuity that in future years will take him to the very top of his profession, earning him the respect not only of his colleagues, but also of those in high office.

Thus, instead of airily dismissing her concerns and resuming what is known universally in police parlance as 'proceeding', he regards her thoughtfully.

"Tell me what is worrying you," he says, getting out notebook and pencil.

So she does. Tells him how she and Sawney Sue (*"She's a bit simple like, but a good-hearted girl, do anything for anybody,"*) had met some time ago and struck up an unlikely friendship. How they'd been standing under a portico in Regent Street, eyeing up the potential clientele.

How a punter had sauntered over and asked her for a bit of a jangle, so she'd taken him down a side alley, telling Sue to keep cave. (*"Coz there's them as would report you for doing it in a public place, dunno why, it's not as if it ain't in the Bible, is it?"*) and when she returned, Sue was gone, which wasn't like her, coz they always looked out for each other, and she hadn't seen her since.

"What did she look like, this friend of yours?" he asks.

She gives him a description.

"What do you fink, Mr Policeman? You fink The Slasher's got her?"

Constable Evans is thinking a lot of things. Some of them are more urgent than others.

"Now look, you wait here, Miss ... I just have to see a man about a dog. When I return, I shall escort you to the nearest Police Station, where you can give a full statement, which I will make sure gets to the detectives in Scotland Yard."

Constable Evans goes to point Peter at a convenient wall. When he returns, the young woman will have vanished. Of course. But he will mention what she told him to his superior officer, who will tell it to the station sergeant, who will relate it to Detective Inspector Stride over a jar of ale in the Dog and Bucket two nights later. Detective Inspector Stride will, in turn, match up the description with the body of an unnamed and unclaimed young woman lying in the police mortuary.

There may still not be a pattern, but the individual threads are beginning to come together.

****

Love and liability. They go together like the title of a novel. For some it involves taking responsibility for finding a place to call home. For others, it is faking a façade of normality.

Thus, here is Hyacinth Clout, in the hallway, with a duster, waiting for the lunchtime post to plop through the letterbox. Since their first meeting ten days ago, she and Lonely Widower have exchanged several letters of an increasingly amicable nature. His always seem to arrive at the same time of day.

This explains her current location, and therefore also her air of agitation. For Lobelia, who generally keeps to her own quarters in the morning hours, is wont to appear from on high when lunch is scheduled.

Hyacinth has on her cleaning apron, all the better to fool her with. She makes half-hearted dabs at the bannister rail, while listening for footsteps on the other side of the front door and at the same time for footsteps coming along the upstairs corridor. Her ability to multitask is truly admirable.

Just when the tension is becoming almost too much to bear, the flap is lifted and a letter is pushed through. Hyacinth falls upon it like a vulture upon its prey. As she straightens up, she meets the stern-eyed face of her sister, who has appeared from the morning-room without her realising.

"What on earth are you doing scrabbling around on the mat?" Lobelia inquires. Coldly.

Hyacinth hides the letter in her hand and the hand behind her back.

"I thought I saw a black beetle," she lies.

"Really, Hyacinth, your current behaviour leaves a lot to be desired," her sister continues. "Have you prepared luncheon yet?"

Hyacinth nods. A cold collation of last night's beef is awaiting consumption in the kitchen.

"I hope you have not forgotten that we are both attending a meeting of the Society for Returning Young Women to Their Friends in the Country. Your absence from the last meeting has been noted and remarked upon."

"Who has remarked upon it?"

"Reverend Bittersplit."

"Well, it's none of his business," Hyacinth declares defiantly.

Lobelia's unplucked eyebrows almost disappear into her straggly hairline.

"I hope I did not hear you aright! Reverend Bittersplit is a man I hold in the highest respect. He is a member of the cloth – a sacred profession. And he was the only man Mama trusted in her final days upon this earth."

More fool her, Hyacinth thinks glumly. She remembers all too vividly his tedious visits to the house, when she was forced to sit at the dying woman's bedside in her role as nurse and chaperone, listening to her mother's choky, rasping breath as Reverend Bittersplit read passages from the Bible interspersed with long invocations to the Almighty.

"And he is the father of Bethica, our dear and trusted friend."

Your dear and trusted friend, Hyacinth thinks. Frankly, the relationship between Bethica and her sister puzzles her. They seem very close – almost unnaturally so – visiting or corresponding with each other daily.

And one evening last week, when Hyacinth had cause to return unexpectedly to the vestry, having once again left her umbrella in the stand, she had found her sister and Bethica clasped in each other's arms in a passionate embrace.

Hyacinth has never seen her sister display any sign of affection towards her, and only dutiful affection towards Mama. The sight had given her a jolt. Of course, they'd jumped apart and pretended they were merely tidying the hymn books, but Hyacinth knew what she saw. And since that day, Lobelia has been extra-sharp with her. It is strange and confusing.

"I shall fetch the luncheon," she says heading for the basement door.

In the safety of the kitchen, she tears open the letter.

Dear Hyacinth (yes, things have certainly moved on apace),

I have so enjoyed your last letter – the descriptions of the committee ladies made me laugh out loud. What a witty way with words you have. I could almost see them in my mind's eye: such a sad solemn bunch of spinsters. How can a bright sunny nature such as yours flourish in such poor soil?

Thank you also for your recipe for mint tea – I gave it to one of the servants and she produced a fragrant cup of it the very same afternoon. 'The cup that cheers

but does not inebriate' as Dr Johnson once memorably wrote.

The reason I am writing to you is to suggest another delightful meeting. I shall be in the vicinity of Hampstead this very afternoon, and intend to partake of tea and cakes at the Lily Lounge, where we spent such a pleasant afternoon a short while ago.

Would you be able to slip away for a couple of hours? I do hope so. There is something rather important that I wish to say to you, and I do not feel that a letter is the correct medium to say it.

I look forward to a merry meeting,
Your
'Not So Lonely' Widower

Hyacinth lets the letter fall to the table ... where it lands face down on the butter. Her heart is pounding like a piston engine in her chest. She feels the room swim and clasps the side of the table for support.

The words *'something rather important'* swim before her eyes. Oh, what could it be? Surely ... no – not after so short an acquaintance? But did not Romeo and Juliet fall in love upon first sight? And what about David and Bathsheba?

Hyacinth reclaims the letter, now greasy and smudged, and places it in her pocket. Then she picks up the serving tray and makes her way to the dining room, where Lobelia is already seated in her place, napkin upon her lap. She eyes the food with relish, helping herself to the best bits of meat before she closes her eyes and folds her hands.

"For what we are about to receive may the Lord make us truly thankful," she intones, before seizing her knife and fork and digging in.

Hyacinth pokes at her plate. Her brain is in a whirl. One thing is paramount: she has to find a reason to be absent from the committee meeting this afternoon.

"You are not eating, Hyacinth," Lobelia remarks, pouring herself a glass of water.

"I am not hungry. In fact, I feel a little nauseous. I have a headache coming on. I think I ought to rest upstairs this afternoon."

Lobelia eyes her narrowly. Headaches are *her* territory. Hyacinth flinches. It is almost as if her sister can see inside her mind, can tell that she is lying.

"Nonsense," Lobelia declares robustly. "A bit of fresh air will do you good. A nice brisk walk to the vicarage will soon get rid of your headache. Now eat up. It is a sin to waste good food."

Miserably Hyacinth forks a miniscule portion of meat into her mouth. The unfairness of her situation is almost overwhelming. Lobelia, upon the slightest pretext, can take to her bed, whilst Hyacinth has to soldier on, suffering in silence. (Although, as a small inconvenient inner voice reminds her, she isn't really suffering at all – merely pretending she is so that she can sneak out and meet Lonely Widower).

Angrily, she clatters the plates, causing further eyebrow-lifting.

"I do not know why you are behaving so childishly, Hyacinth," Lobelia remarks acidly, "I have only asked that you accompany me this afternoon. You missed church last Sunday – and Reverend Bittersplit preached so eloquently upon idleness. Something that seems to be your besetting sin at the moment."

"And what if I do not want to go?"

Lobelia laughs harshly. It is not a pleasant sound.

"Want? What is this sudden 'want'? We are not put on this earth for our own 'wants' Hyacinth. Anyway,

I'm afraid you have no choice. I cannot continue to make excuses for your absence."

She folds her thin lips together and eyes her sister disapprovingly. Hyacinth glares back at her, two spots of colour in each cheek.

"Temper, temper," Lobelia scolds. "Always the way with you. I recall how Mama used to say: *I can beat her and beat her, but the temper will not come out*."

She rises and walks to the door. Turning on the threshold, she says,

"Be ready at 2.30 prompt, please. I do not wish to keep the committee waiting."

Hyacinth returns to the kitchen and rereads her letter. Joy and duty. One of them is going to smash. She washes up the luncheon things. Then she tiptoes upstairs. Lobelia's door is shut – she is probably taking a brief nap. Hyacinth changes out of her morning dress into a smarter one, takes her best bonnet and shawl, and tiptoes downstairs once more.

She opens the front door as quietly as she can and steps out into the street. There will be consequences to face later, and she knows they will be dire, but right now she is not going to think about them. Her heart is singing like a caged bird set free. She almost dances her way to the cab rank at the bottom of the street.

Some time later, Hyacinth alights at the top of Hampstead High Street. She crosses the road, trying to keep her shoes and the hem of her dress from getting splashed by the many muddy dung-filled puddles, and makes her way to the tea-room.

Lonely Widower is already waiting. He rises and smiles at her. Hyacinth feels her heart beating faster. This moment is worth all the scolding she will have to endure upon her return. Blushing, she threads her way between the tables.

"Hyacinth."

He says her name in a way she has never heard it said before. As if he liked the sound of it; as if it were special, not a name to be uttered crossly, or angrily, or scornfully. She feels lightheaded. This must be what being slightly drunk feels like. Not that she drinks; the nearest she has ever got is a tiny sip of syrupy Communion wine once a month.

The waitress pulls out her chair. Hyacinth sinks into it and begins to remove her gloves.

"I am so glad you have come," Lonely Widower says. "And look – I have secured our table once more. I'm afraid I always think of it as 'our table' now whenever I recall that happy first meeting."

"Yes, I think so too," she admits shyly.

"I have also taken the liberty of ordering the identical tea – I hope you do not mind."

"Oh no, that is just what I would like."

"We are very similar in our thinking, aren't we?" he says, sitting back and regarding her intently.

Hyacinth is so overcome that she lowers her head and focuses on the gloves lying in her lap. The waitress brings the tea and cakes. She gives Hyacinth a quick glance as she lays out the plates and pours the fragrant liquid into the two china cups.

"Now, let us eat," Lonely Widower says, passing her the plate of cakes.

Hyacinth takes one, but finds she cannot manage more than a few crumbs. She is too excited at the prospect of what lies ahead. Lonely Widower, however, makes a good meal. Cake after cake vanishes and the waitress refills his cup three times.

Finally, he wipes his mouth carefully and folds his napkin.

"Now, to the matter I mentioned in my letter," he says.

Hyacinth can barely utter a small squeaky "Yes?"

"I have spoken and written often about my dear precious girl Agnes and her delicate state of health, have I not?"

Hyacinth nods.

"Indeed, were it not for her condition, I should have been able to see you far more often, maybe take you to dinner and a concert or theatre performance," he sighs. "But all those lovely occasions have had to be set aside. I must be at her beck and call as much as possible. I know you have understood, and it is greatly to your credit."

Hyacinth smiles modestly and looks down.

"However, a wonderful thing has happened. And I wanted to share it with you, as you are the young lady who is, if I might be very bold, second only in my affections. Agnes has the opportunity of going abroad to visit a spa. It will greatly improve her health and make her pain and suffering so much better."

Hyacinth looks pleased.

"It would also give us the opportunity, in her absence – which may be as long as six weeks, her doctor says – to spend more time together. I should like that so much, Hyacinth, wouldn't you?"

Hyacinth makes a small choking sound.

"But there is one thing standing in the way of poor Agnes' trip and our treats: the cost. Six weeks abroad ...." He sighs, lets his voice tail off and shakes his head sadly. "I so want my ewe lamb to be well enough to dance at ... but no," he hastily corrects himself, "I presume too much; I have spoken too freely."

Hyacinth's throat is so dry and her heart is pounding so loudly that she is sure he can hear it – that the hovering waitress can hear it, that the whole tea-room can hear it.

"What can I do?" she hears herself ask, in a voice she doesn't recognise as hers.

"I cannot ask you for money – that would be too much, and I will not do it Hyacinth, no I will not. Maybe I could solicit your prayers instead? I shall try to raise the necessary amount as best I can."

Hyacinth begins to speak. Stops. Then begins again.

"I have some jewellery left to me by Mama. Perhaps I could sell it?"

He raises both hands in horror.

"SELL your beloved Mother's jewels? Oh Hyacinth, Hyacinth!"

She wasn't that beloved, Hyacinth thinks silently. *And the jewels are very ugly and old-fashioned.* A memory of Mama in her final days rises to her mind. Red-faced, finger-pointing, nit-picking, fault-finding.

"I shall sell them," she says, sticking her chin into the air. "I do not think it will take me long to do so and I will write to you when I have done. The living are more important that the dead. Your daughter shall have her trip abroad."

He reaches across the table and clasps her hands in his.

"I have no words," he says. "None. You have acted exactly as I knew you would do, and I thank you from the bottom of my heart. I shall tell Agnes when I return of the kind, generous precious girl I have come to know, and one day ... if all goes to plan ..." He stops, gets out a handkerchief and mops his eyes.

Hyacinth fixes her eyes on the contents of her teacup, waiting breathlessly for him to regain his composure.

"Ah Hyacinth, you are one in a million – no, one in a million million," Lonely Widower declares. "And now let me settle the bill. I am anxious to go straight back and convey the joyful news to poor dear Agnes. How happy she will be when I tell her!"

He pays the waitress, then helps Hyacinth on with her shawl, before escorting her to the door of the tea room.

"I cannot wait to see you again," he murmurs in her ear as he puts her into a cab. "What a wonderful, wonderful person you are, my Hyacinth – and to think that had I not inserted that advert, and you had not answered it, our paths might never have crossed."

Hyacinth can barely breathe. She feels light, fragile, as if she were made of glass. Touch her and she will fall to pieces with happiness. The carriage clops along the sun-drenched streets. There is nothing I would change about my life, she thinks. The only fly in the sugar-bowl is the prospect of facing Lobelia upon her return.

But it doesn't matter about Lobelia and what she will think, Hyacinth reminds herself, nor what Mama's committee ladies think, nor what Reverend Bittersplit and his sour-puss daughter Bethica think. Because soon, very soon, she will not be there for them to think it.

****

For some, the course of true love runs smoothly. For others, it barely moves at all. Here is Emily Benet sitting at the sewing table, stitching Nottingham lace onto a beautiful peacock blue silk taffeta ball gown. The lace is very fine and she is having to bend close to it to ensure that each tiny stitch is placed exactly against the edge of the lace, so that it will not show.

Her eyes feel as if they have rings of fire surrounding them, the effect of sitting up late last night and the night before that. Her wrists have pins and needles and her fingers are swollen.

Added to this, Emily has been unable to go shopping after work – not that there is any 'after work' at the moment, it is more a case of re-locating work from one room to another. This means that her meagre store cupboard has not been replenished. For the past week, she has existed on the coffee and bread supplied by the store, and a few sips of water.

But it is always like this, and has always been like this, she reminds herself. For the Season is in full swing, society is in town, and balls and evening parties are being held everywhere in fine houses, keeping the sewing-room girls as busy, as they always are at this time of year.

Let us focus for a while on the peacock blue silk taffeta dress. Emily has just put the last stitch into it and bitten off the thread. Now it is hanging on a model while Mrs Crevice subjects it to a minute examination. Being found satisfactory, it leaves the sewing-room for the showroom, where it is carefully packed in tissue paper and placed into one of the department store's distinctive striped boxes.

From there it is dispatched by carriage to a big white pillared house in Knightsbridge, where the ladies' maid carries it straight up to the bedroom of a very pretty and very rich young lady. She has bright blue eyes and blonde hair, and the sort of fair porcelain skin that is enhanced by wearing blue. The lovely dress is taken out of the box and laid upon a white-canopied bed to await its owner's return.

Its owner is out with her Mama right now, choosing some new dancing shoes for the ball tonight. It will be her first ball and she is almost beside herself with anticipation and excitement. Already there have been giggly conversations with her close girl friends, little notes on pressed paper have been exchanged, confidences shared, secrets whispered.

On her return, she will hurry up to her room to see her new dress. She will pick it up, exclaiming how fine it is. Then she will hold it up against herself and look in the mirror. How beautiful she looks! She actually dances a few steps, her eyes shining, a pink flush on her pretty cheeks as she anticipates the effect she will have upon certain young gentlemen's hearts tonight.

Later she will be dressed by the ladies' maid, her hair crimped and fashionably curled. A pearl necklace, a present from her dear kind brother in India, will be fastened round her white swan neck. She will be the cynosure of all eyes as her little slippered feet patter out the rhythms of the music. Her dance card will be full.

After the ball is over, she will be driven home by the big-calved footman who secretly dotes on her, as do all the male staff. In one of those ironic coincidences, the carriage will pass by a close-shaven man walking towards Oxford Street with a fixed and determined expression on his face. His name is Jack Cully, but she will not know this.

Nor will Jack Cully know that just a few feet away, the work of Emily Benet's skilled hands is being driven home. It is the closest the dressmaker and detective have come to each other for weeks.

On her return, the rich young lady will be divested of the peacock blue silk dress which will be hung in a wardrobe alongside a whole row of other pretty silk dresses, all worn only once, until eventually it will be taken out and cut down for a younger sister to wear.

****

Meanwhile, the carriage passes and Cully walks. He has taken to walking the streets after dark, crossing the threshold of the night city, co-mingling with the ghosts of the past and the outcasts of the present. In these night-time wanderings, he passes houses lit like shops, shops lit like theatres, brightly illuminated windows, dance-halls and supper-rooms. Behind these lie stifling alleys and dark courts shouldering one another, cabining and confining whole nests of poverty-stricken inhabitants.

Cully always follows the same route, crossing from pool of light to pool of light like someone connecting dots, his steps unwavering until he reaches his destination: a row of dilapidated lodging houses, their peeling painted doors bearing witness to years of neglect. He positions himself in a doorway, his eyes fixed upon one lighted window high up, where a small candle flickers and burns.

Only when the flame is extinguished does he leave his post, turning up his coat collar against the night chill to pursue his lonely way back to his own solitary lodgings and his own silent hearth. Hard times.

****

For Hyacinth and her older sister Lobelia, it is more a case of interesting times. Prior to Hyacinth's unexplained and defiant disobedience, the hierarchical structure in the Clout household was quite clear, having been established over years and years of verbal attrition. Now the sisters appear to have entered a country where they do not know the vocabulary or the rules of conduct. And there are no guide books to help them.

It is morning. Rain stutters against the windows as if unsure of its intentions. The Clout sisters are seated either side of the breakfast table, over which gloom has settled like a grey fog. Lobelia cuts her toast in a determined manner, her mouth set in a grim line.

Hyacinth toys with a slice of bacon. She is far too nervous to eat.

Today she has arranged to meet her friend Portia Mullygrub in town. Together they are going to take Mama's jewels to a reputable jeweller. When she has sold them, Hyacinth will write to Lonely Widower. Then they will meet for tea and she will give him the money for his dear daughter Agnes' trip abroad.

Her thinking has not progressed beyond this point. She dares not let it.

"I am going to copy out Reverend Bittersplit's sermon straight after breakfast," Lobelia says. "The one he preached last Sunday. I thought it was particularly fine. And most appropriate," she adds giving Hyacinth a meaningful glance.

Hyacinth scrolls back. Ah yes. The sermon on *The Sin of Disobedience*. It had necessitated a lot of lectern-thumping and punitive verses from the Old Testament, uttered in the sonorous drawl Reverend Bittersplit always adopted for preaching, and that worked on Hyacinth's nerves like a fork on a metal saucepan.

A couple of times during the sermon he had stared long and hard in her direction as if he were addressing his words directly at her. Indeed, a few of the simpler members of the congregation had actually turned around and stared at her too. It had been most annoying.

"Well, I am going out as soon as I have cleared the breakfast plates," she says.

Lobelia's head shoots up.

"Oh? And where are you going? Or am I now no longer to be privy to your movements?" she inquires acidly.

"I am meeting Miss Portia Mullygrub," Hyacinth replies. "You remember her mother speaking at a church meeting, surely?"

Lobelia's expression could sour milk.

"I do not understand this constant wish to 'go out'. Mama did not 'go out' except to chair committees or to attend church or church events. I do not 'go out'. Indeed, I consider it totally inappropriate for a young woman to be seen on the public streets without a chaperone."

"I am twenty-two years old," Hyacinth retorts. "Nobody of my age needs a chaperone anymore. Those days have gone. If you came with me you'd see many young women shopping or walking around on their own. Anyway, I shall not be on my own, as I am meeting a friend."

"And since when did you decide to extend your friendship to those outside our own immediate circle of acquaintances?"

Hyacinth feels an intense weariness steal over her. Talking to Lobelia is like holding a conversation in the dark with a black cat. In response, she gets up and walks across the room.

"Wait, Hyacinth!" Lobelia orders. "I have not finished speaking!"

But I have finished listening, Hyacinth thinks. Averting her eyes from her sister's mottled angry face, she walks out of the room. The sooner she sells Mama's jewellery the better; she simply cannot go on living here for much longer.

Some time later a small procession makes its way up Ludgate Hill. The participants are: Portia Mullygrub, Cordelia Mullygrub, Hyacinth, a perambulator and a couple of laggard small Mullygrubs who keep getting terribly distracted by the wagons and horses slipping and sliding on the steep cobbled street.

After some cogitation in the cab, Hyacinth has decided not to tell Portia the true reason for their journey. Lonely Widower and his sickly daughter will remain her secret for a while longer. At least until he has declared, and a date has been set for their joyful union.

With a degree of chivvying, the party reaches their destination just beyond the Belle Sauvage Inn: a jeweller's shop with bracelets and brooches on trays in the curved shop window, and a sign indicating that the owners buy old jewellery and gold.

"I shall wait outside," Portia says, stuffing stray hair back under her bonnet. "My clothes do not bear scrutiny today, and the children are not fit to be seen in such a smart shop."

Hyacinth pushes open the door. A jangly bell summons a middle-aged man from some inner recess. He smiles at her, rubbing his hands together.

"Good morning Madam. How may I be of assistance to you on this bright Spring morning?" he asks. "We have a fine selection of brooches and ladies' watches, if you care to take a look at them."

Hyacinth notes the whiteness of his linen, the gold cravat pin and ruby signet ring. She remembers Lonely Widower's clean and spotless appearance. These things are important. They show that here is someone who takes care of themselves, someone to be trusted.

"I have not come here to buy anything," she says, reaching into her bag. "I would like to sell some jewellery. That is, if you are interested in buying it. The items belonged to my Mama. She died some time ago."

The shop owner takes the corded velvet bag and tips Hyacinth's small share of Mama's rings, bracelets and necklaces onto the counter. He picks up a jeweller's loupe and goes to work.

Hyacinth watches as item after item is held up to the light, then subjected to a minute scrutiny. Finally, the man nods to himself a couple of times in a satisfied manner.

"There are some nice pieces here, Miss. Of course, the settings are a little old-fashioned for modern taste and will have to be altered, but the stones are good. I am prepared to offer you eighty pounds. What do you say?"

Hyacinth catches her breath. It is considerably more than she expected.

"I ... I shall be delighted to accept," she stammers.

While she waits for the jeweller to write out the paperwork and hand her the money, Hyacinth passes the time by picturing Lonely Widower's face after she has told him the good news. How happy he will be! And poor Agnes too. A warm beneficent glow suffuses her heart.

Eventually the transaction is complete. Hyacinth stuffs the notes into her bag and rejoins Portia and Cordelia outside the shop.

"It is done," she says.

Portia gestures towards the window.

"There are some beautiful rings in this shop," she says. "I wish Traffy might buy me a ring, but if he did we would have no money to start out in life."

She takes firm hold of the perambulator handle.

"Now we must return. Ma is supposed to be cooking the dinner, but she is working on her lecture tour, and I worry that the food will burn."

They retrace their steps, Cordelia holding the hands of the small Mullygrubs, as they have a tendency to stray off the pavement and into the road. At the bottom of the hill they pass by a sweetshop. Hyacinth stops.

"May I buy the children some sweets?" she asks.

The small Mullygrubs instantly cluster round their sister, staring up at her, their faces wreathed in hopeful smiles. Portia hesitates, then nods her head.

"You may," she says graciously.

Hyacinth enters the shop. It is one of those old-fashioned shops with wooden shelves containing jars of lovely coloured sweets, softly glowing like jewels. There is a tray of broken toffee pieces on the counter, some brass scales and a small wooden shovel.

The shop reminds her of when she was a girl. There was a sweet shop just like this by the park. What was its name? She searches her memory: *Mrs Gulliver's Sweetshop and Confectioner*.

Hyacinth scans the labels on the glass jars. Bullseyes, fudge, pear drops, humbugs, liquorice comfits. All the old familiar names of her childhood. She glances towards the window. On the other side of the glass she sees Portia waiting with the perambulator. Just as she remembers seeing Lobelia waiting, on a summer afternoon so long ago ...

Past and present elide.

Hyacinth is six years old, standing by the counter in Mrs Gulliver's shop, clutching a penny. It is a hot day. Lobelia is waiting outside with the baby in the perambulator. He has been fractious for days and Mama has had enough: "Take him out," she had commanded. "And don't bring him back until he is quiet."

The baby had cried and cried. Lobelia had rocked the perambulator but he would not settle. Even though they had tried to pacify him with his favourite blue blanket, the one Hyacinth had painstakingly chain-stitched with his name.

So Lobelia had said they would buy some sweets, and give him one to keep him quiet. Hyacinth has been sent with the precious penny to buy the sweets.

Mrs Gulliver waits patiently for her to make up her mind. But Hyacinth cannot choose. There are so many jars, and the responsibility of choosing the right sweets hangs above her like a great weight. If she gets it wrong, Lobelia will slap her and pinch her. Then she will tell Mama, who will send her to her room without her supper.

The young Hyacinth glances through the sweet shop window seeking guidance, and sees Lobelia standing in the middle of the pavement. The perambulator is gone. Her sister's arms are firmly folded and she is smiling and smiling, and looking down the road ...

And all at once Hyacinth cannot breathe. Her heart starts thumping in her chest and her mouth is bone dry. She didn't let go of the perambulator handle. How could she have done? She was in the shop buying sweets. Lobelia must have given it a push, sending perambulator and baby bowling along the pavement until it was out of sight.

All those years of terror, of guilt, of desperately trying to recall what had happened that sunny summer afternoon so long ago, when three went out to play but only two returned. No wonder she could never bring the incident to mind, however hard she tried: she hadn't been there in the first place.

Hyacinth is still standing in the middle of the shop, frozen in the moment, mouth agape and staring unseeingly out of the window, when she feels a tug on her sleeve. Glancing down, she sees Cordelia looking up at her, a worried expression on her pinched little face.

"Are you alright, Miss? Only Porty needs to get back."

Making a huge effort, Hyacinth pulls herself together. They choose the sweets, pay for them, and carry the bags out to the waiting Mullygrubs who receive them with great rejoicing.

All the way back to Holborn, Hyacinth has the sensation of being physically, but not really mentally present. She responds to Portia's remarks in a polite monotone. Finally, they reach Portia's street and say their goodbyes, Portia inviting her to accompany her on a future visit to the West End to buy some material to make her wedding dress.

"For I WILL marry Traffy, whatever Ma thinks," she declares defiantly.

Hyacinth agrees, but for all she knows she might have agreed to accompany Portia on a trip to the moon. She hails a cab and gives the driver directions to Islington.

Anger boils hotly inside her tightly corseted breast. Her mind is racing. To be so lied to and lied about! To have lived most of her life under a black cloud! To be hated and blamed by her own mother for something she never did!

Hyacinth tries hard not to think vengeful thoughts towards her sister – after all, she has been brought up a Christian. But it is difficult. Despite her best intentions, her mind cannot help straying to the kitchen table, and the collection of knives lying in the middle drawer.

****

Meanwhile, back at Scotland Yard, Detective Inspector Stride is suffering from a series of unsolved murders and a blinding headache. The two are not unrelated, though the second is not being aided by a superfluity of strong black coffee.

To achieve a successful outcome in any investigation you have to ask the right people the right questions, otherwise nothing at all useful happens. He has the distinct feeling that he isn't asking the right questions, and is racking his brains trying to work out what the right questions – and who the right people – might be.

Stride has been a policeman all his life, but he still has moments when he wonders what makes him go on fighting other people's wars so that they can have what is perceived as justice. Why has he has been blessed with a stupidity so great that he believes he can achieve something?

Ever since the first murdered woman was brought in, he has been vilified in the press, sworn at on the street, and denied help by people who might have helped him. People who, for their own safety, **should** have helped him.

He picks up Police Constable Evans' report and flicks through it once again. It came so tantalisingly close. If only the girl had returned a few minutes earlier from servicing her client, she might have been able to give them a description. It was the lack of this tangible, flesh on the bones, *I-saw-him-and-he-looked-like-this* evidence that is driving him slowly insane.

Stride is used to letting the facts speak for themselves. The trouble is he has so few of them that they are barely whispering. How could somebody walk the city streets quite openly, abduct and kill without the slightest attempt at secrecy, and yet remain as invisible as the wind?

He has heard people call London the modern Babylon. He prefers to think of it as a gigantic cesspit. Sooner or later all the filth and dregs of humanity wash up in it. Stride stares out of the grimy office window. *You're out there*, he thinks. *You're out there somewhere. And by Christ, I won't rest until I hunt you down.*

****

Spring is in the air, but the air in the sewing-room is anything but springy. The tiny windows do not open, and the proximity of leaky drains and a rotting rubbish heap in the adjacent court are also contributing to yet another bad air day.

It is as if all the goodness has been sucked out of the atmosphere in which the sewing-room girls are forced to spend ten hours a day stitching and cutting.

Thus it is hardly surprising when, with a gentle moan, Emily Benet suddenly breaks off from the silk evening dress she is sewing, utters a sigh as light as a feather falling in a cathedral, and drops to the floor.

There is instant consternation. Everyone leaps up and hurries over to where she lies, eyes closed, her face as yellowy-white as the silk bodice she has been working on. Caro, the erstwhile complainant, bends over her prone figure and places an ear close to Emily's face. She listens intently then glances up, her face ashen.

"She ain't breathing right. Someone run and find a doctor – quick!"

The pattern-cutters exchange a quick meaningful glance, before one hurries away. The rest of the young women stand in a helpless circle. Little Fan begins to cry.

Meanwhile Mrs Crevice, who has been watching proceedings with an expression of alarm on her hard face, now claps her hands authoritatively.

"Girls! That is enough. Back to work, *please* – leave Miss Benet where she lies. I am sure medical help will arrive shortly."

Caro stands. She is a big healthy-looking young woman, newly-married to a butcher, and so has access to the sort of food denied to most of the others. She towers over Mrs Crevice.

"You," she snaps, "can take your fucken '*Back to work*' and stick it where the sun don't shine. And none of us -" she shoots a warning glance round the group, "NONE of us is going ANYWHERE, until Em's been seen by a doctor."

Mrs Crevice stares at her in open-mouthed incredulity.

"I am not used to having my authority questioned, young woman," she says coldly. "Back to work all of you! Or there will be no pay at the end of the week."

Caro's chin lifts a little higher and her eyes flash anger.

"Don't none of you MOVE!" she states. "We all know why Em's fainted. It's 'cause YOU has been making her work all hours, like some of the rest of us has been. Only Em's been working harder and longer than any of us, on account of her being the new superintendent."

She folds her arms across her overall bodice, defiantly outstaring Mrs Crevice.

"You can't take away our pay. You ain't the boss – though you gives yourself the airs and graces. If you even try to do that, we will all walk out. Like those girls did in that factory over Wapping way. Em read me all about it in the newspapers. A strike, it was called. And then where will your precious customers get their fine dresses from? We ain't slaves, even though you think we are slaves and you treat us like slaves."

A few of the sewing-room girls try to slink surreptitiously away at this point, because not everybody has Caro's strength of character, nor her access to food. But they are halted by the entrance of the pattern-cutter and a physician carrying a medical bag. The physician kneels by Emily's side and studies her. He lifts her limp wrist and feels her pulse. Then he puts a listening tube to her chest. Time seems to stand still. The sewing girls hold their breath awaiting his verdict. The physician shakes his head.

"This young woman's pulse is extremely weak and irregular and her heartbeat is too sluggish," he says. "I also notice that she seems quite wasted. When did she last eat?"

A murmur of amusement runs round the crowd.

"We don't eat, Mr Doctor," one girl says. "Look around you. We are far too busy. We has a bite and a sup of tea when we can."

"*If* we can," another girl adds.

The physician stands.

"You were lucky I was passing then," he says. "This young woman has collapsed. Her whole system appears to have broken down. Also, she is also clearly suffering from semi-starvation."

"So when might she be fit to resume work?" Mrs Crevice inquires, ignoring Caro's incredulous expression.

"It is unlikely she will ever be fit for work of this sort again," the physician replies. "Indeed, unless her present situation is swiftly remedied, I do not even see her lasting out the week."

Shocked silence greets his words.

"Is there no medicine you could give her?" Caro asks.

He shakes his head.

"Far too late for that, my girl," he says grimly.

The doctor packs his bag, then glances round the room.

"I was actually on the way to see a very important patient when I was diverted here," he says. "To whom should I send my bill for this consultation?"

"Send it to the owner of the store," Caro spits. "He's the fucken arsehole who did this to her."

She beckons to Little Fan.

"Cut along and get my Davey – you know where he works. Tell him to bring a hurdle or a door – summat to carry Em on. We need to get her out of here and into the fresh air."

She gives Mrs Crevice a steel-capped look.

"And don't think for one minute you're going to dock her pay, or mine. 'Cause if you do, I'll tell my husband. And then you'll have him to deal with. And he's got a right nasty temper on him when his dander is up, so I wouldn't try him if I was you."

Little Fan cuts along as fast as her short legs and her streaming eyes will allow her. Meanwhile Caro fetches Emily's shawl and gently covers her with it. Her eyes are full of unshed tears as she looks down on the limp figure. Then she lowers herself to the floor, gently takes Emily's unprotesting head in her hands, and cradles her in her lap.

One by one the girls return to their work, but there is none of the former banter across the big sewing table. They work in utter silence, grim-faced and not making eye contact with each other. Even Mrs Crevice keeps to her own area and does not attempt to interfere, chivvy or criticise.

After what seems like an eternity, Little Fan returns in the company of two big beefy-armed young men in butcher's aprons. They are carrying a piece of wooden board. They scoop Emily up as easily as if she was a small child and lay her gently on the flat wooden surface. With Caro bringing up the rear, they carry her out of the sewing-room.

As usual, Jack Cully will mount his vigil outside Emily Benet's lodging house that night. He will observe the absence of candlelight, but will deduce that the young seamstress is having a well-deserved rest. It will take him two more nights to realise that something is wrong.

$$****$$

London in 1861 is the capital of leisure and pleasure. It is the Mecca of marvels, the Eldorado of entertainment. There is the Crystal Palace, the Zoological Gardens, Westminster Abbey, the Gallery of Antiquities in the British Museum, to name but a few of the sights.

London embraces you. It takes you to its smoggy foggy heart. It can also pick your pocket, rip you off and leave you with some very nasty intestinal problems, but that is all part of its charm.

All you need is *Bradshaw's Guide Through London And Its Environs* (purchasable at every railway station throughout Great Britain and Ireland), money, and a willingness to be amazed. The city will do the rest.

And here, with a copy of the first and a rapidly declining amount of the second, are Effie McGraw and her husband James, down from Edinburgh on a wee break. It is the first holiday they have taken for years, and she at least is determined to enjoy it.

So far, they have been to visit Tussaud's Wax Exhibition in Baker Street (one shilling each), where she marvelled at the display of Monarchs of England, and he paid special heed to the depraved and bloodstained members of the criminal fraternity.

They have been to the Royal Academy (one shilling each), and the Tower Jewel Office (sixpence each). Here they saw the Imperial Crown, which almost took her breath away, though he seemed more interested in the number of warders and guards, even going so far as to make notes in the green octavo notebook (threepence) purchased from W.H. Smith upon their arrival at Kings Cross railway station.

Now they are sitting at a marble-topped table in a small elegant tea-room, partaking of light refreshments.

"It's an awfu' big place, this London, is it not?" Effie remarks, breaking into a scone.

"Aye, it certainly is that, my dear," her husband agrees.

And awfu' expensive, he thinks dourly, regarding his plate of 'one shilling tea'. There does not seem much on it for the price. Also, he is not one for dainty French creations filled with cream. Give him a good honest slab of his wife's home-made fruit cake any day. Sticks to your ribs, and keeps you going in the dreich Edinburgh weather.

Effie consults the *Bradshaw*.

"I thought we might go back to that nice arcade in Piccadilly after our tea," she says. "I saw a very pretty shawl and mantle shop there."

"Uh-huh, uh-huh. Whatever you want, my love," James McGraw nods.

It is Effie's holiday after all, even though it is his pocketbook that is funding it. He pays the waitress and they sally forth into the crowded noisy thoroughfare. James takes his wife's arm and steers her round the inevitable sandwich-board men and street musicians who ply their trade to the detriment of those who just wish to stroll about in peace.

As they walk, he keeps a sharp eye out for pickpockets and small boys with nefarious inclinations. For James McGraw knows the ways of the street, aye, he surely does that. Progressing in fits and starts towards the Strand, his eye is caught and then held by a newsvendor's board on the opposite side of the street. It bears the ominous words:

Where Will The Slasher Strike Next?
London Lives in Fear! Detective Police Baffled.

James McGraw carefully places his wife in front of a shop window, telling her to remain exactly where she is and not to move or speak to anybody until he returns. Then, with surprising agility for a man of his age and bulk, he darts across the busy street.

A few minutes later he is back, triumphantly bearing a copy of *The Inquirer*.

"Aw Jamie – what would you want with that London paper?" Effie protests. "It'll no be full of any nice news."

"Indeed," her husband agrees. "But it is always interesting to see what the guid folks of London Town are up to."

He folds up the paper and tucks it into his outer coat pocket. Later, after a meat supper in the hotel, and when Effie is sound asleep in the bed that is far too soft for his taste, Inspector James McGraw will sit in the armchair, unfold the newspaper and finally read the story beneath the headlines.

So, my bairn, he'll think, *we meet again. Now, who'd ever have thought it?*

****

Now that she knows the truth, Hyacinth Clout would never have thought she could continue living in the family house with her sister Lobelia without words being said or worse being done. But somehow, she is managing to keep both her temper, and her hands off the kitchen knives.

Instead of confrontation, she has decided to adopt a bright brittle tone when speaking to Lobelia. When she has to speak to Lobelia. Most of the time she tries not to speak to Lobelia if she can avoid doing so. Meanwhile she awaits anxiously for the reply to her letter to *Lonely Widower*.

Three long days have passed since she wrote to him, then sneaked out to the post-box and dropped the missive into its green maw. Three days during which she and tension have become good friends. Surely she cannot have to wait much longer?

"I shall be going out later," Lobelia announces suddenly.

The sisters are seated at their desks in the morning room, dealing with correspondence. Or rather, Lobelia is. Hyacinth is drawing small desperate concentric circles on a piece of blotting paper. She does not look up.

"I shall be spending most of the day with my good friend Bethica," Lobelia continues. "We will be using our time profitably to organise a charitable sale of work for those in need. As dear Mama used to do. You need not prepare any luncheon, as I shall have mine at the Vicarage."

Hyacinth presses her lips together. There is another entire conversation going on here. One she has chosen not to have. For now.

Lobelia gives her a long penetrating stare as if making up her mind about something.

"I am not sure why you are behaving in this silly and childish manner, Hyacinth. I will say that I won't tolerate it for much longer. I suggest in my absence that you reflect upon your current conduct. Maybe read a few chapters of your Bible. I shall leave upon the hall table a sermon Reverend Bittersplit preached some time ago on the subject of Straying from the True Path of Righteousness. I commend it to your perusal."

She gets up and stalks out of the room. Hyacinth tries not to react, but hot tears of anger come unbidden to her eyes. She stabs the nib of the pen into the blotting paper. It breaks.

Later, when she is sure Lobelia has left the house, Hyacinth pens another quick letter to *Lonely Widower*, in case the first one has gone astray. You never know; the post is not always reliable. Then she goes down to the kitchen to survey the contents of the larder. Just because Lobelia is not going to return, this doesn't mean that Hyacinth cannot have a nice luncheon. She uses Reverend Bittersplit's sermon to light the oven. It burns most satisfactorily.

****

A few miles away, Mrs Witchard's lodger has woken late, to bright sunshine shimmering round the cracks in the window blind. He rolls onto his back, latching his hands behind his head, and stares up at the ceiling. Memory sinks its teeth into his spirit and takes him away with it.

He sees a green field, high summer, the sun pouring down like molten butter from an impossibly blue sky. A boy runs across the field. He has a butterfly net. He is laughing, making great ineffective swoops in the air with the net, catching nothing. He jumps for joy, for the freedom to run, for the whole world that surrounds him and awaits him.

The lodger feels something like a sob gathering in his throat. If only he could go back in time, could step into the boy's world and warn him: *One day you will grow up to be a man. People will lie to you and abuse you. You will do terrible things to yourself; you will hurt other people.*

He lowers his legs to the bare faded wooden floor. Already the face that greets him in his shaving mirror doesn't resemble anybody he has ever met. He is a stranger in his own life. His hands reach out for the one thing that remains a constant source of solace. But when he uncorks the bottle and dips in the syringe, it comes back empty.

He stares at his hands, hands that never used to shake but now cannot stop shaking, and wonders whether anyone else has ever noticed that if the sun hit your palm a certain way, you could see right through the skin to the busy tunnels with blood moving around inside.

He rises and shambles into his clothes. No time for breakfast; he is late. Again. He has been warned that if he continues to arrive late, he will find that his current apprenticeship as a dresser to one of London's top surgeons will be terminated. He cannot allow that to happen, mainly because it will deny him access to the precious cupboard where the bottles of opium and laudanum are kept.

He will not steal from his landlady again. It is too risky. And besides, the stuff he had bought from the chemist was of inferior quality. It had not had the desired effect. The thoughts which he was trying to obliterate had reached him before sleep did.

He puts the empty little brown bottle in his pocket. He will refill it later, when there is a lull in proceedings. Today is operating day. He will have to clean tables and instruments, mop up spilt blood. Some of the patients will live; some will die on the operating table. Life. Death. Separated by such a fine thread. And how easily it is snapped.

****

Lunchtime, and Detective Inspector Stride sits alone in his accustomed booth in Sally's Chop House. He is deep in thought, so remains unaware of the numerous pairs of eyes covertly watching him. A detective deep in thought is always a worrying sight for those in the immediate vicinity, in that a detective deep in thought might quickly turn into to a detective hot on the trail.

Having spent another morning poring over crime reports and medical reports, Stride is thinking about the relativity of truth. He is beginning to conclude that it is a fairly flexible concept.

There is the truth of the police surgeon, which is based upon medical observation and digging about in dead bodies. There is the newspapers' truth, which is based upon hyperbole, scaremongering and gross inaccuracy. There is also his truth, which is based on a legal system that draws a clear demarcation line between right and wrong.

Everybody has their own truth, he concludes. And maybe, ultimately, truth is what we make of it ourselves. This, in turn, is just the sum of what is in someone else's interests, balanced by the power they hold.

All this thinking means that Stride is not eating his plate of chops, a fact that hasn't gone unnoticed by Sally, the eponymous owner, who now steps (or rather, given his size, looms) out of the background.

"Everything alright today, Mr Stride?" he asks, wiping his hands on his food-stained apron. "Chops done to your satisfaction?"

Stride stares into the middle distance broodily.

"What is truth, Sally? Do you know?"

"Couldn't say Mr Stride, I'm sure," Sally replies innocently, a lifetime of minor offences and infractions having somewhat blunted his understanding of the concept.

"No, neither can I," Stride replies grimly. "And therein lies the problem."

"Right. Right. 'Nother glass of ale with your meal?" Sally inquires, deciding to err on the side of selective stupidity.

Stride lifts his glass and takes a meditative swallow. He has barely set it down when his field of vision is unexpectedly blocked by a big bearded man in a loud tweed suit and bowler.

"Am I addressing Inspector Leo Stride?" the man asks in an unmistakably Scottish accent.

"I am Detective Inspector Stride, yes. And who might you be?"

Sally glances around swiftly, then discreetly withdraws to a listening but not noticeably intruding distance.

The big man pulls a card case from an inner pocket and hands Stride his card.

"I am Inspector James McGraw, of the parish of Leith in the city of Edinburgh," he says, sliding his bulk into the opposite bench. "Your Sergeant told me where to find you. I believe you may have one of my bairns, as I like to call them. For they were all bairns once, though they have strayed far from their innocence now."

He signals to the not-really-hovering Sally.

"A glass of your best ale and a plate of mutton chops with tatties, if you please."

Stride marvels at the ease of the man as he settles himself more comfortably, spreading his bulk to fill the narrow bench seat.

"Bairns?" he queries.

The Inspector unfolds a newspaper and spreads it out upon the table, stabbing a large tobacco-stained finger at the lead story.

"Here it is now – yesterday's newspaper: ***When Will The Slasher Strike Again?***

"Ah. I see. You don't want to believe everything you read," Stride says knowledgeably. "They make a lot of it up – especially the reporters that write for that particular rag."

McGraw leans forward, bringing his face within a couple of inches of Stride's, and lowers his voice to a confidential level.

"So, let us compare notes, Inspector Stride: We are talking about young lassies – yes?"

Stride nods.

"Each discovered sitting upright, with her throat cut? Head bashed in? No theft of personal property? No hanky-panky?"

Nods again.

"And has the bairn tried to cut out the heart of each one with a sharp knife?"

Stride sucks in his breath.

"How did you know that? It isn't in any of the newspapers. We deliberately kept it quiet."

McGraw sits back and smiles.

"I didn't know for sure. You just told me."

Stride pulls a face. Caught by the oldest trick in the book!

McGraw nods.

"Aye, it is him. For certain. He murdered two lassies, then disappeared completely just as we were closing in on him. The newspaper reporters called him the Monster of Morningside. They also like catchy headlines in my part of the world. Looks like he pitched up here in your fair city."

McGraw pauses as his meal is put on the table. He picks up his knife and fork, examining them carefully for smudges.

"For God's sake man, tell me what you know!" Stride exclaims, raising his voice without realising it and causing several diners to set down their cutlery and glance apprehensively in his direction.

"Weesht, Inspector. We don't want the whole world kenning our business," McGraw says, shaking his head. "Now then, let me taste this good London food, and after, I shall tell you all about your *Slasher*."

By the time Stride leaves the chop house, it has started to rain. Stride likes rain. Street crime goes down when it rains, because people stay indoors. Some of the best nights of his career have been rainy, when he's stood in doorways, or in the lee of a building, or under a pillar or portico, his collar pulled up, hat pulled down, and just listened to the silver rustling of the rain.

Once he'd been standing so still, so not there as it were, that a fleeing pickpocket had actually leaned against him to catch his breath. And it was only when Stride laid a quiet hand on his shoulder and whispered, *"Police. You're nicked,"* that the pickpocket realised what had happened. And wet himself.

There were few joyous moments in the life of a beat constable. That was one of them.

Stride heads back to his office, mulling over what the Scottish inspector has told him. Clearly, they had got it wrong. They had made assumptions based on false premises. Now he feels better. He had been having doubts. Not a good thing. Doubts are like cold water, and you don't want cold water when you are trying to apprehend a murderer.

He quickens his pace, hoping that Jack Cully will be waiting for him when he arrives. He has much of interest to impart.

****

But Jack Cully is not going to be there. Twenty-four hours have passed since he managed to gain entry to

Emily Benet's lodgings, and discovered that not only was her room empty, but that it had been re-let to another tenant. Twenty-four hours since he had learned from her workmates that she had collapsed, and, close to death, been carried away by Caro Wilson's husband and one of his friends.

Where she is now remains a mystery. Caro has not returned to the sewing-room, and Little Fan, the only other source of information, has not been seen since the day Emily collapsed. It is as if Emily Benet has simply vanished from the face of the earth – a conclusion that Cully just cannot bear to contemplate.

So he is attempting not to contemplate it, and to get on with his job. And while Stride is being enlightened over a plate of mutton shops, Cully is walking briskly towards the Corinthian-porticoed edifice that is University College Hospital. He thinks better when his feet are moving. The mere activity helps him to order his thoughts.

Cully is following up his own line of inquiry. He has conflated the police surgeon's comments about the knife used by the murderer to excise the hearts of his victims, together with the murderer's possible medical expertise, and has realised just how close the crime scenes are to one of the seven London teaching hospitals.

Cully enters the University College Hospital and looks around for someone to question. He is just wondering what might happen if he ventures through the double doors and into the bowels of the hospital, when the double doors are opened and a man in a porter's uniform bustles through. He stops short at the sight of the visitor.

"Yes, can I help you?"

Cully introduces himself, a move that inevitably results in the man taking a few steps back and assuming an innocent expression, as people always did, much to Cully's secret amusement.

"I wonder whether I might speak to one of the doctors," he says. "It is about the series of murders that have been taking place," he adds, lest the man assume it is a personal or medical matter.

"Do you mean one of the physicians, or one of the surgeons?"

"Exactly," Cully nods, not having a clue what the differentiation means.

The man rubs his chin.

"I'm not sure. Mr Featherstone is off today. He usually says who can or can't come into the building. Bit of a stickler for the rules and regs, he is. If you know what I mean. And it's operating day today too, so Mr Bliston is in theatre."

"I see."

Cully folds his arms, plants his feet firmly apart and adopts the *I'm-not-moving-from-this-spot* stance beloved of all police officers of whatever rank. It generally achieves its purpose.

"Oh, all right. I'll show you up to the gallery – you might be able to have a quick word in between operations. Or maybe one of his assistants could help you. As it's a police matter. Only please don't tell Mr Featherstone, will you, it's more than my life's worth."

Promising not to divulge anything to anybody, Cully follows him up the stone steps. As he does so, the reason why this isn't a good idea shuffles from the back of his mind to the front, but it is too late. He pauses on the threshold.

"Can I ask you a quick question – have you had a young woman admitted recently? Her name is Emily Benet. She collapsed at her place of work from exhaustion."

The man shakes his head.

"Only people who come here are those who needs operations. Did she need an operation?"

Cully shakes his head.

The man shrugs.

"In there," he says, waving him through the wooden door. He hurries off.

Cully enters a whitewashed brick-walled room with a bare-boarded floor area at the centre and wooden galleries all around. The word 'theatre' seems wholly appropriate: the galleries are packed with medical students leaning over the rails and peering down.

Beneath, and the focus of their gaze, is a table with a box of sawdust under it. A man lies strapped to the table, a tube in his mouth. His left trouser leg has been cut back to the thigh, revealing a bloody mass of flesh and bone.

Cully winces. It is one thing to see a dead body being prodded by the police surgeon; but this is a live individual, though the strange noises he is making right now as the surgeon approaches him carrying a sharp knife are more animal than human.

"Train guard," the student nearest him whispers, getting out his pocket watch. "Crushed his leg in a fall between the train and the platform at King's Cross. Bliston's going to amputate below the knee. Fastest surgeon in England."

The surgeon grasps the man's foot with one hand and lowers the knife to just below where his knee would have been located. There is a breathless hush, followed by cries of: "Heads, heads," directed at those nearest the table from those further back.

Cully scans the eager focused faces, trying to locate the odd one out, the one whose expression doesn't quite match that of his fellows. He barely hears the sound of the saw, the moans of the patient.

Suddenly there is a muffled cheer, followed by applause.

The surgeon glances up and calls: "Time, gentlemen please?"

"Forty-five seconds, sir," comes back the reply.

Bliston nods in a satisfied way. Wiping his hands on his frock coat, he gives instructions to the two surgical assistants, who begin swabbing and bandaging the stump. Another glance round the room and he strides majestically towards the door.

Cully hurries back downstairs, catching up with him as he crosses the foyer.

"Sir, a moment please."

Robert Bliston turns, frowning.

"If you are a member of the press, I shall not speak to you," he says coldly. "I have told you I have nothing to say. Whatever stories that woman has concocted, I shall neither confirm nor deny. You are wasting your time."

"I am Detective Sergeant Jack Cully from Scotland Yard," Cully says.

"Are you here to arrest me, detective sergeant? For God's sake! Has it come to this?" Bliston's voice rises as his black brows come together in a frown.

Cully explains his mission. Briefly.

The surgeon listens, then shakes his head.

"I know nothing of these matters. My students are all of the highest calibre – many of them were educated at Oxford or Cambridge. None would stoop to such bestiality. Now if you will excuse me, my carriage awaits."

He sweeps out, a couple of students holding the door with an air of reverence.

Cully stands helplessly in the centre of the foyer. He is just about to leave when one of the two assistants comes out of the operating theatre, his apron bright with blood.

He holds something wrapped in a cloth. Blood stains the material. For a moment, their eyes meet. The young man gives him a searching glance. Then, as the hallway fills with loud chatting students, he lowers his gaze and hurries away.

Mentally crossing University College Hospital off his list of harbourers of potential suspects, Jack Cully goes to find a cup of strong coffee and a ham sandwich. After consuming them he will visit St Thomas's and St Bartholomew's, two more local London hospitals (the outcomes will be the same, and neither will have any record of an Emily Benet). He will then make his way back to Scotland Yard, where he will be awaited by Stride and an interesting revelation.

****

There are very few revelations, interesting or otherwise, to be found in the laundry room of the Strand Union Workhouse in Cleveland Street. Here it is all soiled bedding and crusty garments. The air smells of damp, drains, stale sweat, and unwashed clothes.

A young girl with an old face stands on the top step of a high stool. She holds a wooden paddle in both hands and stirs the water in a big copper boiler. Once it has attained a modicum of heat, it will be decanted into a series of wooden tubs, each provided with a bar of cheap lye soap and a couple of washboards. A group of older women wait patiently by each tub. None of them is the mother of the young girl.

"You want to watch you don't fall in, my gal," one of the women jokes.

The girl ignores her. Face set in a venomous expression, she stirs and stirs, watching the bubbles rise. As she stirs, thoughts rise to the surface of her mind. She remembers a family scrabbling to get by, small brothers and sisters playing in the dirt. A mother who occasionally smiled.

The young girl with the old face stirs and stirs. She remembers damp walls, a leaky roof, windows stuffed with rags to keep out the draughts, a bare cupboard. A landlord without pity. A rat-faced street-hard landlord's lackey who took her father's last link to his past and broke his spirit. The bubbles rise faster.

From her perch, she can see the overseer's room. The door is open. On the table is a steaming mug of tea. She sees a plate of cold meat and bread. A box of lucifer matches. No overseer. She stops stirring and climbs down.

"Water's hot enough now," she says.

The girl walks swiftly, her bare feet cat-quiet, to the office. Pauses on the threshold. Glances over her shoulder to where the women are busy filling the tubs. Then she darts in and seizes the box of matches. Her face wiped of any expression, she re-crosses the laundry floor and goes out. The box is hidden in her hand. Her fingers stroke the sandpapered back.

The bubbles rise faster and faster.

****

Detective Inspector Stride spends the afternoon in his office rewriting his report on The Slasher in the light of the new evidence he has received, while waiting with barely concealed impatience for the return of Jack Cully. Luckily, the completion of the report and Cully's arrival in his office dovetail neatly.

Barely is Cully through the door, when Stride thrusts the report at him.

"Where have you been, Jack? Never mind, don't answer – read this. We have had a breakthrough. Finally!"

Cully stands in front of the desk and reads in silence:

New Information Received upon the Suspicious Deaths of Violet Manning, Cora Thomas, Annie Smith and Susannah Higgs

The man suspected of killing the above, known colloquially in the popular press as 'The Slasher,' has been identified by Inspector James McGraw of the parish of Leith in Edinburgh as possibly the only son of a Scottish baronet, Sir William MacKye.

The young man, baptised Edward, is living in London and likely to be using a different name. He is 24 years old, of above average height, thin build and with dark hair. He has very deep-set brown eyes and a scar on his left hand, the result of a fall in childhood.

The young man came to the attention of the Edinburgh Police when a report of harassment of his daughter was made by Mr David Balcombe, a city wine merchant, in September 1860. Mr Balcombe said his daughter Harriet (18) had met Edward MacKye, then a student at Edinburgh Medical School, at a ball in the city in the previous spring.

There was some mutual attraction; meetings and an exchange of correspondence followed, but the lady had many suitors and her interest soon waned. Also, her father's wish was for her to marry elsewhere. Upon being informed of this by Mr Balcombe, MacKye fell into a great rage and tried to remonstrate violently with him, having to be restrained by a servant and ejected from the house.

There then followed a brief period when, according to Mr Balcombe, MacKye consistently followed his daughter in the street, stood outside the house every night into the small hours, and bombarded her with letters telling her of his love for her and imploring her to run away with him.

Such was his persistence that Miss Balcombe for a short time became a prisoner in her own house, unable to leave for fear of being followed or importuned by MacKye. Even upon her engagement to another, he did not stop his unwelcome attentions. Eventually, Miss Balcombe, on the advice of her medical physician, left the family house and went to stay with relatives in England.

Miss Balcombe's rejection of MacKye's advances coincided with a number of brutal murders of young women in the city of Edinburgh. Each victim was killed in precisely the same way: the throat being cut, the head struck with a heavy object, the victim left propped up in a sitting position, and, most strikingly, deep cuts being made around the heart of each young woman with what the police believe to be a straight-back amputation knife, commonly used in surgical procedures.

The association with MacKye came to light when Mr Balcombe made his allegations to the police and supplied a description of his daughter Harriet. Inspector McGraw immediately observed that the height, fair hair, facial features and colouring of the lady was remarkably similar to those of all the victims. The Edinburgh police immediately attempted to bring MacKye in for questioning, but he evaded them and has not been seen at his lodgings or in the city environs since.

Cully finishes reading and glances up.

"So, the police surgeon was right about the medical connection."

"Yes, damn him," Stride says.

"What about the man's parents?"

"Dead," Stride says. "Estate entailed upon a distant cousin. Apparently MacKye received his inheritance when he reached the age of majority and promptly severed all contact with the family."

"Why London?"

"McGraw thinks he may be under the mistaken impression that Harriet Balcombe has moved to London. So, what do you think?"

Cully is thinking that as Emily Benet is small and dark-haired, she is safe – in one respect. In all other respects ... But he has steeled himself not to think about other respects.

"Should we continue to visit hospitals and make enquiries?" Cully asks.

Stride shrugs.

"We have no other leads. But he might be working for one of the private physicians. The whole of Bloomsbury is awash with them. Or he may have left the medical profession altogether. Who knows?"

Cully decides to ignore this. Visiting hospitals suits him. It gives him the chance to ask whether Emily Benet has been admitted. He makes a mental note to rise early and begin his enquiries afresh.

Something else is also nagging away at the back of his mind. He tries to foreground it, but to no avail. It has been a long day, he reminds himself.

Stride pinches the bridge of his nose, then pulls out his pocket watch. "Sometimes I wonder whether we are all equally deranged," he remarks, getting up and reaching for his hat. "Is the difference only who lets the monster loose and who doesn't?"

****

Much to Hyacinth Clout's surprise, Lobelia returns home from the Vicarage in a very good mood. So sunny is her temper, that the painful events of earlier in the day seem to have vanished away, like morning mist.

Indeed, Hyacinth actually hears her humming a hymn tune – one of the more positive ones – as she divests herself of her outer garments.

"Ah there you are, Hyacinth," Lobelia says, entering the parlour.

"Where else would I be?"

"Who knows? Tartary? Timbuktoo?"

Hyacinth eyes her narrowly. There is a flush on Lobelia's normally pallid face and her scrimped-back hair is escaping from its pins. Very strange.

"Did you have a good lunch at the Vicarage?" she asks cautiously.

"Oh. Lunch. Yes. I believe it was excellent."

"And how is Bethica Bittersplit? Did you organise the charitable sale of work?"

Lobelia's eyes take on a dreamy faraway expression.

"She is a wonderful friend," she declares, a little too vehemently.

Lobelia places the tips of her fingers against her mouth in a gesture that Hyacinth recognises from their childhood. It was the same gesture she used to make whenever Mama was interrogating them closely about some act of defiance or perceived misdemeanour.

The young Hyacinth had decided that she did it to stop the words from coming out, so that Mama would not get upset, and rage and shout and threaten to beat them with a stick. But there is no Mama now. Mama is dead. She eyes Lobelia curiously.

"I think I shall go up to my room," Lobelia says. "You will call me when supper is ready?"

Humming happily, she walks out. Hyacinth hears her heavy tread going up the stairs. Then along the top corridor. A pause, and a door closes. She rises and goes down to the kitchen to begin supper preparations.

Something has clearly taken place this afternoon, but what it was she cannot imagine. Mama never returned from planning a sale of work in such a mellow mood. Quite the opposite.

Still, why should she care? Hyacinth smiles a secret smile. Her hand strays to the pocket in her apron wherein lies the letter from *Lonely Widower*, finally delivered this afternoon.

She has read it so often that she almost knows it by heart.

Dearest, dearest Hyacinth (he writes),
I was so full of joy when I read your letter. How good you are to this lonely undeserving man and his poor helpless little girl. Who but an angel such as yourself would stoop to aid and succour us in our hour of greatest need?

I cannot thank and bless you enough. May I suggest that we meet tomorrow at the usual hour and in the usual place – our place, as I think of it now. I have taken the liberty of reading your precious words to Agnes. Her eyes filled with tears and she too raised her hands in blessing. 'Just think, dear father,' she said in her innocent girlish way, 'I shall now be able to get well. And when I am well, the first thing I shall do is meet and thank my benefactress for giving me back my health and strength.'

You see Hyacinth, how much your generous gift is truly appreciated.

Until tomorrow.
Your
Lonely Widower

Once again Hyacinth's eyes well up. To be so appreciated. For doing so little. It is almost too much to bear. Resolutely, she puts the contents of the letter behind her and concentrates on the task in hand. It would not do to cut herself or scald her arm. Nothing must get in the way of her leaving the house tomorrow afternoon.

She lights the oven and puts water on to boil. She can barely contain her excitement. How is she going to live through the long hours until tomorrow arrives?

****

Early evening, and the lamps in Bow Street, Covent Garden have been lit. Tonight the Royal Italian Opera is giving a performance of *Don Caspare*. The great Portofino will sing the Don. The rich and famous, the rich and infamous, and the just plain rich, are lining up in their carriages.

They are looking forward to an evening's entertainment that will have less to do with what is happening upon the stage, and more upon what is happening in the boxes that surround the stage, for the opera is always an occasion to be seen and to see.

Meanwhile, as they wait to be de-carriaged, the less rich sidle in through the ornate golden-scrolled foyer doors, trying not to brush against their better-dressed (and therefore worthier) brethren.

Look more closely. Just descending from a polished barouche is a pretty young woman barely out of her teens. She is wearing a pale-yellow silk evening gown. Diamonds glitter at her neck and on her wrist. Her black evening velvet cloak perfectly sets off her fair complexion. Her blonde ringlets bob and dance as the footman hands her down. Mama and Papa wait for her on the pavement.

It is her first opera. It is her nicest and newest dress – you may recognise it as the one Emily Benet was working on when she collapsed. Another hand has finished off the fine sewing, and here it is on its first (and possibly only) outing in the giddy social world that is the London Season.

Mama and Papa shepherd the silk dress and its wearer through the noisy pre-performance crowd in the theatre foyer. The heat from all these captive bodies is overpowering. Fans are being plied like tremulous butterfly wings.

White-gloved hands surreptitiously pat shiny faces with lace handkerchiefs, because of course a lady must never display publicly any sign that she is too hot, too cold, or too anything else.

Their progress is not going unmarked. A face at the edge of the pavement crowd has noticed the pretty one the moment she alighted from the carriage. As she enters the theatre, a man enters also. As she is borne aloft up the crimson carpeted stairs that lead to the black doors of the boxes, the man elbows his way through to the ticket seller's booth and demands a seat for tonight's performance.

He is informed there are no seats left. He requests a box. He is told there are no boxes left either. He presses his case. Again, the reply comes back, with the addition that the only empty box is number 13.

He expresses his desire to purchase a seat in this box. And is informed that for various reasons to do with superstitions around the number 13, and a rumour that it is haunted, this box remains locked at all times. Orders of the Management.

The man turns abruptly and makes his way back through the crowd. A little while later, as the first chords are being played, he will enter the theatre once more, ascend the stairs and make his way to the seat he has chosen.

Meanwhile the young woman is staring down at the magnificent gold proscenium arch and the rich red stage curtain. Light from gas lamps falls upon white shoulders, sparkling jewellery. Exotic plumes and feathers bob and sway in this very urban jungle.

The orchestra enters the pit and the musicians begin to tune their instruments. Mama hands her a playbill and a pair of opera glasses. The first notes of the overture begin. She is instantly transported. She has never heard an orchestra before. The sheer grandeur and glory of so many instruments all making a noise at once!

The audience settles down. The curtain rises. She leans forward, drinking in the music, the singing, the spectacle. Meanwhile her Mama carefully studies the occupants of the neighbouring boxes, then nudges her sharply.

"Charlotte! Mrs Rankin is bowing to you – and you with your eyes on the stage! Young George Osborne has been waiting to catch your eye this quarter of an hour ... and now you're looking at the playbill! I am mortified!"

Reluctantly, Charlotte tears her eyes away from the stage and performs her social duties. She has barely returned to her former position when she feels a strange sensation, as if someone is looking straight at her. She turns her head. It takes her some minutes to track down the source of the sensation but eventually she locates it to one of the boxes on the opposite side of the stage.

She lifts her opera glasses. The box is in total darkness, but she can just see the faint outline of man's face with a pair of glittering eyes that are watching her intently. Suddenly the watcher realises he has been spotted, and melts into the shadows at the back of the box. She waits to see if he will reappear. He does not.

The interval arrives. The yellow-silked girl slips out of the stuffy box on to the landing to get some air. She stands at the half-open door, fanning herself with her playbill, while watching the well-dressed audience promenading to and fro. People she does not know, or only knows slightly, arrive at the box and enter, to be greeted by Mama and Papa.

Nobody notices that she is missing until the second act begins, and then it is assumed that she has met up with some young friends and has gone to sit with them.

Eventually the opera reaches its inevitable conclusion: the heroine sings and dies tragically; the hero sings and survives hopefully. The orchestra plays the final chord. The audience applaud politely. The curtain falls.

Mama and Papa make their way down the crimson stairs to the foyer to await the arrival of their daughter. It will take them a while to realise that she is not coming, even longer to ascertain that she did not leave the theatre with another family.

It will be several days before the theatre staff become aware that the lock of Box 13 has been broken. Upon entering the box, they will discover the propped-up body of a young woman, her throat slit, wearing a blood-encrusted yellow silk dress, cut about the bodice. Her left hand will still be clutching a copy of the playbill.

****

But before that happens, there are other revelations. Let us return to Islington where Hyacinth and Lobelia Clout are enjoying a nicely-prepared breakfast in the sun-dappled dining room. Crisply fried bacon, poached eggs, toast cut into neat triangles and divested of its crusts, fresh butter, homemade raspberry jam and hot coffee, all await consumption.

Hyacinth has excelled herself this morning, as Lobelia herself remarks, unfolding her napkin and eyeing the groaning board with approbation. And last night, Hyacinth made an apple pie whose crust was so light it melted in the mouth.

Little does Lobelia suspect, as she helps herself to the crispest of the rashers, that it is not sororial affection that is producing this veritable feast of good things. Hyacinth is mentally preparing for this afternoon.

She is sublimating her nerves by running through her culinary repertoire, even though Lobelia is the only fortunate recipient. Cooking is a calming occupation. It fills up the time leading to her meeting with *Lonely Widower*.

After breakfast, Hyacinth descends to the kitchen to make the suet pastry crust for a steak and kidney pie, which is soon wrapped in a checked pudding cloth and placed on a trivet over a pan of boiling water. A bottled cherry pie is also placed in the oven beneath, and a pink strawberry-flavoured shape cools on a larder shelf. Time positively whizzes by.

Almost before she knows it, luncheon o'clock rolls around. Cold beef, some boiled potatoes and a glass jar of pickles are placed on the table, together with the rest of the apple pie (which, Hyacinth notices, is now somewhat smaller than it was when she put it away last night). Lobelia makes a hearty meal, scarcely seeming to notice that Hyacinth just picks at her food.

As soon as Lobelia has retired to her room for an hour or so of Bible reading and meditation, Hyacinth tiptoes upstairs and begins her preparations. She has a new dress, purchased ready-made. She bought it when she and Portia Mullygrub went shopping for the material for Portia's wedding dress. It is a nice bright blue poplin, with cream lace around the collar and cuffs and on the front bodice seams.

Hyacinth has never bought a new dress in her life – she has always made her own clothes. But she decided a disbursement from the money she'd received was justified. And Portia had agreed, though Hyacinth had not told her what occasion the dress was for.

Now she slips it over her head, struggling with the back buttons, and regards herself in her mirror. She looks so different! The blue poplin brings out the blue colour of her eyes, and the subtle tailoring of the bodice gives her figure unaccustomed curves and a tiny waist.

Hyacinth puts on a pair of bronze kid boots (another recent purchase) and arranges her hair in two side bunches and a back bun. She folds the banknotes and places them at the bottom of her bag. Then she tiptoes back downstairs to complete her outfit with shawl and bonnet.

Checking that she has her door key and a clean pocket handkerchief, she opens the front door and slips out. She picks up a hackney carriage and gives the driver precise instructions. All the way to Hampstead, she sits with her hands tightly clasped in her lap, marvelling that the people and traffic passing by are unaware that inside the cab is someone whose world may be about to change forever.

Alighting at her destination, she pays the driver two shillings, then makes her way to the Lily Lounge. She enters, sits down at the accustomed table and composes herself. Minutes pass. The door to the tea-room opens and shuts, opens and shuts, but the man she is waiting for with bated breath and beating heart does not appear.

Hyacinth checks her watch. *Lonely Widower* is late. He has never been late before. She takes out his letter and rereads it. No, she has not mistaken the time, nor the day.

So, where is he? Concern turns to anxiety as the minutes tick by and he does not appear. Then, just as anxiety lurches into panic, the waitress who served them tea upon her last visit approaches the table.

"Excuse me for troubling you, Miss," she asks, "but are you possibly waiting for the gentleman with the beard?"

Hyacinth glances up, surprised.

"I might be ..." she stammers, "why do you ask?"

The waitress hands Hyacinth a card. It reads:

The Lily Lounge (select tea-room)
12 Flask Walk
off Hampstead High Street
London
(Wedding Breakfasts and Supper Parties catered for)
Mrs L. Marks, proprietress

"I am Mrs Lilith Marks," she says simply. "And I have to tell you that if you are waiting for the '*gentleman*' with the beard, he won't be coming."

Hyacinth feels the colour draining from her face. The room spins.

"How do you know this? Has he had an accident? Did he leave a message?"

The woman's dark eyes flash.

"He won't be coming because I have sent him packing. Him and all his nasty tricks."

Hyacinth's jaw drops. She stares at Lilith Marks in bewilderment.

"I'm sorry, I don't understand," she falters.

Lilith Marks signals to one of the waitresses.

"Pot of strong tea please, Mabel. I think we're going to need it."

She pulls out the chair opposite and sits down.

"You have been wickedly deceived, young lady. And you aren't the only one. Now then," she continues as the tea is brought, "I suggest you drink this while it is hot – and it's no good you looking at the door. As I said, he isn't coming."

Bewildered but obedient, Hyacinth swallows a mouthful of tea.

Lilith Marks settles herself more comfortably.

"I noticed your gentleman friend just before Christmas – soon after we first opened. He started coming in for tea regularly, always the same time, but different days. He was nicely dressed, but there was something about him that just made me suspicious. I have a very suspicious nature, you see. Especially where men are concerned. So, I made sure I was always the waitress that served him. He never noticed – men don't tend to notice waiting staff. More fool them."

She nods at Hyacinth.

"Bit more tea ... I'm sorry, I don't know your name."

"Hyacinth Clout," Hyacinth whispers.

Lilith Marks nods.

"And what name did the gentleman go by?" she asks.

"John Smithson."

Lilith smiles grimly.

"Not his real name, you can be sure of that. And where did this 'Mr Smithson' tell you he lived?"

Poor Hyacinth's lower lip is beginning to tremble.

"He did not tell me exactly, but I had the impression it was Muswell Hill."

"Clever of him then, for he also lives in Highgate and Hackney. At least, that's what he told the other two."

Hyacinth is aghast!

"The other two?"

"Janet Dunbar and Nora Barlow. Both single ladies, a bit older than you, not nearly as pretty, but very respectable. Both met him through an advert he placed in the newspapers. Both handed over their life's savings thinking he was going to make them an offer of marriage. They never saw him again."

Hyacinth's head is spinning.

"No, surely that can't be true?"

"True as I'm sitting here. Did he tell you the story about the sick daughter? Yes, I see from your face he did. There is no sick daughter, Miss Clout. And there would have been no marriage either. Once you'd handed over the money, he'd be gone like the west wind. And you'd never be able to trace him."

Hyacinth's hands are gripping the sides of the chair. It is the only way she can still remain upright.

"Both ladies returned several times, hoping to find him, for he'd stopped answering their letters and this was the only place they knew he frequented. That was how I found out what had been going on, right under my nose. I was very sorry for them, but there was nothing I could do, for he never came in again.

"Lying low spending his ill-gotten gains, I guessed. And then, a few weeks ago the door opened and in he walked, bold as brass. He'd dyed his hair, and grown a beard, but I recognised him. And then you came in."

"I was going to give him eighty pounds," Hyacinth gulps. Tears are dripping down her face now and plopping into her lap. "I sold my dead Mama's jewellery. I have the money here in my bag."

"Well, at least you'll leave with it still in your bag," Lilith Marks says. "And think yourself lucky. I sent 'Mr Smithson' packing with a flea in his ear, and the promise that if I ever saw him again I'd lock the door and contact the police. You've had a very fortunate escape, I'd say."

She pours Hyacinth a fresh cup of tea.

"We have a saying where I come from: *The heart doesn't have any bones. So it can't be broken.* Now dry your eyes and finish your tea. It's on the house."

Lilith Marks pushes back her chair and goes back behind the counter. Hyacinth mops her eyes and tried to grasp what has happened. All her hopes have just been shipwrecked. Her beautiful castle of dreams has been tumbled about her ears. Her lovely future is a thing of the past. She finishes her tea, then makes her way unsteadily back out into the street.

Even here, even now, even after all that she has been told, she still looks round hopefully before hailing a passing cab. Just in case. But he is nowhere to be seen. It is over. And before her lies a desert of life with Lobelia, a life of endless cooking and cleaning, and committee meetings and sermons and the horrible Bittersplits.

Hot tears scald her cheeks. Oh, how is she going to bear it?

****

Life is made up of variables. Whilst Hyacinth Clout (eighty pounds in pocket) is attempting to compose herself on the back seat of a hansom cab, Tonkin (hands in pockets) is strolling along Gower Street. He has spent the day extracting rent from people who are only one meal away from destitution.

Tonkin feels no pity for the hapless victims of Morbid Crevice's avarice, even though he has observed that many are so sunk in despair and apathy that they are quite unable to pull themselves up by their bootstraps. If they had bootstraps, which most do not.

Tonkin's opinion is that they deserve everything they don't get. He is working hard to better himself. He does not have much sympathy for those who choose to sit around on their ragged arses, bewailing their lot in life.

Tonkin is deliberately delaying his return to his place of employment. It is a fine afternoon, fresh air and sunshine are free, and he has siphoned off enough from the top of the rents to buy himself a meat pie.

Now replete, he saunters across Queens Square, passing the Ladies' Charity School, and the National Hospital for Nervous Diseases. Black dust blows in the air like ebonised pollen.

Tonkin stares up at the tall plane trees. The wind ruffles the branches. He imagines what it might be like to climb to the top of one and view the city from its branches. He is so engrossed with his dendrology that it takes a few seconds before his brain registers that a commotion has broken out on the other side of the street.

Glancing to his left, he sees people running towards an elderly man who has just collapsed onto the pavement. Never one to allow the slightest opportunity for possible gain to pass him by, Tonkin hurries over and joins the onlookers, who are engaging in the traditional London pastime of hanging around to see what's going to happen next.

What happens next is that someone emerges from one of the houses and starts examining the fallen man. Tonkin uses his sharp elbows to push to the front of the crowd. He uses his sharp eyes to spot that the man's leather bag and his top hat have rolled, unnoticed, into the gutter. He uses his sharp fingers to scoop them up and then his nimble legs to bear him swiftly away from the scene.

Once around the corner and out of sight, Tonkin opens the bag. Inside he finds a collection of medical instruments and a number of glass bottles full of what he soon realises, from sniffing their contents, must be medicines. A veritable treasure trove! He does a swift mental calculation – and a broad smile crosses his sallow underfed features. Here is riches indeed. Here is meat and drink and a future.

Placing the top hat at a jaunty angle on his head, Tonkin sets off to liquidate his ill-gotten gains. Not so much working his way up, as working his way along. And as Morbid Crevice is soon going to discover, the more money Tonkin obtains, the less of Tonkin's presence there is going to be.

****

London. Metropolis of narrow crooked streets, running in all directions with the spatial logic of a maze. A city built on layer upon layer of other ancient cities, which still maintain a fearful and ghostlike presence. London promises adventure, power, joy, transformation. But at the same time, it can destroy everything you are, everything you know.

Mrs Witchard's lodger rests with his head on his pillow, arms crossed heavily on his chest. The skin of his face is tight against the cheekbones, and reddened where he has shaved without water. First he is sleeping, then he is not sleeping.

He can hear the tick of his watch, separating the dark into measured time. A short while ago, he injected himself with the last of the reddish-brown liquid. He feels the calm descending. He feels himself crossing the threshold where it is too late to go back, where conscious thought stops. He doesn't want to think. He doesn't want to admit that nothing he does will ever dull the pain that comes with jealousy, rejection and humiliation.

He has no need to count his heartbeats to know that his pulse is at rest. He closes his eyes and waits for release. And then it comes, just on the brink of falling away into darkness. That feeling. The one he has come to dread more than any other: the fear. The same fear that he sees mirrored in their eyes, in all of their eyes, as they stare up at him in those last vital seconds. The murderer's fear of his own reflection.

****

Day dawns bright and clear, and the streets are bombarded by bustle. The busy throng of men, the tramping of feet on pavement, the crushing sound of cartwheels on cobbles, rattle of omnibuses, cries of costers and street vendors, and all the bewildering din that goes to make up the diurnal rush hour.

Look more closely. Here are Detective Inspector Stride and Detective Sergeant Cully, heading towards Bow Street. They have received an unusual summons. The body of a young woman has been discovered in a box at the Royal Italian Opera. Arriving outside the building, they are met by a phalanx of reporters. Stride's jaw tightens at the sight of them, more so as he spies a middle-aged couple standing in the foyer, the woman's shoulders shaking with sobs, the man's face set and ashen.

"Oi, Stride," a well-known and equally well-loathed voice calls out as the two detectives prepare to enter. "You going to sing for your supper?"

There is a ripple of laughter from the assembled hacks. Stride spins round and faces them.

"I'm sorry you find the subject of murder so amusing, Mr Dandy," he replies, each syllable etched in acid. "Perhaps if it was a member of your family, or one of your friends – if you have any, that is – you might be able to feel some compassion."

He marches up to Dandy Dick, his face a mask of blazing fury.

"The girl's parents are in there," he spits. "Have a modicum of respect, for God's sake!"

For a second, the two lock eyes. Then Dandy takes a step back. Stride nods curtly to Cully. Together they walk up the steps and into the foyer, where they are immediately accosted by the proprietor.

"Ah. The police, finally," he murmurs, leading them quickly across the foyer and to the foot of the balcony steps before the victim's parents have time to register their arrival. "The incident took place three nights ago during a performance of *Don Caspare*. The great Portofino was singing. It was a glorious triumph! I cannot believe such a thing was actually happening while the opera was being performed."

Stride gets out his notebook.

"Three nights ago?"

The proprietor leads them up the stairs to the dress circle.

"The circumstances are very unusual, Inspector." He speaks in a lowered tone. "The poor unfortunate young lady was killed – or rather was found – in a box that is always kept locked. We have our little traditions in the theatre, you see. The number thirteen is considered unlucky. It was only the comments of some patrons who reported a peculiar smell, and the presence of flies, that alerted my staff to the fact that the box had been broken into."

They have now reached the second landing.

"The parents supplied us with a very detailed description of the young lady the day after they realised she was missing. It was from this that we were able to identify her body, and then subsequently send them word to let them know."

The proprietor leads them along a red-carpeted gallery, finally stopping outside a black painted door bearing the number 13 in faded gold. He gestures.

"She is in there."

"Have any of your staff touched or moved the body?" Stride inquires.

"I cannot say for sure. Obviously, I wasn't here when she was found. Certainly, nobody has been allowed up here since I arrived."

"And the parents?"

He shakes his head.

"We thought it best ... in the circumstances, and given the nature of the young woman's demise, to wait until you arrived and to take your advice on the matter."

Stride nods. His mouth is set in a grim line as he unlatches the door and steps inside. Cully follows. The body of a young woman sits propped up against the side of the box. It is clear from the fixed and rigid position of the limbs, and the hand still clutching the playbill, that cadaveric spasm has already set in.

The blonde curls are dishevelled and matted. The face has taken on the lividity of death, and there are signs of purplish bruising under the skin. Flies buzz languidly in the heat.

Stride turns his head, whips out his handkerchief and holds it in front of his mouth. Cully stares all round, mentally taking in every aspect of the grim scene. Then he starts making notes, after which he bends down and gently picks at the dark coagulated mess on the front of the pink dress.

"There are cuts," he says. "It is him."

The two detectives quit the box. Stride leans against the wall, mouth open, breathing in the warm stale air.

"I hate this, Jack," he says quietly. "It never gets any easier, however long you've been in the job. Down there are two people, probably never done a day's harm in their lives, and their daughter's been murdered by some evil bastard purely because she looked like some woman who rejected him in the past."

He turns to the proprietor.

"I shall make arrangements for the body to be removed to the police morgue for an autopsy. In the meantime, nobody is to enter this box or touch anything. The parents may apply to Scotland Yard for the return of their daughter's body for burial, once the necessary procedures have taken place."

"But they are waiting downstairs to take her home; what shall I tell them?" the proprietor spreads his hands helplessly.

"Tell them what I've just told you," Stride says grimly. "And nobody – NOBODY, I tell you – is to talk to the reporters from the press waiting outside the theatre."

He glances round.

"I presume there is a back entrance? If you would show us where it is, we'll be on our way."

The proprietor leads the way back downstairs. They enter the stalls and head for the stage area, where members of the opera chorus, carrying their scores, are gathering by the pit piano for a rehearsal. They look round apprehensively.

"The stage door is through there, inspector," the proprietor says, gesturing towards the left-hand side of the stage.

"Oh – before I forget," Stride says, "I'd like you to contact all the staff who were in the theatre three nights ago. One of my officers will be back later to interview them. Hopefully somebody may have seen something."

He eyes the chorus.

"What are you rehearsing?"

"Act One of *La Bella Ragazza*," one of the chorus tells him. "It's a tragedy. The beautiful young heroine is killed by a false lover."

"Indeed. That is a tragedy," Stride murmurs. "Please – don't let us stop you."

They cross the stage and leave, just as the chorus-master plays the opening bars.

****

Sometimes Art imitates Life, sometimes the reverse. The tragedy of Hyacinth Clout is being played out not in a beautiful theatre but right under the noses of her nearest and dearest. Well, the nose of her nearest. The dearest has proved himself as false as the hero of *La Bella Ragazza*.

Physically, Hyacinth has moved on from the astonishing revelation of Lonely Widower's duplicity. The daily task, the monotonous routines, have been resumed. But emotionally, she is far from over it. Her nerves and her confidence have been badly shaken, and there is nobody in whom she can confide.

In addition to this, Hyacinth's plan to confront her sister Lobelia with the truth about the loss of their little brother has had to be shelved. She was only waiting until she was sure she had another home to go to. Now she has also lost the chance to expose her sister's lies and cruelty.

Hyacinth sits alone in the morning room. She is sewing a new dress. As her needle darts in and out, she remembers how Lobelia was always the one who had the new clothes. Hyacinth had her sister's hand-me-downs until she was old enough to make her own dresses – never very successfully, but good enough for the church circles in which the Clouts moved, where finery of dress was looked down upon with deep suspicion.

However, the dress she is currently sewing is not for her, though she wishes with every tiny stitch she makes that it was. Hyacinth has agreed to help her friend Portia Mullygrub with her wedding trousseau, because the chances of a white dress retaining its pristineness in a house where cups are overturned, ashes are spilled, and small children with grubby hands and faces run riot, are slender to say the least.

Added to this, Portia has currently little time to spare: Mrs Mullygrub is in high demand as a speaker, and Portia is either accompanying her, writing letters, or keeping house for her brothers and sisters.

Also, the small Mullygrubs have big mouths – and Portia does not want Traffy to know anything about the dress until he sees her in it, walking down the aisle on their wedding day. (Which IS going to happen, even though they still have nowhere to live and therefore Ma is still refusing to give them her blessing.)

It is the least Hyacinth can do, and she is doing it willingly, though the irony of the task does not escape her. As she sews the cheap white cotton material, she cannot help but compare their two situations. It is a tale of two kitties. Portia has no money, but the love of a good man. Hyacinth has eighty pounds and a lucky escape from a bad one.

The clock in the hallway chimes the half-hour. Hyacinth sighs, sets down the sleeve she is working on and goes down to the kitchen to put the kettle on. Portia will be coming over shortly to help sew. She wonders briefly what Lobelia is up to – she left the house straight after breakfast wearing her hat and mantle, without saying where she was going or when she'd be back.

Hyacinth sets out a tray with the best china cups, and cuts generous slices of sponge cake. Portia will be thirsty and hungry after her walk, and Hyacinth is not sure that she gets enough to eat at home. The tiny waist of the wedding dress bears witness to that.

She is just pouring boiling water into the warmed teapot, when the front door bell rings. Answering it, she finds a windswept Portia Mullygrub on the step, her face flushed, and her bonnet slightly askew.

"Ah, I expect I am too early and have disturbed you," she says, frizzling her hair with her fingers.

Hyacinth lets her in and helps her off with the battered bonnet and lumpily-knitted shawl.

"I am quite worn out today," Portia tells her, pulling a face. "I have been writing letters for Ma till two this morning, and my head aches. And I have had to get Pa to mind the little ones for me, without telling him why. I hate keeping secrets, but what can I do? Ma is dead set against me marrying Traffy, but if we do not marry soon, I fear he might break it off and find someone else."

Privately, Hyacinth doubts this. Underneath her slightly prickly exterior, Portia has a heart of gold. And she is very pretty, when she isn't scowling.

"You have timed it perfectly," she says. "The tea is just drawing. Now come and look at the dress – I think it is getting along very well."

She leads the way to the morning room, where the future Mrs Moggs' bridal attire is laid out on the table.

"Oh, you have got on with it since last time," Portia exclaims, cautiously lifting the basted dress by the shoulders. "And how well you have done. I should never have managed to get so far."

"I'm sure you would," Hyacinth responds.

Portia shakes her head, scattering hairpins in all directions.

"You know what the house is like. It is nothing but dirt, waste, papers, noise, confusion, and tumbling downstairs from week's end to week's end. There is no time to do anything worthwhile, and if it were not for your infinite kindness, Hyacinth, I should have to be married in my old frock. Not that Traffy would mind, for he has said many a time that it is me he is marrying, which is just as well, but even so I should not like to let him down."

She holds the dress up against herself.

Hyacinth feels a catch in her throat. Unbidden tears well up in her eyes.

"I think we should have some tea," she says quickly. "Then you can try the dress on and we will be able to see how it fits."

"Oh, it will be perfect," Portia says. "See how neatly you have set the sleeves – I wish I had learned to sew like that."

She lowers the dress carefully back onto the table and smoothes out the skirt. Then noticing Hyacinth's face, she remarks,

"But you are looking rather pale, Hyacinth, if I may be so bold as to remark. Is anything amiss?"

Hyacinth is almost tempted. But she resists. She recalls Mama's stern face whenever she approached her to confide some childhood grievance. The harsh voice telling her that *Nobody is interested in a tattletale, especially a lying one.*

She remembers Lobelia's bright triumphant little smile as she stood in the doorway, waiting for Hyacinth to pass by with her lips pressed tightly together to hold in the sobs. She has had a lifetime of suppressing her feelings. It is too late now to break habits ingrained by such an upbringing.

"I think I may have a slight head cold," she says.

Portia eyes her narrowly.

"If you say so."

Hyacinth smiles back bravely.

"A cup of tea will soon sort it," she says. "And then we must get on; we have a lot of work to do."

They descend to the kitchen. Hyacinth pours the tea, reflecting that Lobelia, were she here, would never countenance entertaining a friend in the kitchen. Common, she would call it.

Portia blows on her tea.

"This is a pretty big house to run all by yourself," she remarks.

Hyacinth explains the reasons why Mama refused to employ any domestic staff.

"But now ..." Portia begins.

But now there is the sound of the front door opening. Hyacinth shakes her head quickly. Portia gives her a knowing glance. Next minute, Hyacinth's name is called in a peremptory tone. Sighing, she gets up and ascends the basement steps.

Lobelia stands in the hallway removing her hat and blowing on the feathers.

"I observe that we have an afternoon caller," she remarks, glancing towards the shabby bonnet with its chewed strings hanging askew from the hat-stand.

"It is Portia Mullygrub. She has come to help me to sew her wedding dress."

Lobelia purses her thin lips.

"I do not think Mama would approve of taking in sewing, even if it is for a good cause."

Hyacinth presses her lips together. They eye each other in silence.

"You do not ask me where I have been, I notice," Lobelia says.

"Do you want me to ask you?"

Lobelia sniffs.

"I have been to a meeting of the Overseas Missionary Society for the Conversion of the African Heathen. Bethica Bittersplit accompanied me."

"How nice for you."

Lobelia's expression ices over.

"Your lack of interest in the work of the church, work that our dear Mama so championed while she lived, and exhorted us both to continue after her death, has been noticed."

"Has it? By whom?"

"Reverend Bittersplit has commented several times upon your absence at church prayer meetings. He has even inquired discreetly about the state of your soul."

Hyacinth fires up.

"My soul is perfectly fine, thank you. I do not need you or the Reverend to concern yourself about it."

Lobelia regards her with the expression of someone whose patience for the simple-minded is wearing thin.

"Ah. You never change, do you Hyacinth? Same today as you were when a child. Always quick to anger, quick to accuse others of fault finding when, in reality, it is you that are at fault."

Now, Hyacinth's inner avenging angel whispers, *now*. But before she can open her mouth, Portia appears in the hallway, carrying Hyacinth's teacup and her slice of cake.

"I took the liberty of bringing this up from the kitchen," she says. "I cannot spare much more time, as Ma will be back from her meeting shortly and there will be letters to write."

Hyacinth pulls herself together. What was she thinking? She cannot have a blazing argument with her sister. She has a guest. Social conventions must be followed.

"I am so sorry, Portia. I have neglected you," she says, reaching for the tea and cake.

Lobelia gives the cup and plate a hungry look.

"Ah. I see there is tea and sponge cake," she says.

"So, let us get on immediately," Hyacinth says, ignoring her.

Lobelia can get her own tea and cake. Hyacinth is not her sister's slave. Chin in the air, she sweeps past her and enters the morning room.

Portia's face is a mask of innocence as she follows her.

****

By contrast, not much work is being done in the sewing-room at Marshall & Snellgrove, despite Mrs Crevice's command to 'get back to your sewing at once!' The reason for this unexpected cessation from toil is the reappearance of Little Fan, who has just tiptoed quietly in, looking even more confused and anxious than before her absence.

Her arrival provokes an instant down-needles as the girls gather round, questioning her about the whereabouts and the fate of Emily Benet. Little Fan, overwhelmed by the unexpected attention, is initially reduced to silence.

Eventually, after much prodding and probing, she stammers out that as far as she heard it, Emily Benet was taken away, all of a suddenly, in a carriage which had problems navigating the narrow back streets and knocked over Mrs Towler's fruit stall. She hasn't seen her since.

Having imparted this information, Little Fan picks up the broom and begins sweeping under and around the tables, as if she has never left. The sewing-room girls exchange glances. Someone circles a finger at the side of their temple. There are nods of agreement, some shrugs. Then, at Mrs Crevice's repeated command, the girls return to their sewing.

"At least she isn't dead," one of the pattern-cutters murmurs to her neighbour.

"You don't know that for sure. Maybe she was being taken away to be buried," remarks the neighbour, who isn't known for her cheerful disposition.

"If she was dead, Caro'd have told us, surely?" a finisher adds.

"If she remembered," the gloomy neighbour answers. "We aren't exactly top of her visiting list any more are we? Gone a bit high and bloody mighty now she's moved on."

For the redoubtable Caroline has quit the sewing-room and joined her husband in his butcher's business, the ability to stand up for oneself and confront authority both being very transferable skills.

"So, you reckon poor Em's dead and buried?" the pattern-cutter sighs.

"We all seen the state of her, didn't we? We all heard what that quack said?" Miss Cheerful replies. "Why would she be taken off in a carriage if she was alive and well? Anyway, management seem to think so, since they've filled her place pretty quickly."

The remark 'Dead man's shoes' hovers in the air, looking for somewhere to land. All eyes swivel to Emily Benet's seat, and to the new girl sitting there, who is keeping her head down and concentrating furiously on her sewing.

Silence falls, heavy as a brick. The sewing-room girls stare at the new girl. They exchange meaningful glances. Then they bend their faces to their work once more, for when all is said and done, they each have a living to earn. Nobody speaks. The only sound is the tuneless humming of Little Fan as she chases tiny bits of cloth and thread around the room, an expression of fixed intensity on her simple childlike face.

****

Over at Scotland Yard, there is definitely more fuming than humming. For Detective Inspector Stride, it is turning out to be one of those days, in other words, the sort that he endures most days.

Another tranche of hostile press coverage lies spread out before him on his desk. The early evening headline writers have had a field day, some focusing on the **Slasher Still At Large, Police Baffled** angle, others indulging in witty wordplay around singing and dancing.

One wag of a reporter has even got hold of a copy of a police poster and issued his own version, featuring a picture of Stride himself, under the heading **Wanted for Wasting Public Money**.

Was it any wonder that the general public were so backward in coming forward, when they were fed a constant diet of presumed police incompetence? If Stride had his way, all journalists would be boiled alive stuffed with their own copy, then fed to any passing pig.

A knock at the door heralds the entrance of Jack Cully, his expression warily hopeful.

"Come in Jack. Seen these?" Stride barks, gesturing angrily at his desk.

"Not all of them," Cully says.

Cully sincerely hopes Stride also hasn't seen all of them. The level of shallow innuendo indulged in by some of the lower order of hacks makes a puddle on the pavement look deep.

"We are dealing with crimes of unbridled brutality, and these bastards are making light of it! Would they take the same line if it was one of their daughters who'd been murdered? I think not."

Cully agrees.

"What do you think, Jack?" Stride says wearily. "Are we barking up the wrong tree?"

Cully shrugs.

"But I've heard back from the Opera House," he continues. "They've got hold of the ticket seller who was on duty the night of the murder. Apparently, he remembers something about that evening. I'm on my way to interview him now. I'll take Leonard with me in case he gives us a description."

"Don't know why they employ that useless lump of a police artist," Stride mutters. "Never produced a good likeness since I've been here."

Cully keeps his face expressionless. Leonard's cartoons, including a couple of really good portraits of Stride, feature prominently on the junior constables' notice board.

A short while later, Cully and the police artist step into the foyer of the Royal Italian Opera. Here they are introduced to the ticket seller, a small limp-haired man with an old-fashioned walrus moustache, gold pince-nez glasses and a crumpled suit.

The three men repair to the back row of the stalls where, at Cully's prompting, the ticket seller tells the two policemen what happened on the night of the murder.

Cully writes it down, stopping every now and then to check or confirm a fact. Finally, he asks:

"Was there anything that struck you about the man who wanted a seat in Box 13? Anything out of the ordinary?"

"Yes. Yes, there was. He had a very penetrating stare. Didn't blink once. I found my own eyes watering in sympathy. And his clothes weren't what you'd expect from a regular patron. More what you'd wear to go for an evening stroll. He didn't even have a smart top hat."

"Would you be able to supply my artist with an exact description?"

"Pretty much. I have a good eye for faces. And there was another thing struck me as odd. I was just closing the booth. I'd put the shutters up, because after the first interval you don't get many people wanting to buy a ticket for that performance.

"Anyway, I was sorting the money into bags when I heard the sound of footsteps. So, I looked though the slats and there he was, the same man I'd seen earlier. He came running across the foyer from the balcony stairs direction as if all the fiends of Hell were at his tail. Never seen anything like it. Face pale as death, coat tails flying, hair all over the place, eyes staring out of his head.

"I remember thinking: *I say, how did you get up there without me noticing?* Next thing he'd pushed open the street doors and he was gone. I thought I must have dreamed it – until I finished work and was leaving. I like to get out before the end of the opera, miss all the crowds."

He dips into an oilcloth bag by his feet and brings out an ivory-handled knife.

"I found this just on the other side of the doors. Thought nothing of it, until Mr Cryer contacted me and told me about the murder."

He hands the knife to Cully.

"Do you think this is the murder weapon, sergeant? Because it don't look like something you'd use to peel fruit."

Cully handles the knife gingerly. Its bright steel blade glints wickedly up at him.

"It seems suspiciously clean," he remarks.

"Ah. Yes, sorry about that. I did give it a bit of a sluice under the tap when I got in. Thought it might come in useful. You can never have too many knives, can you? And I like to do a few bits and bobs around the house, help the wife out."

Cully sucks in his breath sharply, then asks,

"I don't suppose you happened to notice while you were 'sluicing it' whether the knife had any stains on the blade? Red stains .... possible of a blood-like nature?"

The man shakes his head.

"Can't recall. Like I said, I'm sorry. Mind on other things – our youngest has just gone into service and the wife is fretting about it."

Cully wraps the knife in his pocket handkerchief and places it gingerly in his coat pocket.

"Thank you very much, Mr Pinkerton. You have been most helpful."

"Is there a reward?" the man asks eagerly, his small eyes gleaming behind the pince-nez.

"Not as yet. Perhaps you'd like to work with the police artist now. Let's see if he can draw the face of the man you saw."

"Will there be a reward when you catch him? If it is him?"

Cully feels a great wave of tiredness wash over him. Over the past week he has visited hospital after hospital asking the same questions, getting the same answers. He has stood outside Emily Benet's lodgings, just because it was the last time and place he saw her. For all he knows, she could be anywhere on God's green earth. Or possibly under it.

A few hours ago, he had stood over the decomposing body of another young woman whose life had been snuffed out like a candle in a gale. And now he has to deal with greedy little men like this.

"I am sure the Metropolitan Police will be very grateful for any information you can supply," he says, wooden-faced.

He turns to Leonard, who is preparing his sketchbook and lining up his pencils.

"Do your best," he murmurs. "This could just be the break we're all waiting for."

****

Sadly, there is no break for the dressers in the operating theatre. From early morning, an endless procession of badly-wounded individuals has passed in a horizontal stream through the theatre doors, leaving again shortly afterwards minus some part of their anatomy, some nearer to their Maker than others.

The sawdust box has been changed, the table swabbed down, the watchers in the gallery have been amused or amazed. Finally, the surgeon calls a halt, mainly because he has luncheon waiting at his club. The students stream out into the spring sunshine, exchanging the fetid air of the operating theatre for the slightly better air of the city street.

At the news-stands, the afternoon papers have just been delivered. Mrs Witchard's lodger glances at the headlines, pauses, and walks on. He buys apples and yesterday's bread, a heel of dry cheese and a bottle of cheap wine, and trudges towards his lodgings hugging his purchases to his chest. There is much to be done before the summer exams, which will free him from the tyranny of student life with its daily humiliations, and allow him finally to set up practice in his own name. Whatever that name will be when the time comes.

He passes Rhymer's, one of the apothecary shops he frequents when he cannot gain access to his usual source of supply, and pushes open the door. Inside the dark unlit interior, bottles of tincture of digitalis and saffron, tar ointments, liquid aloe and iron tonics line the shelves.

He waits while the elderly, stooped apothecary makes up his opium, his cough loud and rasping. The man should make up a tincture of something for himself, the lodger thinks. The apothecary has had that cough ever since he first started coming into the shop. It is not as if he does not carry the remedy. There are drugs here for diseases, for dreams, for fighting dragons and for keeping demons at bay. Surely there must also be something for coughs.

He pays, and carries the bottle and the food back to his room, placing everything on the table. Then he walks to the window, opens it and gazes unseeingly out across the crooked tiled roofs. Today the air is so clear he can see for miles. He has heard it said there are millions and millions of people living here. Restless. All, like him, needing what they do not have.

Sometimes he forgets the present; there is so much of the past to keep clear. He blinks, closes his eyes. When he opens them again he is crying, but there is nothing he can do about it. His life swings on its turning point. He feels a melancholy tug inside him, as if his body had its own tides and currents.

Life isn't something that takes care of itself, he has learned that through pain and suffering. There are big black holes you can fall into, with long sharp spikes at the bottom. He shudders. Outside his window, the air is sweet with the scent of blossom.

****

Time rolls relentlessly along, and eventually it reaches eight o'clock, and all is well. Mrs Crevice has seen the sewing-room girls off the premises. Most of them are carrying extra work that means they will get very little rest tonight.

Now she takes a last sharp look round her domain to make sure everything is ship-shape. She has already counted the scissors and checked the needles. No pilfering of store property on her watch. Oh no.

Mrs Crevice turns down the lights and locks the side door. She places the keys in her basket and sets off. Tonight, she will dine solo. Morbid Crevice is working back at his shop. It is stocktaking time, which also includes perusing the contents of the big black safe. So secret are these contents, that Tonkin has been sent off without any supper, and told not return until morning.

Mrs Crevice stops at one of the many food shops still open. She orders an eel pie, hot. The proprietor is in his shirtsleeves, a clean white apron protecting his waistcoat and trousers from damage. He lifts the lid of the metal receptacle in front of him, whips out a hot pie, runs a knife round it inside the dish and turns it out on to a piece of paper.

Mrs Crevice takes the pie round to the dolly shop and knocks on the window. She has to knock several times before her beloved opens the shop door.

"Watchoo doing here?" he snaps, his eyes hostile and unwelcoming.

"Brought you a nice pie," his *inamorata* says.

Crevice snatches up the pie, cursing as the hot pastry burns his fingers. He nods a thank-you, then closes the door once more. His wife hears the sound of the key turning in the lock. She is also aware of the strong smell of brandy fumes. These things will be important later on.

Night wears on. There is sound everywhere, none of it close. Background noise of people, echoes of whispers, whispers of echoes, the clatter of traffic. The metal voices of church clocks chime the passing hours. Ten. Eleven. Twelve.

A lone figure suddenly steps out of the shadows and scurries towards the shop. It is the girl from the workhouse. She carries the box of matches, holding them in her hand as if they were a talisman. Round the back of the shop she goes, down an alleyway so narrow that she has to hold her breath, until she reaches the door to the back shop.

There she pauses. Her nose wrinkles. What is that smell? It seems to be coming from within the building. She reaches out her hand to grasp the door handle, pushes open the unlocked door, and strikes a match. The sulphur flare reveals a sputtering fire in the grate, a suffocating vapour in the air. The match goes out. She strikes another. The walls seem covered with a thick greasy sooty coating. She sees a chair, a table full of papers, an empty brandy bottle, an unlocked safe.

The match goes out. She strikes another. The last. She sees charred floorboards, a puddle of thick yellow liquid, a pile of grey ash, something round and black, a half-burned hand, two blackened feet. The match goes out. She turns and runs back to the street, feeling the scream rising, rising until it fills her mouth with its horror.

In the grey light of a grey dawn, Mrs Crevice will make her way to the shop. Getting no answer to her knock, she too will go around the back. The police, who will arrive some time later, will take the body – or what they can find of the body – of Morbid Crevice to the police morgue, where it will be pored over by the police surgeon and his colleagues in the Metropolitan Police.

It will be noted that the front door of the shop had remained locked throughout the whole proceedings. The empty spirits bottle will be taken away for examination. It will also be observed that no other parts of the room or the furniture were burned or destroyed, save for the body of the hapless victim.

The condition of the body parts will be the subject of careful scrutiny. It will be seen that the head, hands and feet have been burned to a black mass, while other parts have been reduced to a carbonaceous foetid unctuous ash. The thick greasy soot and the foul odour will be discussed.

In the final outcome, due to the lack of any logical explanation or reasonable evidence to the contrary, it will be concluded by the experts brought in to consult upon the case, that the fire originated within the actual body of Morbid Crevice, and therefore the cause of death will be pronounced a 'death by spontaneous combustion'.

But before all these events take place, there will be another visitor to the shop. Tonkin, having tramped the streets all night, will return to his place of employment very early, before dawn has broken. He will enter the small fetid room. Finding an unlocked safe and no employer, he will help himself to certain items of jewellery, which he will tie up in a bundle of old clothes before taking to his heels.

Also in the bundle will be his current ill-gotten gains, together with the only thing he has left from his past: a ragged blue baby-blanket, taken from the cupboard in the Foundling Hospital where the children's few pitiful keepsakes are stored. It has the remnants of a name, no longer legible, chain-stitched in one corner.

****

Meanwhile, in Detective Inspector Stride's office, the tottering piles of paperwork are slightly less alpine. There are even occasional patches of desktop visible. Stride sits behind the desk. He is humming happily.

He looks up and grins as Jack Cully enters. Cully has learned over the years that when Stride grins in that shiny sort of way, it means that someone is trying to play a game without realising that Stride has the only copy of the rules.

"The game's afoot, Jack," Stride says smugly, thumping his fist on the desk and causing a minor avalanche.

Cully wishes his boss wouldn't quote the meaningless gibberish that gets put out from time to time by *The Police Gazette*. Also, he hopes it is more than just one foot – or rather one set of two feet. And preferably not his two feet. He has worn down his boots walking from hospital to hospital. And he fears his constant hospital presence means he is beginning to smell like one.

"That police artist has done us proud," Stride declares. "I always said it was a good idea to employ him. Once we get the posters placed in the areas where the murders took place, someone is bound to recognise our man."

"Hopefully they will do more than just recognise him," Cully adds. "Is there a reward offered?"

"I'd have thought assisting the police to bring a vile murderer of innocent females to justice would be incentive and reward enough, wouldn't you, Jack?"

Probably not, Cully thinks, being slightly more in touch with street sentiment.

"Are we supplying any newspapers with the portrait?" he asks.

Stride sucks in his breath sharply.

"And have a repeat of the *'I am The Slasher's Mother'* letters? I think we'll keep the popular press out of it."

Cully opens his mouth to disagree. Stride cuts him off at the pass.

"Remember that *'Gigantic Hound'* story? As soon as the press got hold of it, we were inundated with sightings. Took all our resources to check them out. Meanwhile, the real criminal was getting away with murder right under our noses."

"If you say so."

"I do. Can you imagine what our friend Dandy would do with it? We'd be harried from pillar to post. My God – I wouldn't even put it past him to offer a reward just to spite us! And I bet he wouldn't be the one who ends up having to pay it."

Stride picks up a folder of reports. Cully recognises them as his hospital ones.

"Very thorough work, Jack. Well done."

For Jack Cully, the unexpected praise is tinged with the knowledge that he has still been unable to ascertain the whereabouts of Emily Benet. The memory of her awakes with him, accompanies him wherever he goes, and goes to sleep with him at night. The sense of loss is palpable, as painful as an open wound.

Meanwhile Stride rubs his hands.

"Right," he says, reaching for his coat and hat. "I'm off. A cup of coffee from the coffee stall, and then onward and upwards. The show must go on, as they say."

****

And indeed, the show must go on, for people want to be entertained. And wherever there are people wanting to be entertained, there are other people willing to entertain them. Police Constable Tom 'Taffy' Evans is only too aware of this, especially as his leave has just been cancelled and he has been put on extra duties.

He has scribbled a hasty letter back home to inform his sweetheart Megan of the change in plans, and now, as he patrols his beat, he is mulling over a strategy to deal with the expected response. She is a fiery one, his Megan, and this is the second time in two months that his leave has been cancelled.

Constable Evans knows the reason why all police leave has been cancelled. He may not read the newspapers but he passes various news vendors boards constantly. He sees the gory headlines on a daily basis. He hears the boys shouting the latest news on *The Slasher* – the fearsome killer who stalks the streets by night.

He has heard London compared to great cities of the past like Imperial Rome.

Constable Evans (who has been brought up Chapel) thinks it is more like the city of Babylon mentioned in the Book of Revelations: *'a great city dressed in purple and scarlet, glittering with gold, precious stones and pearls,'* but at the same time *'a home for demons and a haunt for every evil spirit.'*

He is just proceeding down Regent Street and wondering whether he could afford any of the merchandise displayed in the shop windows, and whether a present from London might smooth his path with Megan, when he finds himself being addressed by a young woman. You will no doubt recognise her as Estelle, the 'French' lodger whom Stride and Cully encountered upon their fruitless visit to Mrs Desiderata Tightly's Rooms for Professional and Visiting Ladies.

Constable Evans does not recognise her of course, never having crossed the threshold of that establishment. But from her scanty low-cut attire and boldly painted face, he recognises what she is. His heart sinks. He hates giving offence, but really, this fatal attraction he seems to possess for ladies of the night is beginning to get on his nerves. And it is making him the butt of his fellow constables' jokes.

"Oi, you – copper," Estelle says, launching herself from the doorway in which she is loitering with intent.

Constable Evans halts, folds his arms. Looks down. Hastily averts his gaze.

"Yes Miss, what can I do for you?"

Estelle eyes him up and down.

"Well ... now there's a question, innit?" she drawls.

Constable Evans folds his lips disapprovingly.

"Soliciting an officer while he is on duty is a criminal offence and might result in a Prosecution for Public Indecency," he repeats woodenly.

Estelle sniggers.

"Yeah, right. Like I haven't ever been asked to give one of you lot a quickie dahn a dark alley? Chief constables, inspectors, sergeants, I've had you all. Lit'rally."

Constable Evans pretends he has not heard. He finds this the best approach.

"Is there something you want, Miss?"

"Apart from a thousand pounds and a rich old 'usband with a dicky heart? Yeah, there is ... I want you to come with me."

Constable Evans opens his mouth to decline the invitation, but Estelle grabs him firmly by the sleeve and hauls him towards one of the colonnades. She is surprisingly strong, and he finds himself following her unprotestingly. She leads him to a pillar.

"There," she says, pointing.

He follows her finger. Affixed to the pillar is a Police '*Wanted*' poster, bearing the artistic endeavours of Leonard.

"I seen him," she says triumphantly.

"Where?"

"Soho. Last Wednesday evening. He was standing outside the bazaar, watching the ladies going in and out."

"You are sure it is the same man?"

She nods.

"Oh, it's him alright. No mistake. Recognised him the moment I saw his picture. Almost a speaking likeness. Not that he was speaking. More staring."

Recalling his last encounter with a lady of negotiable affections, Constable Evans does not hesitate.

"You need to come along right now and talk to my superior officer," he says.

Estelle regards him frostily.

"In your dreams, big boy," she says, moving a few steps away from him. "I ain't going dahn to no rozzer shop. What if word got out? Bad for business."

But Constable Evens is a quick learner. Besides, his time on the beat has accustomed him to dealing with members of the public who treat their memory as only a rough guide to events.

"I shall accompany you every step of the way, Miss, to make sure you arrive safely and tell my sergeant exactly what you told me," he says, moving a few steps towards her. "After all, we wouldn't want you to be attacked by anything. Like a sudden loss of memory, for example."

He tucks her hand firmly under his arm and begins to walk towards Bow Street.

"You come along with me all nice and quiet like, and I'm sure there will be a cup of tea for you," he smiles. "Maybe even a biscuit. Now, I can't say fairer than that, can I?"

****

There are no biscuits being handed out to the medical students learning their surgical trade in the Dissecting Room at University College. There are quite a lot of dead bodies though. Each cadaver has been neatly laid out on a long oblong wooden table, with four sets of dissecting instruments in wooden boxes placed around.

Mrs Witchard's lodger is working with three other students. He slices open a parchment-coloured leg, being careful not to cut himself with a scalpel. (The high death rate amongst medical students is always blamed on dissections, or the putrid emanations from bodies.)

He has managed to gulp down some tasteless watery porridge before leaving his dismal lodgings, and now his stomach grumbles embarrassingly. He remembers the advice of his Edinburgh professor: *Eat a solid breakfast before dissecting, and avoid the company of women and tiring activities, such as dancing, the night before.*

He'd like to treat himself to a hot lunch, but he may not have enough time. Many students just grab a sandwich or a pork pie and eat it on the benches outside the lecture theatre. The trouble with dissection is that it gives you a hearty appetite, but as soon as you enter a chop house, the smell of cooked meat takes it away. Sometimes he thinks the dishes even taste of the body he has just dissected. He is sure that he reeks of mortality. Maybe that was why she ... The dissecting knife slips, clatters to the ground. He stares down. Despair shifts within, half-awake to its own strength. His heart goes falling away inside him.

"Butterfingers, old man," remarks one of the students.

He shrugs, does not respond, goes on working numbly, separating veins and arteries. This is the last class of the term and he needs his certificate of attendance to add to his final qualification. He cannot falter now. He is not one of the lucky ones. He has no rich parents, no degree from Oxford, no favoured status within the University.

Life will not fling wide its golden gates and beckon him through. Faugh! He has to scrimp to find the £90 fees – which he still hasn't paid in full. He has decided to grow a full beard in the hope the bursar will not recognise him as he slides past his office, jacket collar pulled up as high as possible.

He blinks, then goes on slicing with clinical detachment. He feels dazed, halfway to sleeping. His head aches. When he has done, he slides the dissecting knife into his pocket before leaving the room. He crosses the wide atrium and opens one of the main doors. The smell of rain blows in. He walks out into it.

****

London in springtime. A white-skied day. Blossom in the parks. Everything is in bloom. The small female flower-seller on the corner of Tottenham Court Road has bunches of violets in her basket. There are geraniums in pots on sills. Even the canaries and linnets hanging from first-floor windows in their tiny wicker cages seem chirpier.

It is certainly not a day for bombshells and blow-ups, you would think. But you would be wrong. Unaware of what is about to descend upon her, Hyacinth Clout has decided to embark upon the annual spring-clean.

When Mama was alive, this was the only time servants were employed, albeit temporarily. The prospect of one of her daughters down on all fours scrubbing was a concept too appalling for even Mama to stomach.

For the past two years Hyacinth has applied to a certain agency, and a reliable woman has been sent to help with the onerous task of taking up and beating the carpets, washing the net curtains and cleaning the paintwork with soda.

The subject has been broached with Lobelia, who seemed somewhat distracted by the request and merely responded with an airy wave of her hand that she would 'think about it' in due course.

At the time, Hyacinth was surprised. Usually Lobelia took grim pleasure in pointing out every smudge and smear and commenting disparagingly upon Hyacinth's slapdash attitude to housework.

However, the weeks have gone by, and in the absence of any positive response from her sister, and currently in the absence of said sister, Hyacinth has decided to begin the process herself. So here she is, down on all fours with a bar of lye soap, a bucket of scalding hot water and a brush, scrubbing the hall tiles.

She has just reached the door that separates the kitchen stairs from the rest of the house when the front door opens and Lobelia enters. Hyacinth gets to her feet, wiping her red soapy hands on her apron.

Lobelia spots her. Her eyes widen in shock.

"What on earth are you doing, Hyacinth?" she exclaims.

"I'd have thought that was fairly obvious. I am scrubbing the floor."

Lobelia removes her bonnet and places it on one of the wooden pegs. She regards Hyacinth, head on one side.

"Look at the state of you! You are soaked! And your hands! What would Mama say if she could see you?"

"I do not know. The question is immaterial in any case as Mama is dead."

Lobelia purses her thin lips.

"Indeed, she is. Driven to an early grave by a broken heart. And who broke her heart?"

"The heart has no bones so it cannot be broken," Hyacinth repeats automatically.

It is a phrase she has found particularly comforting over the past few weeks.

Lobelia stares at her. She frowns.

"So, if you will excuse me, Lobelia, I should like to get on," Hyacinth says.

"Wait!" Lobelia commands.

Hyacinth pauses.

"I have something I wish to say to you. You may not be aware that I have recently written to the Overseas Missionary Society for the Conversion of the African Heathen, asking to go out to Africa as a missionary. As has my dear friend Bethica. Today we heard that we have both been accepted. It is our intention to unburden ourselves of the onerous responsibilities and duties imposed upon us both. We are called to fulfil a higher and more noble calling."

Lobelia smirks complacently.

"I see," Hyacinth answers. "How will you manage financially?"

"The church will fund us – Reverend Bittersplit is going to take up a collection. Bethica has a small inheritance from a deceased relative. And as I shall not be returning to this country, I shall sell the house."

Hyacinth feels the ground under her feet sliding sideways.

"Sell the house? But where shall I live? I have nowhere to go."

Lobelia shrugs.

"Mama left the house to me in her Will. It is up to me to do with it whatever I want. You are not my concern. You are no longer worthy of my concern."

"You would be happy to see your own sister made homeless?"

Silence. It would appear to be so.

Hyacinth takes a deep breath. She is not sure where all the terrible anger piling up inside her is coming from, but she is powerless to stop it now.

"If you try to sell this house," she says, the words issuing forth fast and hot, like molten lava, "then I shall write to your *Christian Missionary Society* and tell them that you have turned your own sister out into the street to starve. Once they know that, I do not think they will be quite so keen to take you on. And I shall write to the newspapers and expose you for the hypocrite you are. And I shall write to every member of the church too, and tell them what you have done."

Lobelia's jaw drops.

"I do not believe you! You wouldn't dare."

"Oh, I would dare," Hyacinth continues recklessly. "Believe me, it'd give me no greater pleasure. Because, you see, I have remembered what happened when we were children. That day when Billy disappeared.

"It was YOU who let go of the perambulator, Lobelia, not me. I was in the shop buying sweets. When I came out, you told me a nice lady had taken the baby away because she didn't have a baby of her own. I was too small to understand what you had done.

"When we got home, you went straight to Mama and blamed me. You both blamed me. Over and over again, until I too came to believe your lies. You are a vile, evil woman, Lobelia Clout. You were jealous of the baby, and you got rid of him. Jealous, nasty and cruel.

"I think I might even go to the police and tell them what you did all those years ago. I expect there is some law about abandoning babies. You could go to prison."

Lobelia staggers back, the colour draining from her face.

Emboldened, Hyacinth takes a few steps towards her.

"So, this is what I suggest: go out to Africa as a missionary. Good riddance. I will stay in the house and look after it. Otherwise, I will take up my pen and ruin your precious reputation forever."

The silence between them is so thick you could cut it and serve it in slices.

Then without a further word, Lobelia Clout sweeps past her sister, her eyes spitting hatred. She mounts the stairs. Hyacinth remains in the hallway. She is still shaking from the violence of her outburst. She hears the sound of something heavy being dragged along the floor. Time crawls broken-backed. She finds herself unable to move. Eventually Lobelia appears on the landing dragging a trunk behind her.

"I have packed my belongings," she announces stiffly. "I will not remain in the same house as you a moment longer. I shall stay with Phyllis and her dear mother, until such time as I quit these shores."

Hyacinth waits until the front door closes on her sister, until the sound of the cab's wheels fade into the distance. Only then does she let out her breath in one long sigh. Quietness envelops her.

After all the shouting and tension the silence is almost tangibly calming, as if relief could be breathed in on air. Her arms close round herself like those of a lover. She catches sight of her reflection in the hallway mirror and is surprised to see that she is smiling.

****

Hyacinth Clout awakes next day to a sunny morning and a clear conscience. She has done the right thing in confronting her sister. The absence of said sister from their shared home cannot be laid at her door. And the joy of no longer having to feel guilty about something she didn't do is almost overwhelming.

No longer at the mercy of the daily routine, she takes her time getting up. She breakfasts in the kitchen, on leftovers from the night before, and still wearing her morning wrapper, her hair bundled carelessly into a net. The house is totally silent. A whole glorious golden day lies ahead of her, just waiting to be filled with whatever she decides to do. She is not bounded by having to shop, or clean, or prepare meals.

Hyacinth decides to explore the city of her birth, its highways and byways, nooks and corners. She has lived in London all her life, yet she knows less about it than she does about the exciting places she has encountered in her reading of fiction.

Today she will begin her journey, starting with Westminster Abbey. She would like to see Poets' Corner and read Milton's *Ode to Shakespeare* for herself. And she can treat herself to a nice luncheon in a tea-room after her visit as she doesn't have to hurry home to prepare food. In the afternoon, she has an important appointment to keep. One that she hopes will determine the course of her future life. She goes up to her bedroom and dresses carefully.

****

The office of Raven & Rooke, Solicitors, is situated in one of the old quiet courts off Chancery Lane. So old and quiet is the court, that the noise of the city seems to have passed it by entirely. Even the trees in the old square rustle quietly in the breeze, blowing dust quietly into the still air as afternoon sunshine streams down from a silent sky.

Mr Juniper, the old lawyers' clerk, sits behind a high wooden desk under a dusty skylight in the outer office of Raven & Rooke, an array of quills in a jar and a bottle of black ink to hand. He is copying a Will. His pen wanders along the fine manuscript paper, scribing bequests and withholdings in flowing copperplate.

The lives of the living are predicated upon the lives of the dead, which always lead back, never ahead. Once you grasp this detrimental mastery, you understand all there is to know about the human condition. Mr Juniper understands it completely.

The front door bell rings. He gets up creakily from his work and goes to answer it. Standing outside the brass-plated door is a young woman. Of no particular beauty, or fineness of attire, but with a grim and purposeful expression on her face.

"I am here to see Mr Raven. I have an appointment," she announces, smoothing her gloves.

Mr Juniper bows and shows her to the inner office. She sits in the cliental chair, which is placed next to Mr Raven's chair, high-backed black horsehair with rows of brass rivets.

"Mr Raven is in Court at present, but I expect him imminently," he says.

"Then I shall sit here and await his return."

Mr Juniper returns to his copying. The quill pen scratches its way across the paper. The clock in the outer office ticks loudly. Who knows what the client is doing. Eventually Mr Raven arrives, is informed that the client is waiting, and strides into his office, closing the door.

Mr Juniper dips his quill into the ink-bottle.

The clock ticks. The quill pen scratches. Then the door to the inner office opens. Mr Juniper rises to his feet politely. The client emerges, her expression even more grimly determined. She barely acknowledges the presence of the clerk as she sweeps across the outer office and goes out into the bright sunshine.

Mr Juniper takes his seat. He reaches for the blotter and rolls it across the lines of flowing copperplate writing. Another task completed. He wipes the nib on a flannel and begins the next copying task.

Meanwhile the client hails a hansom and gives the driver instructions. Arriving home, she pays the one shilling and sixpence fare, alights and goes quickly inside, untying her bonnet strings and throwing off her shawl as she passes through the door.

Hyacinth makes her way straight to the morning room, where she seats herself at the writing desk. She takes a sheet of notepaper and a pen, and after chewing the end of the pen for a couple of seconds, writes the following:

Dear Lobelia,

Today I paid a visit to Mr Raven, Mama's trusted solicitor. As you may recall, I was not present at the reading of Mama's Will as I remained at home, indisposed with a headache. Afterwards you were kind enough to relay the contents to me. Like the fool I seem to have been, I believed what you told me.

But now, having studied the Will for myself at Mr Raven's chambers, I know what Mama's actual last wishes were. As you know, the ownership of the house was indeed bequeathed to you, on the understanding that you would live in it continuously during your lifetime.

But if you chose, for any reason whatsoever, to quit the house, the ownership then passed to me. Mama was quite clear about this. I have consulted Mr Raven and he is of the opinion that, should you decide to leave England to work as a missionary in Africa, you would no longer be 'living continuously in the house'.

Indeed, you are currently no longer living in the house, having chosen to move out and abide elsewhere. Therefore, by default, I am now the sole owner. Mr Raven has been kind enough to put all this in writing, so that it is quite clear and irrefutable should anybody try to contest it.

You are not now or at any time in the future, in a position to sell the house, nor to turn me out into the street.

Your sister,
Hyacinth

Two days later, just as she is beginning to settle into her new life, Hyacinth returns from Mudie's with a new novel to find a letter lying face downwards in the hallway. Even after all this time, even after all that has happened, her heart suddenly misses a beat and she finds it hard to swallow.

She picks up the envelope and turns it over. She recognises the handwriting instantly. With a sinking feeling, she carries the letter into the morning room and opens it.

Dear Hyacinth (she reads),

*I have been made aware of the departure of your
sister from the family home and the sad events leading
up to it. It is my duty and intention to call upon you this
afternoon with the purpose of discussing this, and
certain other matters arising from it.*

Yours,

In His Name,

E. N. Bittersplit (Revd.)

A large chunk of gold flakes off the day. It is clear
that Lobelia has not wasted any time. She has been
gone for less than a week, and already she is calling up
reinforcements. He is going to lecture her, Hyacinth
thinks gloomily. He is going to harangue and harass
her. He is going to bully and browbeat her. He is
probably going to quote obscure verses from the Bible.
He is certainly going to take Lobelia's side. She
wonders what the N stands for. Nuisance is rather too
obvious.

And how typical of him not to state an exact time.
As if she has nothing better to do but remain in the
house awaiting his arrival. Hyacinth is just preparing to
mount the stairs to her room to tidy her hair, when the
doorbell rings. She recognises Reverend Bittersplit, a
tall shadow behind the stained-glass panel. His head is
framed in a yellow semicircle, like a malign halo.

For one mad moment, she toys with the idea of
hiding somewhere until he goes away. But this would
only be putting off the inevitable. Reminding herself
that she has already won the primary skirmish with
Lobelia, and that whatever happens, this is her house
now, she takes a deep breath and walks slowly to the
front door.

A short while later Reverend Bittersplit is sitting,
very black and upright in what was once Mama's

favourite chair, then Lobelia's, but is definitely now going to be given away to some charitable concern.

He folds his arms and regards Hyacinth with an expression of quelling disapproval. She notices there is a droplet of water on the end of his beaked nose. She focuses on it, trying to keep her expression blank as she awaits the tirade.

"I am pleased to find you at home, Hyacinth," he begins. "From what you sister tells me, home is a place where you have rarely presenced yourself."

"If that were so, my sister would probably have starved," Hyacinth counters. "As we do not have a servant and Lobelia cannot cook, I am forced always to be here to prepare the food and cook our meals. Did she look starved to you when you saw her last?"

Reverend Bittersplit's bushy eyebrows rise up sharply, like two black crows in a stubbled field.

"I do not understand this attitude, Hyacinth. Ephesians 5, verse 11."

Hyacinth pinches her lips together to stop the words from falling out. She recalls reading somewhere that every person living in London is only a few feet away from a rat. She guesses it is, like most things, a matter of interpretation.

"What has my sister said?"

Reverend Bittersplit's face takes on a sad and sympathetic expression.

"She has explained, fully and frankly, the circumstances leading up to her departure from the house. She blames herself, of course. Had she been more aware of the way your dear Mama's death had affected you, she would have taken steps to provide you with the medical help you so clearly need much earlier, whatever the cost to herself."

Hyacinth gapes at him.

"Lobelia thinks I am ILL? What did she say?"

"She described the way you were ranting and raving at her in such a frightening manner that she felt for her own safety that she could not stay in the house a minute longer. She has also mentioned your many disappearances from the house for long periods with no explanation as to where you went.

"Is this the behaviour of a normal person? It is your sister's opinion that the death of your dearly beloved mother has affected your mind to an alarming extent causing it to become unhinged.

"I, too, have noticed the sad changes in you, as have several members of the congregation who have privately expressed their concern. Your sister believes you may be suffering from melancholia of the spirit and that you should not be left unattended to stay here on your own, where you might become a danger to yourself."

He leans forward and regards her earnestly.

"There are places, Hyacinth. Good, kind places where one may go and be, in the fullness of time and with the right treatment, restored to health. I know of one such place in Sussex. A fine Christian place run by Catholic nuns. They are very kindly souls and the regime is not too strenuous. No cold baths and locked rooms. No indeed. We live in a modern age after all."

"I see," Hyacinth says woodenly.

So, Lobelia is putting it about that she, Hyacinth, has lost her mind. Which, if proved, would also mean losing her liberty and her freedom, and being incarcerated in some private lunatic asylum where she'd be left to rot away for the rest of her days.

Hyacinth has recently finished reading *The Woman in White*, thus she knows exactly what might happen to her. If she allows it to happen. Presumably the upside of any such diagnosis would allow Lobelia to sell the house and pocket all the money from the sale.

"I think I should like to have a word with my sister," she says grimly. "Several words, actually," she amends.

Reverend Bittersplit tweaks his collar, as if it is suddenly too tight and is constricting his breathing.

"I'm afraid that will not be possible. She and my daughter will be sailing for Africa shortly and they are both entirely engrossed in their preparations. She has left it up to me to reason with you and see whether you are willing to comply with her wishes."

"And if I am not?"

Reverend Bittersplit stares at his hands. Kneads his thighs. Twists the gold signet ring on his little finger a couple of times. Then he rises and stands in front of the empty hearth, swaying to and fro without speaking for several minutes. His lips are compressed and his eyes seem to be almost starting out of his head. It is most disconcerting.

Hyacinth is about to suggest some tea – if she can be trusted to make her way to the kitchen without falling into a fit and attacking herself – when he suddenly bursts out,

"I cannot but speak now. What I am about to say, Hyacinth – nay, to ask, is something that I have been mulling over in my mind for some time. I have indeed been wrestling with my soul, praying about it and seeking guidance from a Higher Power."

Reverend Bittersplit's face is twisted, as if the agony of the struggle between his inner vicar and the Almighty has all but overpowered him. Hyacinth watches him in great alarm. There is something unreal about what is unfolding. She glances at the poker and wonders whether she ought to lay hold of it.

"You know my situation. I am alone, and have been for many years. Bethica has grown up without the guiding hand of her mother who was taken from us soon after my daughter entered this world. It was God's Will to inflict this suffering upon us both and I accepted His Yoke and shouldered His Burden without complaint.

"But now Bethica is a grown woman, and about to embark upon her own life. Which brings me to what I wish to say to you, Hyacinth."

To Hyacinth's complete horror, Reverend Bittersplit suddenly lurches forward, and grasps one of her hands, almost hauling her to her feet.

"There is so much that I could accomplish with the right companion at my side. I have observed you for many years, Hyacinth. You are still very young and you have some strange and foolish ideas, but with my guidance and firmness, I believe I could instruct and correct your waywardness, so that together we might both approach the Heavenly Throne and stand hand in hand and side by side in His Holy Presence."

Horrified, Hyacinth snatches her hand out of his cold, dry, talon-like grasp.

"You are asking me to MARRY you?" she gasps.

Reverend Bittersplit smiles complacently.

"Male and female created He them, dear Hyacinth. Genesis 1, 27. I trust that though this may be an unexpected request, it is not an unwelcome one. I am aware of several ladies in the congregation who would envy you your position as my future helpmeet. And given your present circumstances it is not acceptable that, as an unmarried young woman, you continue to live alone in this house. I have sought the Lord's will in prayer on this matter and I believe that marriage to me would be the best solution all round."

Hyacinth's head is whirling.

"But wait – I thought you just told me earlier that I was mad, and needed locking up in an asylum."

He regards her evenly.

"That is the opinion of your sister. I do not entirely concur with her."

"So ... either I agree to marry you, or I will be sent to an asylum?"

He frowns.

"You have a rather unfortunate way of expressing yourself."

Hyacinth rises to her feet. Some things need to be expressed standing up.

"Firstly," she begins, "I am NOT mad. No doctor in London would pronounce me mad, of that I am sure. I was with Mama's lawyer a couple of days ago, and there was nothing in his demeanour to suggest he thought I was behaving in an irrational or uncontrolled manner. I am, however, very angry with the LIES, for they are LIES, that Lobelia has been spreading about me.

"And as for your proposal of marriage – I cannot think of anybody I should less like to marry. I do not love you. I have never loved you and I would not ever love you. And without love, I believe such a marriage would be utterly loathsome to me. And now I should like you to leave, please."

Reverend Bittersplit stares at her in complete bewilderment.

"You are rejecting my offer? Rejecting it? And this is your final word?"

"I am. And it is. Now, please go."

Hyacinth walks to the door, opens it and stands meaningfully on the threshold. Reverend Bittersplit glares angrily at her, then claps his hat onto his head and stalks out into the hallway. She hears the front door being wrenched open, then slammed shut.

Hyacinth collapses onto the sofa. Laughter bubbles up inside her. She gulps it down. She does not know whether to laugh or cry. She feels as if she has been teetering on the edge of a precipice. She is giddy with relief. With an enormous effort of will, she pulls herself together and goes down to the kitchen, where she makes herself a very strong and very sweet cup of tea.

****

The Mother's Arms has not undergone any sort of makeover since the last time Stride and Cully drank there. If anything, it has slipped even further into a decline, like some aged relative who is gently sliding towards senility.

The bar counter seems duller, the glasses cloudier, the beer, more watery. Only the patrons remain the same. Solid, cloth-capped, hunched at their tables, staring gloomily into their pints as if they can see their future at the bottom of the glass, and it is not good.

Stride picks his way round the tables and leans his elbows upon the bar.

"Detective Inspector Stride, Scotland Yard," he says. "I gather you wished to speak to me."

The landlord glances unhappily over Stride's shoulder, pulls a reluctant face, then instructs the languid barmaid (who is drying glasses with the same cloth she has just used to mop up spills) to 'watch the bar, while I'm out the back with the gent'lm'n.'

Stride follows him through to a small shabby sitting room at the rear of the pub. It reeks of stale cigar smoke and the walls are stained yellowy-brown.

"It's like this," the landlord begins. Then stops.

Stride folds his arms, leans against the wall and waits. You can learn a lot by listening to the spaces between the words. He'd once managed to piece together an entire case from what one of the witnesses hadn't said.

"I don't normally do this," the landlord continues, biting his thumb awkwardly.

No, none of you do, Stride thinks. *We're the enemy, aren't we? Until something bad happens to one of your own. Then it's a case of: my enemy's enemy is suddenly my friend.*

"That man," the landlord says.

Stride nods encouragingly.

"You know which man I mean: the one on the poster. He was in here t'other evening."

Stride focuses in on the landlord's face.

"Go on."

"Well, I was just setting up for the night's session when he came in. On his own like. Ordered a brandy and water. Swallowed it down in one. The he just sat there. Watching the door. As if he was waiting for someone to come in."

Stride frowns.

"Are you sure it was him?"

The landlord nods.

"He'd grown a bit of a beard, wot he didn't have on the poster. But yeah, it was him. I'd seen him before so I knew. He comes in every now and then with some other young gents. I think they're all students from one of the 'orspitals, because they brought a whole skellington in one night for a joke. Put it in a chair. Tried to buy it a drink. Sometimes they start out here and then go on to other pubs. I guessed that was why he'd come in."

"And did the others join him eventually?"

The landlord shakes his head.

"Sat there for an hour. Didn't buy another drink. I was jist going to go and say summat, when he suddenly got up and left."

Stride processes this.

"You don't happen to know which hospital?"

The landlord shakes his head.

"'Nother time they brought in a jar with a pickled baby. Made a great joke about it being too young to drink beer. Very ... *amoosing* young gents, they are. If you find that sort of thing amoosing."

"Quite."

The landlord eyes him speculatively, his rheumy eyes glistening in the pale gaslight. He lowers his voice.

"I heard there was a reward?"

"For bringing underage medical specimens into public houses? I doubt it."

"Nah – you know what I mean. If this is *The Slasher*, isn't there some sort of reward for catching him?"

Stride glances round the shabby room.

"Have you caught him? Is he here somewhere?"

He pushes himself off the greasy wall.

"Thank you for your information, Mr ... it will be added to all the other information we receive."

Stride turns his back on the landlord's crestfallen face and walks through into the bar. Silence falls as he crosses the floor and follows him out as he leaves.

****

Another day dawns, bright and rain-washed, and once again we find ourselves in the narrow street of tall run-down houses just off Holborn. We pause outside the shabbiest and most run-down of the run-down houses. A couple of very grubby children are playing in the gutter. They have a battered hoop and are laughing as they bowl it along the street.

A cab turns the corner, causing the two to scatter in alarm. Their alarm is increased when it halts outside the shabby house. The cab door opens, and a young woman descends carrying a long flat box. There is a squeal of recognition and she is greeted rapturously by the two children who jump up and down with excitement and look hopefully at the box.

"Good morning Horatio and Fortinbras," she says, smiling.

The small Mullygrubs rough and tumble up the steps, and bound and bundle into the house, yelling at the top of their voices. Hyacinth Clout (for it is she) follows them, stepping carefully over and around the usual assortment of miscellaneous objects that litter the dark hallway.

She enters the parlour, where Portia sits at the table, scribbling assiduously. Cordelia is making ineffectual dabs at the mantelpiece with a cloth, not so much cleaning as moving the dust to a different location. Both look up, their eyes swivelling to the box.

"Yes, it is finished," Hyacinth says. "I put the final stitch in last night."

Portia rises, sticks the pen into her hair and clears a space for her. Cordelia picks up armfuls of papers and distributes them amongst the saggy chairs. The small Mullygrubs gather expectantly round the table.

Portia lifts the lid. Everyone peers into the box. There, folded neatly on a bed of apricot satin and wrapped in striped tissue paper, is the wedding dress. A collective "Aaah!" goes up on all sides.

"I packed it in an old dress box of mine. I hope that is all right."

Portia's eyes are bright with tears.

"I cannot believe that it is actually going to happen," she says. "We have been engaged for so long and dear Traffy has been so patient. And now the church is booked, and the wedding breakfast is arranged, and my dress is here, and all we need is somewhere to live, and I'm sure Traffy WILL find us somewhere for he is searching day and night, he tells me, and then Pa and Ma MUST give us their blessing."

Hyacinth purses her lips. She has been mulling over an idea for the past few days, ever since her rejection of Reverend Bittersplit's unexpected marriage proposal. Now seems exactly the right moment to suggest it.

"I may have found you somewhere to live after you are married," she says hesitantly. "How would you both like to come and live with me? The house is quite big enough for all of us."

Portia stares at her, mouth agape.

"But your sister ..." she stutters.

"She is on a boat to Africa," Hyacinth says firmly. "And as I now own the house, it is entirely up to me whom I invite to share it. I would expect you to pay some rent, of course, and maybe help out with the housework, but I'm sure we could come to an accommodation, if you think Mr Moggs would agree. Cordelia can visit whenever she likes. And of course, Horatio, Fortinbras, Juliet and Ophelia would be welcome to come and play in the garden. There is a summerhouse."

The small Mullygrubs' faces brighten immediately at this delightful prospect.

"Shall I leave it to you to mention it to Mr Moggs and to your Mama and Papa?" Hyacinth says.

"She is speaking at a meeting of the Ladies' Association for the Benefit of Gentlewomen of Good Family, Reduced in Fortune Below the State of Comfort to Which They Have Been Accustomed, but I shall speak to her as soon as she returns. And I shall tell Traffy tonight," Portia says, her eyes dancing. "Are you quite sure about this, Hyacinth?"

"Oh yes. Quite sure," Hyacinth nods.

The chances of Hyacinth being carted off to a lunatic asylum, when Portia and her husband are in residence at her house, are almost negligible. Also, she is beginning to feel the want of companionship, especially in the evenings. And she is growing rather fond of Portia.

Unexpectedly, Portia hold out both hands. Hyacinth takes them in hers.

"I am better and happier for meeting you, Hyacinth," Portia says. "And so is Traffy. And when we are married, I shall try to be the best of wives. And if you will let me, I shall try to be the best of friends as well."

And having made this heartfelt declaration, Portia Mullygrub wipes her eyes on her sleeve, runs her fingers through her tangled hair, and then shows Hyacinth out with as much grace as if she were a highborn lady living in a fine mansion.

****

Meanwhile, not too far away from this happy scene, Detective Inspector Stride is wrestling with demons. In particular, one demon, whose habitation is Fleet Street and whose name is Richard Dandy, chief reporter on *The Inquirer*.

Barely had Stride crossed the threshold of Scotland Yard that morning, when one of the day constables had handed him a morning copy of *The Inquirer*. There, on the front page, was a rather poor copy of the police artist's drawing, under the banner headline:

50 Golden Guineas to Find This Man!

With a sinking heart, Stride had carried the offending journal to his office, knowing before he'd even started reading the accompanying article exactly what he would find. Criticism of the detective police.

Personal attacks on his competence. Suggestions that 'The Man in the Street' was being short-changed. Praise for the investigative powers of *The Inquirer's* reporters.

He is just contemplating the letter he intends to fire off to the editor of *The Inquirer* when there is a knock at his door, and the desk sergeant sticks his head round. His expression is inscrutable.

"Sir, there are some people in the waiting area. Quite a lot of people actually, sir. They all want to see you about *The Slasher*. They say they have conclusive evidence of his whereabouts and have come to claim the reward money, sir."

Stride groans.

"Take their names and addresses. Get a brief statement from each of them. And don't offer anybody anything."

The desk sergeant disappears. Stride lowers his head into his hands. Then he picks up his pen and begins writing furiously. A couple of times the vehemence of the words causes the nib of his pen to break and he has to replace it.

He has just sealed up the letter when Jack Cully appears.

"Did you know—" he begins.

"Yes, I knew. Did you know who started this?" Stride snarls.

He waves the sealed envelope in the air.

"This should settle his hash once and for all. Damn his arrogance! Just when we were hoping for a breakthrough."

Cully casts a quick glance down at the desk, where the offending article is laid out, facing Stride. Then he pauses. Focuses his gaze more intently upon the picture. He has not viewed Leonardo's artistic efforts yet as he has been too busy chasing dead ends.

Now he finds himself looking down at a man's face. He remembers where he has seen this man before. University College Hospital medical school. He was looking down at him then, from a wooden gallery. The gallery was full of students. An operation was taking place. The man was one of the dressers. A few minutes later, he had seen him again – carrying away the bloody remains of an amputated leg.

Jack Cully pulls up a chair and sits down.

"I think we may have our breakthrough," he says.

****

Mr Horace Featherstone has portered at the University College Hospital medical school for so many years that it seems as if he has always worked there. He remembers when all anatomy classes had to take place in Winter because of the bodies going off in the heat. He remembers when Mr Jeremy Bentham, philosopher, was a real live person as opposed to an Auto-icon in a wooden cabinet, whose head and eyes are constantly being 'borrowed' by prankish students.

He remembers when the study of Classical Languages was considered an essential part of medical training. He remembers various students beginning their careers as timorous young apprentices and ending up confident physicians at the top of their game. What he does not remember is the sudden and precipitous arrival of two detectives from Scotland Yard, accompanied by three constables armed with handcuffs and truncheons.

Mr Horace Featherstone is a short, portly porter, with thinning grey hair smarmed back with Macassar oil – and a stickler for the rules. He is the sort of person who refers to his place of work as 'my little kingdom'.

Right now, his little kingdom is being invaded. He is not a happy porter at all.

"I'm afraid I cannot allow your policemen to go any further into the building, inspector," he bleats, folding his arms and blocking their entry. "There are rules about entering a medical establishment while bearing arms. They date back to 1789."

In reply, Stride waves his copy of *The Inquirer* at him.

"Never mind that. Do you recognise this man?"

Mr Featherstone is faced with a dilemma. If he takes his eye off the main door, there is a chance the constables might sneak round behind him in a pincer movement, thus disobeying his clearly iterated orders. On the other hand, he has been asked a question and like most men of his ilk, the chance to show off his knowledge is not to be thrown away lightly.

"Let me see now," he says, pulling out a pair of spectacles.

He adjusts them on his veiny nose and peers at the newspaper.

"Why, that looks just like one of our students," he says.

Stride and Cully exchange triumphant glances over the top of the little man's head.

"Where might I find the young man?" Stride asks.

Mr Featherstone hesitates.

"I'm afraid I cannot allow you or your men to proceed further than the atrium," he says. "This is a medical school. There are rules about non-medical people being allowed in. Especially armed non-medical people. At the end of the day it's more than my job's worth."

Stride and Cully exchange exasperated expressions.

"We are on police business," Cully says, before Stride loses his temper and starts shouting and they get ejected. "It is very important that we speak to this man. If you cannot allow us in, could you find someone in authority who might be able to answer our question?"

Mr Featherstone cogitates for a few seconds.

"I could go and ask the Bursar, I suppose," he says reluctantly.

"Yes, why don't you go and do that," Stride suggests drily.

The little man fusses off. Stride and Cully and their escort adopt poses of casual nonchalance, while carefully scrutinising everybody who enters or leaves.

Eventually Mr Featherstone returns, accompanied by a gaunt saturnine middle-aged man with a lugubrious expression on his face.

"Inspector. You have a question you wish to ask me, hmmm...?" he says, clearing his throat.

Stride shows him the newspaper.

"Ah. Yes. My, my. That is a very good likeness of young Mr Johnson. Very good."

Stride and Cully exchange bemused glances.

"His name isn't Edward MacKye?"

"Not this young man, I assure you. Samuel Johnson ... hmmm. Joined the medical school last year."

"That fits with what we were told," Cully murmurs. "He must be using a false name."

"We'd like to talk to Mr Johnson, if we may," Stride says grimly.

"Ah. That might be a problem."

"Why?"

"The Winter term has just ended. The Summer term will not begin for another three weeks. The students are not required to attend until then."

Stride utters an exclamation of dismay.

"Can you give us his address then?"

The Bursar shakes his head, "I'm afraid —"

246

"No!" Stride cries. "You are NOT afraid. You will give us the information, or I will have you arrested on a charge of obstructing a senior police officer in the pursuit of a criminal."

Mr Featherstone gasps in horror.

"You can't say that! You are talking to the Bursar."

Stride rounds on him, his face ablaze.

"I don't give a tuppenny damn if I'm talking to the bloody Archbishop of Canterbury. I will not have my inquiry impeded!"

"What I was *going* to say, inspector, before I was interrupted," the Bursar resumes calmly, "was that I do not know where Mr Johnson is currently residing. Indeed, I wish I did, for he has not paid a penny in fees. I have written several letters to the address he supplied, but they have all been returned unopened. If you manage to track him down, you might remind him of this fact ... hmmm?"

****

The word serendipitous was coined in 1754 by Horace Walpole to describe a chance event that occurs in an unexpectedly happy way. Detective Sergeant Jack Cully, who has parted from Stride and his posse and is taking the scenic route back to Scotland Yard, has probably never heard either of Horace Walpole, or his verbal invention. However, he is going to experience a serendipitous event. Very shortly.

Cully steps off the main thoroughfare of Tottenham Court Road, where the lunchtime crowds of shoppers and street-sellers mill and throng in noisy abundance, and enters the anonymous footstreets of small shops and old traders.

He finds himself on familiar ground. This area of the West End is close to where the body of Violet Manning was discovered. Where Annie Smith lived her short life. The urge to take one last look at the building where Emily Benet lived proves more than he can resist.

Cully is just about to enter the side street where the shabby lodging-house is located, when he spies walking towards him a sturdy young woman in a no-nonsense bonnet and a butcher's apron.

She is supporting a much smaller, frailer female companion who picks her way gingerly over the rutted uneven pavement. Jack Cully stops and stares, suddenly feeling the breath leave his body. Then without a moment's hesitation he leaps forward, arms outstretched, crying,

"Emily! My God, Emily – you're alive!"

And Emily Benet, frail and wasted but very much alive, takes one look at his radiant, overjoyed face, utters a gentle sigh, and drops down in a faint at his feet.

There is instant commotion. Somebody brings out a chair. Emily is placed gently upon it. A second chair is brought out for Cully. Somebody else brings a glass of water, a sugar bun. A dog turns up.

And in the midst of it, and utterly oblivious to the chaos erupting around them, Emily Benet and Jack Cully sit holding hands and staring at each other as if neither of them can quite believe what they are seeing.

Gradually the street empties out of everyone except Caro, who stands at a discreet distance. When only the three of them remain, Cully gently coaxes her story from Emily.

"I do not remember much of what happened after I fainted at work," she tells him. "I was so weak from lack of food and the long hours. I am told that Caro and her husband carried me to their home and there I lay for many days."

"She did, Mr Detective," Caro inserts. "I fed her teaspoons of good beef tea to build up her strength."

"As soon as I was able to sit up and hold a pen, I wrote to my parents in St Albans and they came in a hired carriage and took me straight home. And that is where I have been, regaining my health in the lovely Hertfordshire countryside."

"But you have returned?" Cully says hopefully.

"For now," Emily says. "There is no possibility of work for me back home. So, I have come to see what I can find here."

"Tell him about Ma Crevice," Caro interrupts.

Emily throws her friend a smile, shakes her head.

"Well, if you won't, I shall," Caro declares. "Ma Crevice's old man died in a fire at his shop, and she has been so overcome with grief that she ain't been seen in the sewing-room for days. So Em and I, we went to the management and suggested that we might both be reinstated as joint supervisors, because she is the best dressmaker they've ever had – and they know it. And I am good at organising people. We'd make a great team."

"And what did they say?"

Caro sniffs.

"Huh! Said they'd 'think about it.' But we went down to the sewing-room and saw the girls, and they're getting up a petition to say they don't want Ma Crevice back and they do want us. And if the management don't agree, they will walk out. So I reckon we'll be back by next Monday."

Cully smiles, then turns his attention back to Emily.

"Where are you living? I know you have moved out of your room."

"I'm staying with Caro and her husband just for now," Emily tells him. "They have kindly made me up a bed in their front room. But it is only a temporary arrangement and I hope to find a room to rent as soon as I am back on my feet."

"You're welcome to stay at my place for as long as you likes, and you know it," Caro declares, tossing her head. She lowers her voice, "I'm getting as much good red meat down her as I can, Mr Detective. But I reckon running into you like this is the best tonic she could have, if you'll pardon the liberty."

Reluctantly Cully lets go of Emily Benet's hands.

"I have to get back to Scotland Yard. Detective Inspector Stride will be expecting me," he says. "But I shall return after work to call on you. If that is alright with your chaperone here?"

Caro gives him a good-natured grin.

"I ain't no chaperone. If Em wants to see you, you are welcome. Only could you try and not look like a policeman when you arrive? Bad for business, if you know what I mean."

She helps Emily to her feet and they set off again, Cully watching Emily Benet's slight figure, until it passes out of sight. Then, his step lightened and his heart rejoicing, he retraces his steps. The hubbub of the crowd rises and falls, peaks and troughs all around him. He is barely aware of it. The sun is shining. The nightmare is over. For Jack Cully, it feels as if the whole world is on holiday.

****

Meanwhile, back in his office at Scotland Yard, Stride is attempting to come to terms with the latest setback. A cup of coffee, delivered hot sometime earlier, remains untouched and cooling on his desk. He was on the brink of catching him. He felt it in his bones. He was so close to success that he could almost taste it. It feels unreal, the way everything has crumbled into dust so fast that nothing can be done about it.

A carriage goes by outside the window, iron wheels tumbling, hoof beats hollow on the cobbles. Stride narrows his eyes, his mind boiled down to one thing. There are three weeks until the university term begins. In that time, how many more innocent women might be murdered?

****

Mrs Witchard's lodger sits on his bed, his face turned towards the window. He thinks about how his time has pivoted away from him almost without him knowing it. How his life has fallen away into itself without plot or premonition.

Mainly, he thinks about the events of earlier that evening. He had been sitting in his usual seat at the foot of the dining table, spooning up greasy soup. The rest of the lodgers were also present – except for one, who was late. Mrs Witchard did not like late, and there was an atmosphere of expectation as his key was heard in the door.

Ears straining, the lodgers listen as words are exchanged. Then the man enters the room, bringing the cold sour smell of the streets with him. He takes off his hat and sits down. His eyes swivel to the lodger. His mouth is hard and sly.

"Seen something interesting in the newspaper today, I have."

The lodger keeps his head down, hunches over his bowl.

"Picture on the front page. Spitting image of you, old boy. Did you see it?"

The other lodgers put down their spoons and wait expectantly.

"It isn't me."

The words come out thick as old blood. Even he does not believe them.

"If you say so, old chap," the man grins.

The door opens to admit Mrs Witchard carrying a bowl of soup. The two exchange a meaningful look. Then the man picks up his spoon. The room is absolutely silent, except for the slurping sound of his eating.

The lodger sets down his spoon, wincing as it cracks against the side of the bowl. He pushes himself out of his chair and leaves. As he mounts the stairs, he hears the man's voice, loud and boastful, hears the other responding.

Now there is a knock at his door. The lodger's heart beats like a hunted animal. His hand reaches for the brown bottle. Not bothering with the rituals of strap and syringe, he uncorks it and gulps down the entire contents.

He opens the door. A thin girl stands outside. He recognises her as the maid of all work. He has seen her lugging buckets of water up and down the area steps. She stares up at him.

"Yes?" he says.

Her voice, when it comes, is a whisper barely audible.

"You need to go."

He steps back.

"She's seen your pitcher. She knows who you are. Tomorrow first thing, she is going to the police. I heard them talking about it, her and the fat man. They will share the reward money between them."

He feels the room spin, feels sweat trickling down his spine.

"Why are you telling me this?"

She shrugs. No reason.

"It wasn't me," he says, his voice dropping to the level of hers.

Again, the shrug. Then she is gone, leaving him alone at the open door.

He goes back inside and sits on his bed. He thinks about what he has done for love, what he has felt for it. The way the doing was bound up in the feeling, the feeling blind to whatever he has done.

It is four steps from his bed to the door. He gets up, takes one step, takes another step. He feels his whole life twisting down to this point. He is surprised it has taken so long to reach it.

Outside it is a moonlit night. But the moon, being past the full, is only now rising over the wilderness of London. Everything is still. Still in gardens and parks, still upon smoky house tops, upon high hills and highways, still upon steeples and towers, and trees with a grey ghost of bloom upon them.

He walks the commoner streets, now emptied of the roar and jar of many vehicles, many voices, many feet. He no longer recognises his surroundings. Everything appears cramped and close. There are strange ghostly shapes in the smoke, the chimneys make threatening gestures. Invisible bodies with restless souls chase after him. The windows glare as he hurries by.

Eventually his steps take him to Waterloo Bridge, known colloquially as the English Bridge of Sighs, where the outline of St Paul's looms dark in the distance. He leans upon the stone parapet and stares into the black pit of water that rushes fearfully and secretly beneath him to the unknown ocean. Moonlight shines like a white pillar through a tear in the sky.

As the clock strikes one, he climbs the parapet. The lights upon the bridge burn dim. Life. Death. Only jumping-off points. When he jumps, will there be angels waiting to catch him? For a moment, he is statue-still, poised between earth and sky, between Heaven and Hell, knowing that things must end like this.

Then the air rushes past him and the darkness rushes towards him. He thinks about places he has never been, people he has never met, tears he has never cried and words he has never heard said. Briefly his pale face rises out of the dark water, ghosted with moonlight, before the current takes him and bears him away.

****

Stride and Cully stand in the empty room. It is early morning. Outside, a sudden shower is raining itself out in the empty streets. A small untidy servant girl watches them dumbly from the landing.

"He was here last night," the unpleasant woman says sullenly. "I saw him with my very own eyes. And I didn't hear him go out."

"But he is not here now," Stride says.

Cully picks up an empty glass bottle and sniffs at it.

"Opium," he murmurs.

Stride circles the room, observing, making notes.

"And you say his name is William Smith?"

The woman purses her mouth.

"I think that was what he said. Never spoke much. Just came and went. He was at the University, I know that. Learning to be a doctor. I don't let my rooms to any old riffraff."

Cully lifts the thin mattress. Finds the dissecting knife. Beckons Stride over.

"So where is he now?" he asks the landlady.

"He must've gone out early. But he'll be back, won't he? Stands to reason. He hasn't taken anything with him."

Stride opens the chest of drawers and rummages inside. His hand comes out with a silver locket on a chain. Inside it, a curl of fair hair.

"I shall arrange for some of my officers to wait inside the house," he says.

"So, it is him!" the woman's eyes light up. "When do I claim the reward?"

Stride's expression is so frozen it could have started another Ice Age.

"The 'reward' is nothing to do with the Metropolitan Police, madam. IF this is the man we are after, and IF we manage to apprehend him successfully, then I suggest you apply to *The Inquirer*. Tell them I sent you."

He puts the locket down, turns on his heel and stalks out. Cully follows. The Foundling stands on the landing. She watches the two men descend the stairs, hears their footsteps in the hallway, hears the sound of the front door closing.

Next minute Mrs Witchard comes sailing out of the room, her face flushed with triumph. When she has gone, the Foundling steals into the empty room and picks up the locket, turning it to the light the better to see the rich blonde curl of hair, the shiny silver of the chain. Then she lifts it to her mouth, brushing its brightness against her lips. Her face is desolate and lost.

****

Summer in the city. Cherry blossom and lilac. Bands in the parks. Cholera in the slum courts. London was not built for heat. It is a place built on the image of rain, façades of ashlar stone designed for short cool days and long cold frosty nights.

Nevertheless, it is Summer. A fine morning. And here is a church. Here is a steeple. Step inside, and here are some people. It looks very much, from their best clothes and air of suppressed excitement, that something nice is about to happen. Why not slip into this box pew at the back and await developments?

You will not have to wait long. At the front of the church a tall, thin young man in a very shiny new top hat has just got to his feet. He is wearing very new gloves, and a very new suit that is a tad too big for him, but very smart none the less. He glances towards the back of the church, and his face lights up with radiant happiness.

And here comes the object of the radiance. Portia Mullygrub, transformed from dowdy drab into beautiful bride by a simple white cotton dress, a short veil and a garland of fresh flowers. She holds onto Pa's arm with one hand and a spring posy with the other. Behind the pair walk Cordelia and the small Mullygrubs, tricked out in their finest, with solemn faces as behoves their newly elevated status as their big sister's bridesmaids and pageboys.

Now the minister steps forward and begins to recite the familiar service, the words echoing round the church, as they have done over the centuries. And before you can get out your pocket handkerchief to wipe away your joyful tears, Trafalgar Moggs, bachelor of that parish, and Portia Mullygrub, spinster of this one, are pronounced husband and wife together for as long as they both shall live.

Upon which all the small Mullygrubs throw their hats up in the air and shout "Huzzah!" and the new and blushing Mrs Moggs is kissed by Mr Moggs, before being passed round the assembled company as if she were a sugarplum. After which the whole company, including Ma, bustle noisily out of the church and head off for the wedding breakfast.

****

And here is the new bride a few days later, seated at the kitchen table of her newly-rented house with her new landlady. The dishes have been cleared away, the new 'man of the house' has departed for the city.

They are now awaiting the arrival of the painters and decorators, for Hyacinth has decided to decorate the whole house. There are too many vestigial memories of Mama and Lobelia for her liking.

And she has made other plans too. Plans that she wants to share with Portia.

"I have decided to sell some of the furniture and the paintings, and the rest of Mama's jewellery, and use the money to go travelling," Hyacinth tells her. "Just think: I have never set foot outside London in my whole life. There are so many places I have not seen. I have read about Paris, Rome and Venice in books. Now I should like to visit them for myself."

Portia Moggs' eyes sparkle.

"What a wonderful plan, Hyacinth!" she says. "I dare say I should like to travel the world some day too – when I am not needed by Ma to do all her letter-writing, and Traffy to keep house for him. And then there are the little ones to supervise.

"But I shall look forward to hearing all about these wonderful places when you return. And perhaps one day as you are travelling, you will see a handsome stranger and your eyes will meet across a crowded room, or a railway platform, or somewhere similar."

Laughing, Hyacinth shakes her head.

"I doubt it."

"You never know," Portia says, looking wise. "Meanwhile we will take good care of your house for you while you are gone. If anything needs mending, Traffy is handy with a hammer and nails, and I shall keep it as spick and span as it is now."

"Oh, I would not entrust the care of my house to anyone else," Hyacinth says earnestly.

My house, she thinks, savouring the words. *My lodgers. My future.* And she realises that she regrets nothing, and has nothing to regret. For the first time in her life, Hyacinth Clout is utterly and blissfully content.

****

The great heart of London beats in its giant breast. Draw a circle above the clustering rooftops and you will have within its space everything with its opposite extreme and contradiction. Vice and virtue, wealth and beggary, surfeit and starvation, all treading on each other and crowding together.

Look more closely. Here is Jack Cully, proceeding (as they say in police parlance) along Regent Street. He wears a purposeful expression, redolent of a man on a mission. But he is not wearing his customary work suit, and he has just bought a bunch of violets from the small flower-seller outside the tobacconist's shop, so it is a fair deduction that whatever enterprise he is engaged upon, it is not of a criminal nature.

And here, in his cramped paperwork-strewn office at Scotland Yard, is Detective Inspector Stride, composing the finishing sentences to his report on '*The Slasher*'. His men have staked out the lodging house and the medical school for weeks, but there have been no further sightings.

But nor have there been any further murders. Stride has therefore decided that the man must have either left London, or given up his nocturnal prowlings. Thus, Stride has decided to close the case. Now he signs his name to the report, blots it, and places it in a folder ready to be filed.

In twenty-seven years' time, London will be threatened by an even more deadly killer – somebody whose nickname will become the stuff of fear and legend. By then Stride and Cully will have both left the detective division of the Metropolitan Police, and the investigation will be in the hands of others.

But all this is yet to be. For now, why not stand in the shadow of this awning, and watch as Jack Cully and Emily Benet approach. See how she slips her hand inside his arm and how he leans protectively towards her.

They go quietly along the roaring streets, past the noisy and the eager, the arrogant and vain, the simple and avaricious, until they pass you by without registering your presence, and turn the corner, disappearing forever into their own future.

Finis

Thank you for reading this novel. If you have enjoyed it, why not leave a review and recommend it to other readers? Any review, however long or short, helps me to continue doing what I do.

Printed in Great Britain
by Amazon